Armoires and Arsenic
A Darling Valley Mystery

Cassie Page

To sign up for your free gift and updates about the goings on in Darling Valley, go to this webpage:

http://www.cassiepage.com/?page_id=30

TABLE OF CONTENTS

Chapter One: The Big Move...........4

Chapter Two: Special Delivery...........9

Chapter Three: Just The Facts, Ma'am...........16

Chapter Four: The Crime Scene...........29

Chapter Five: Tuesday's Child...........35

Chapter Six: George Clooney Arrives...........39

Chapter Seven: The Doctor Is In...........44

Chapter Eight: Gimme Jimmy Choos...........57

Chapter Nine: Paymoors...........74

Chapter Ten: A Vision of Tuesday...........79

Chapter Eleven: Speak of the Devil...........88

Chapter Twelve: The Darling Valley Bills...........93

Chapter Thirteen: Downtown DV...........107

Chapter Fourteen: The Widow and the Doctor...........125

Chapter Fifteen: She Did It...........132

Chapter Sixteen: Reading Tea Leaves...........138

Chapter Seventeen: The Auction...........156

Chapter Eighteen: Dinner at Hugos...........168

Chapter Nineteen: Sons of Anarchy...........173

Chapter Twenty: Banking Day...........184

Chapter Twenty-One: A Change of Heart...........195

Chapter Twenty-Two: Another Theft...........199

Chapter Twenty-Three: Tummy Trouble...........203

Chapter Twenty-Four: The Memorial...........213

Chapter Twenty-Five: The Leaves Don't Lie 224

Chapter Twenty-Six: Free At Last 227

Chapter Twenty-Seven: Hands Behind Your Back
.... 239

Chapter Twenty-Eight: The Heist 244

Chapter Twenty-Nine: Going Fishing 254

Chapter Thirty: The Catch 261

Chapter Thirty-One: Sold 271

Chapter Thirty-Two: BFF's 278

About the Author 283

Cassie Page Books 284

Free Gift and Updates About Future Books 285

Contact The Author 286

Follow The Author 287

Fiction Disclaimer 288

Chapter One: The Big Move

What Olivia liked best about moving to sleepy Darling Valley from LA was the absence of crime. No worrying about parking her car on a side street because it might get stolen. Nobody slipping sticky fingers into her purse and lifting her wallet while an accomplice distracted her at the sale rack at Neiman's. Not having to trip over a dead body blocking the doorway of her office building while the LAPD took their sweet time locking down the crime scene. But the best part of living in Darling Valley was never having to find herself sitting across from Brooks at a dinner party while he romanced his new girlfriend and referred to Olivia as a client.

What she hated about Darling Valley was the 400 miles between its pristine mansions and gritty but happening LA.

Olivia sat in her office in the immaculately restored Queen Anne Victorian that housed her two bedroom loft, her design and antique business and a possibly illegal mother-in-law in the basement. The dream house compensated for leaving what she considered the center of the universe, Los Angeles, California.

The mother-in-law housed a regal, but reclusive little old lady who barely gave Olivia the time of day, but paid her rent on time. Wait a minute. If the apartment was not up to code, did that qualify as crime? Why didn't she ask the previous owners when she signed the loan documents containing a contingency that Mrs. Harmon remain ensconced down there for life at the same ridiculous rent? When she thought about it, which she did now over coffee gone cold, that low rent was definitely criminal. And her own fault for overlooking the code issue when renovation was her stock in trade.

Olivia studied the dismal P&L statement that stared back at her from the Excel file on her MacBook. Darling Valley was breaking her bank. But enough S&M. She needed to finish up her impossibly long to-do list for the weekend sale before Cody arrived with the armoire. The success of the sale would determine her future, and the armoire would be the centerpiece of the well-publicized event.

The French boudoir phone rang, startling her out of her catastrophic ruminations. Her arm shot sideways into her coffee mug, splashing her favorite Jamaica Blue Mountain over her desk. This was becoming a cartoon of a morning going very wrong.

 She barked, "Cody, you're late," while she sopped up the coffee with the sleeve of her hoodie.

"Only by an hour," Cody replied in an offended tone that Olivia knew masked a grin spreading across his apple cheeks. "How'd you know it was me?"

"Cody, no customers call about a furniture order at 7:00 in the morning. So it was either you or Elgin Fastner from the bank harassing me about my about to be late mortgage payment if we don't get to work."

Cody was her twenty-one year old delivery guy and right hand everything. They both knew he got away with murder, but he was Olivia's only true friend in this strange, new town. As Cody apologized for his tardiness in a nasal but passable Wolf Blitzer imitation, she fingered one of the three antique netsuke she had unpacked earlier, another source of disappointment. Because of her connection to Brooks, Edward de Waal, the famed ceramicist, had appraised them for her. After ignoring them in his studio for over a month, he finally returned the pieces yesterday with a note saying the inch-long, carved ivory toggles for a Japanese gentleman's purse were indeed late 17th century, but would only command $1,500 each, tops. The shunga, an erotic figure with the iconic nine-tentacled octopus embracing the naked woman, might fetch $2,000. But only from a serious collector. Her dashed hopes for a number three times that raised the stakes on the sale.

"When are you getting here, Cody?" A committed multi-tasker, she checked the time on her laptop while she playfully harassed Cody and winced. Where did two hours go? "There's work to do. I'm in big trouble if this sale isn't a blowout. So get cracking, my friend."

"Are you going to have the cat and nine tails waiting for me?"

She laughed. If she were fifteen years younger she could have a thing for Cody. But she wasn't into boy toys.

"You'll wish that's all I have waiting for you if you don't get those beauties over here. Like yesterday!"

She meant the French armoire, library steps and bergère chairs Cody had picked up from Blackman Furniture Restoration and Imports.

"Seriously, we need to get set up to push merchandise this weekend. Unless you've been doubling down on your Wheaties, it's going to take us the rest of the day to sling everything around and make the showroom pretty.

"OMG! What are you worried about?" Olivia could hear the wind whistling in the open driver side window over his voice. "I can rearrange the goods in the showroom with one hand tied behind me. You gotta believe, woman. Believe!"

He said the last like a preacher at a prayer meeting, a place Cody had never frequented in his life. Then he added in all seriousness, "Of course, there is that one armoire that almost broke my back getting it into the truck. What do you have in there, O? Boulders?"

At first, Olivia winced at Cody referring to her stock and collateral, her beloved treasures as mere goods, as though she sold discount plastic patio furniture. Hers was an enviable collection of mostly 17th, 18th and 19th century French and English antiques she had transported up from Los Angeles earlier this year.

Cody racked up his share of screw-ups on the job, but he was her first friend in Darling Valley, and his loyalty to her soon convinced her to cut him some slack. Sure he marched to his own drummer. But so did she.

"What's your ETA?" she asked.

"I'd say fifteen, maybe twenty, minutes."

"Does that include stopping for coffee at the shop with the cute new barista? Or is that why you're already an hour late?"

"Coffee and Danish," Cody said, slapping his head so Olivia could hear. "I knew I forgot the most important thing. See you in less than an hour, O.

Cody called her O or OMG most of the time, and ma'am when he was innocently flirting with her—neither of them was interested in bridging the 10 year age gap, so the occasional sexy teasing was just fun. Cody reserved her full name, Olivia, though, for those serious times when he had gotten himself into trouble. Like spilling his coffee on the Aubusson carpet in the front of the showroom when he was gesturing about how he had maneuvered into Mrs. Gotrock's driveway without hitting her prize peacocks who had suddenly decided to display right in front of his truck. Gotrocks. That's how he referred to her few wealthy clients. If only she had more of them. Of course, he had nicked a lawn ornament when he swerved to avoid the birds, and Olivia'd had to replace it.

He said, "I'll pick up the usual for you," and before Olivia could object, the line went dead.

She knew he wouldn't answer if she called back to remind him to hustle. Oh well. It would give her time to get dressed, a ritual that could extend beyond Cody's arrival if she wasn't paying attention to the clock.

Wait a minute, she thought as she shut down her computer. What was that about boulders? And he never explained why he was so late. They had agreed on 6 a.m.

Chapter Two: Special Delivery

She stretched her neck to loosen tight muscles for a moment before she headed for the large loft over the shop, the main draw for picking this location on Angel Row, a side street off the highly trafficked Darling Boulevard. She had been at her computer since five a.m., right after her shower, but long before the sun broke through the trees outside her office. Normally, that wasn't such an early hour for her, except she had turned off the computer at three. Now, at shortly after seven, the small space behind the showroom that she used as her office brightened with the natural light coming through the French doors and bay windows overlooking the Garden Center in her back yard. With chronically sleep-deprived eyes, she had watched the rising sun marble the sky with layers of pink and lavender. Traces of rose and ivory still streaked the clouds and cast a faint glow over the room. To get to the window to view the spectacle, though, she'd had to climb over the bedlam of sample books stacked to the ceiling, her enormous stock of gilt drapery hardware and plastic wrapped bolts of very expensive French toile.

She loved her little office, the paned windows and pine floors that she finished in a soft ash gray to compliment the putty walls and white woodwork. She felt at home in there, even though it was where she faced her most odious challenge, her P&L sheet. She'd left a lot behind in LA, but some of the best parts were still with her. The two framed illuminated manuscripts said to be from the hours of a forgotten Medieval duchess, a splurge when she earned her first commission; the old, cheap desk from her student days that she had hand rubbed one winter to a dark sheen, her photographs. The Belleek collection that had belonged to her grandmother. These things resonated with warm memories when homesickness and doubt chilled her to the bone. Not like the items on the showroom floor that she bought for a song from an antiques dealer under water on real estate investments. Beautiful pieces to which she was trying to have no personal attachment. But when it came to antiques, she had to admit, she was an easy bounce.

Before she headed upstairs, she entered the showroom through the French doors connecting to her office and arranged the three netsuke on an 18th century cherry wood table that had once resided in the Duchess of Devonshire's bedroom, the scandalous Duchess, not the modern Mitford one turned shopkeeper. She ran her thumb over the satin finish on one of the ivory trinkets. Are you kidding? Only $1,500 each? Almost worthless, considering her financial needs at the moment. She might as well just add them to her personal collection. Still, fifteen hundred each was nothing to sneeze at these days. She put them back. Oh, how the mighty have fallen. Grasping at a measly 5K.

Olivia's closet was as organized as the rest of her life could be chaotic. She had given up a small alcove overlooking the back garden to have it made into a repository for her supersized wardrobe, the spoils from her once thriving design career in LA.

This morning she picked out an indigo lace top lined with nude chiffon that gave the illusion of exposed ivory skin. Next, a pair of skinny jeans—she grabbed one of the 7 For All Mankind first, then decided on

Armoires and Arsenic

Joe's Jeans. 7FAM was becoming the Beverly Hills uniform, while Joe's hadn't made much of an inroad in Darling Valley. She just felt like taking the road less traveled today. And, because she would be moving furniture, she chose a pair of orange patent leather Valentino flats instead of one of the two hundred odd pairs of mile-high stilettos jammed into the still too-small closet.

Tuesday, the best friend she reluctantly left behind in LA, had said as she helped Olivia pack, that if the design business tanked, she could open a dress shop and sell off all the outfits, purses and shoes she owned but had yet to wear.

Olivia laughed and said, "I can't help it. I like my threads."

Olivia loved all beautiful things, man-made and Nature made. That was one of the reasons she chose Darling Valley when she realized she had to get out of LA or lose her sanity after the breakup with Brooks. Her first vision of the small, affluent village took her breath away. Nestled in the hills separating the town from the Northern California coastline, it also boasted a pristine lake big enough for boating in the summer.

It's home, she had said to herself as she headed back to LA. And six months later, home it became, despite the hazing she took from her sophisticated LA friends about the name.

"Really, Olivia? DARLING Village? How impossibly Angela Lansbury."

She corrected them. "Darling Valley."

This morning she accessorized with four inches of bracelets and a clunky lapis and jade necklace, an original piece of wearable art for which she had traded a cut glass decanter of unknown provenance because it matched this particular Versace top. As a bonus, Xavier, a jeweler with a pricey shop on Darling Boulevard, had become a valuable reference in Darling that she not yet been able to sufficiently leverage.

Oh, yes. Earrings. In a flash, cascading loops of gold dusted her shoulders. Makeup was quick. She didn't need more than a flick of the blusher, some mascara, and a pale gloss. Hair was even quicker. After her shampoo it dried into natural soft, golden waves women paid hundreds of dollars to have permed and colored into their tresses.

In grad school, where she had majored in art history before switching to architecture and interior design, one of her professors compared her to an obscure Botticelli in a private collection he knew of in Florence. She once swore to Tuesday that they would both visit it one day.

Cody's truck crunched over the gravel driveway just then, earlier than expected. She'd better hustle. She took a quick glance at herself in the ornate wardrobe mirror before she headed back downstairs. All she could see was the small hook in her nose and too small chest that could make do with a pair of Band-Aids instead of a bra.

"If you're so blinking gorgeous," she hissed at the mirror, "why can't you keep a man?"

She tiptoed down the wooden stairs so the click of her leather soles on the wood planks wouldn't disturb Mrs. Harmon. She grabbed an oilcloth work apron from the hook by the back door, and tied it around her waist as she threw open the screen to greet Cody.

At the sight of his auburn floppy mop peeking out around his 49er cap and two-day beard, a look that to Olivia's taste looked grubby even though young girls found it sexy—Olive Oyl style, she liked a clean-shaven man--her spirits lifted. She wasn't alone in this cockamamie folly of hers, a feeling that often kept her awake at night. She had Cody, if only for moral support.

"What are you doing," she said, puzzled as she watched him try to wrestle a French oak armoire down the ramp of the truck. Usually, Cody tied the bulkier pieces on his back with straps, a trick from his days as a furniture mover for a real estate staging company. He claimed it was easier than trying to lug it with his arms. But nothing was working for him this morning. The piece wouldn't budge. Cody gave it a troubled frown, an expression that rarely crossed his typically grinning face.

"What did you do, O, tell them to pack this thing with pig iron?"

Olivia jogged across the driveway and hiked herself up onto the bed of the truck.

"What do you mean? I moved this armoire by myself when we dropped it off at Blackman's. It has pine shelves and backing. It can't be that heavy. You're not hung over are you, bad boy?"

She gave him a friendly jab on his arm, the rock hard biceps under his ratty leather jacket giving her an unexpected jolt in her belly. How long had it been since she had felt a man's muscles? She refused to visit that house of pain and focused her attention on moving furniture.

"O, I'm not kidding. It killed me to get this onto the truck in the first place. The other stuff was easy, but this was like a dead weight."

Olivia tried to rock the armoire to walk it over to the ramp. It barely moved, but she sensed a shifting weight inside.

"Something's in there," she said. "I wonder if they used it for temporary storage and forgot to empty it out. Let's open it up."

The armoire was tightly bound with heavy ropes secured with nautical knots. Cody scowled at the setup. "This rig would tie down a battleship. Why the overkill?"

The knots were so tight that Cody had to cut them off with hedge clippers Olivia dug up in the garage. Cody cleared the rope away, then tugged and pulled on the door, but with no luck. He threw up his hands.

"What are we going to do, O? I can't use a crowbar or it will damage the doors. How we are going to open it?"

Olivia tried the door herself with the same result. "Are you sure it isn't locked? Did you pick up the key?"

Cody pulled an ornate iron key from his jacket pocket and dangled it by its rose-colored tassel, then worked it into the lock. "Nope. I can get the lock to turn, but this old wood is all swoll up. This door won't budge."

Armoires and Arsenic

Olivia had a light bulb moment. "Let's tip it forward and see if whatever is inside pushes the door open. I'll stand in front. Do you think you can tip it, Cody?"

"Worth a try. I'll go easy so it doesn't fall on you."

Cody pressed his massive shoulder against the back of the armoire. It started to get away from him, so he grabbed the sides to guide it. Olivia held onto the front. Suddenly, she heard a loud thunk and something inside shift. The door flew open, smacking Olivia in the forehead. She jumped back and the door widened. It gained momentum on creaking hinges as the object inside pushed itself free.

A scream erupted from Olivia's throat. "Oh my god, Cody! There's someone in there."

Cody resettled the armoire and ran around to the front. He stared openmouthed at a man in an expensive sport coat and slacks slumped half in and half out of the armoire. Cody reached over to catch him as he started to slide toward the floor of the truck. He touched him, then jumped back.

"Olivia, it's Mr. Blackman! Holy shit. I think he's dead!"

Chapter Three: Just The Facts, Ma'am

A few minutes later, Olivia and Cody watched Detective Richards park his unmarked car in the driveway and walk back to Cody's truck without acknowledging them, scanning the front porch, side yard, and hedges like a bloodhound sniffing for clues. Cody had parked the truck at the end of the driveway in plain view of passersby on the street and any neighbors poking their heads out their windows to see what the new *vendor* was up to now. That was the dismissive title Xavier told her had been unofficially assigned behind her back. She'd said, *TMI, Xavier. Did I need to know that? Seriously? I'm just a vendor?*

Richards took out a handkerchief and blew his nose before he finally flashed his badge at Cody. "You call this in, son?"

Cody nodded.

"You the owner of this place?"

Olivia did not know which insult to react to first. The condescending *son* he levied at Cody, or his assumption that this twenty-one year old owned Olivia's business.

Olivia walked in front of Cody so the detective would have to look at her directly. "I'm the proprietor. And you are?"

She matched the snarky tone Richards had used with Cody. The detective trained his velvety coal-black eyes at Olivia for a moment, then sneezed again.

"Roses. I'm allergic to roses." He gestured to the bank of fragrant pink and yellow heirlooms that lined the rock garden along the hedge separating Olivia's property from the house next door.

"Detective Gurmeet Richards." He flashed his badge at Olivia this time, stuffed his handkerchief back into his flannel woodsman jacket and gave her an appraising look that she couldn't interpret. Personal or professional? Olivia knew that all interactions between men and women carried an element of sex, if only speculations about what might be under different circumstances. Before she could decide, he turned his back on her and without further word, walked over to the truck.

Gurmeet. Punjabi-American. That explained his gorgeous looks. But where did the attitude come from, mother, father, or was it an occupational hazard? Except for the rare traffic ticket, Olivia was a virgin when it came to dealing with law enforcement personality traits.

Another man walked up behind Richards and gave Olivia a frigid smile. She took the offensive and asked, "Are you the assistant detective?"

He sneered, "I don't assist anyone. Ma'am. Detective Johnson. Detective Richards' partner."

Olivia was not in a conciliatory mood. She was fighting nausea from the shock of seeing the dead man and fighting the guilt of worrying about what this tragedy would do to her weekend sale. But she couldn't separate the two in her mind and took out her mixed emotions on Johnson in his Target-chic sport coat and shiny slacks that had been ironed once too often.

"Do I have to take you at your word, Mr. Johnson, or do you have identification?"

Johnson put his hands on his hips, which pulled his coat open to reveal a sizeable spare tire tumbling over his belt. "Look, ma'am, we have a nasty job to do here. Let's cut the attitude and show a little cooperation. Here's my ID and it's DETECTIVE Johnson if you don't mind. And your name, please?"

He fished an electronic device from his pocket and keyed in her name, Olivia Mariah Granville.

"OMG," he said, smirking. "That's easy to remember."

"I've heard every variation of that joke, detective. Can we get on with this and remove the . . . the . . . ." She didn't know what to call the man still half in and half out of her armoire. She just knew she couldn't look at the inside of the truck again.

"I am a very busy woman." She put on her authoritative voice, if only to give herself a sense of control. This was all too shocking. She wasn't going to lose it in front of these two arrogant men. Cody didn't count. She could be herself with him.

Johnson said, "We have a lot to do before we can transport the body to the ME's lab over in San Rafael. And we'll have to work according to her schedule. She may have a few cases stacked up so it could be a while to arrange the transfer."

"Why San Rafael," Olivia asked, puzzled. It was twenty corkscrewed miles away.

"Darling Valley's a pretty small town. Not much call for murder investigations. San Rafael takes care of autopsies for us."

"Murder?" Olivia said, her voice rising as shock pasted itself on her face in an owl-eyed mask. "How do you know it's a murder?"

Johnson poked at his device, which evidently had jammed. Then he shook it, tried to enter something again, gave up and stuck it in his pocket with a scowl.

By now, Detective Richards had made a cursory examination of the body and came over to ask some questions of his own. He pulled out a small spiral bound note pad and black Bic. No electronics for him, Olivia noticed.

"Can you think of a reason this man might have locked himself in your chest there?"

Olivia avoided his eyes so could concentrate on her answers. She guessed him to be her age, early thirties and younger than Johnson by about a decade.

First, she corrected him. "It's an armoire, Detective. Early 17th century. French."

Richards looked puzzled. "A what? Never mind. Locked himself up, tied the straps around the, what did you call it, armory?"

"ArmOIRE," Olivia repeated. "A wardrobe if you like. For back when houses were built without closets."

Richards stopped her, apparently he knew about living without amenities. He continued. "And loaded himself onto your truck for a special delivery? And then died on the way? That would be a neat trick if he didn't have help. And help means . . . "

"Yes, of course." Olivia said, her cheeks reddening. She was used to being a step ahead of everybody else, but this morning had left her dazed as well as out of sorts. She absolutely hated to look stupid.

"I'm an idiot not to have put two and two together. It's just that I've never seen a dead body before, much less a murdered one."

That wasn't exactly true. There was the guy that time in the West Hollywood Japanese restaurant. The detective seemed to sense her embarrassment and softened his tone.

"I understand, Miss . . . I need your name."

Johnson interrupted. "Miss Granville. Olivia Granville."

He omitted giving Richards her middle initial. Olivia assumed he probably figured there was plenty of time to have a laugh at her expense back at the station.

"So what have we got, Matt?" He used Richards' nickname. "Any ID on the guy?"

"Nothing." Richards's head bobbed around as he answered, a curious cat taking everything in. "Stripped clean of wallet, credit cards. Do you recognize him Miss Granville?"

"Me?" Olivia was curt, wanting this over. "How would I know him? I've never seen him before in my life. But Cody recognized him. Didn't he tell you? It's Mr. Blackman, the owner of the restoration shop I use."

"Yeah," Richards said. "That matches up."

Her back stiffened as she answered, indignant. "Who didn't you believe, me or Cody?" This detective certainly knew how to get under her skin.

"We have procedures, ma'am. Any idea why someone would send his body to you? Pretty gruesome practical joke, don't you think?"

Suddenly, Olivia was overwhelmed with it all. The murder, her money worries, the sale, the dislocation from friends and family in LA. Her longing for Brooks. Her voice cracked and blinked back tears. "His family," she said. "His poor wife."

Johnson stepped in, keeping the interrogation on track. "Cause of death, Matt?" He pulled out his device and punched in some notes. This time it worked.

Richards turned contemplative as he tried to make sense of the scene. "Hard to say. No obvious cause of trauma. No blood, no weapons, no marks of violence that I could see, though I haven't moved the body to have a good look."

Johnson speculated suffocation but Olivia jumped in with, "Not likely. The inside isn't a tight seal. There are openings between the back slats that would let in plenty of air." The practicalities of solving the puzzle diverted her from dwelling on the widow's grief. From past experience she knew her grief could sneak through that opening and reemerge.

Richards shook his head. "Well, whoever did this wasn't going for the perfect crime. We'll have to let the ME figure it out. Has anybody called her office? Johnson, I'll take care of notifying the next of kin when we finish up here."

By now, the entire police force of Darling Valley had converged on Olivia's property. It consisted of a lone squad car and a second unmarked car that was used for drug busts. Exclusive as Darling Valley was, it could not avoid the encroachment of drugs by kids with too much money and time on their hands. Olivia tried to keep up with Darling Valley news, and she had read the three-part exposé in the Marin IJ about the dealers setting up shop near the yacht harbor on the lake, and Darling Valley's small police force completing a crash coarse on drug abatement procedures. Darling Valley or DV, as the locals called it, liked to think the problem was, therefore, under control. Coming from Los Angeles, Olivia knew that was pie in the sky. Murder, however, was just beginning to raise its ugly head.

Johnson and Richards took statements from Olivia and Cody as the police draped yellow crime scene tape all over Olivia's driveway, back yard, and Cody's truck.

Horrified, Olivia spluttered, "Is that necessary? Everybody in town will see that. Can't you just remove the, the," she forced herself to use the ugly word, "body . . . ," just saying it made her stomach churn, "and let us get back to normal?"

Richards folded his arms, Colombo-like and stared away as if to gather his thoughts. Then he turned to Olivia. She felt an unexpected lurch in her throat, and she had to tear her gaze away.

"Miss Granville."

"You can call me Olivia."

He gave her an odd look. "Miss Granville. We only have your word and Mr., I'm sorry, I didn't get your name."

Cody said, "White. Cody White."

Before Richards could continue, a car pulled into the driveway behind the police vehicles. The passenger jumped out wielding a huge shoulder cam and the driver started questioning the nearest police officer. Soon another vehicle followed.

Olivia blurted out, "Reporters? Really? You've been here, like two seconds. Did you call them, Detective? This is all I need, to be on the 6 o'clock news."

Richards' expression showed that he shared her disgust. "The Marin IJ, among others, has police scanners. Prepare yourself for the press, bloggers, amateur paparazzi and anybody too bored by their own lives to stay out of yours."

The quartet, Richards, Johnson, Olivia and Cody, watched the officers push the press back behind the crime tape and then ignore the questions being hurled at them, the agitated pleas for information and photo ops.

Richards gestured for Olivia and the others to move deeper into the yard out of sight of the cameras. "Let's get on with this. What was I saying? Oh, yes. Our procedures. We only have your story and Mr. White's account of what happened here."

Olivia's mouth dropped. "Surely you believe us. You don't think we had anything to do with this horrible crime?"

Richards turned a page on his pad. "Miss Granville, we are a long way from putting all the pieces together. We arrive and see a dead man in very suspicious circumstances in your truck. On your property. You two have been with him for an undetermined amount of time during which you could have committed any number of acts on the body."

This time Cody exploded. "Acts on the body! What do you think we look like? Monsters? We did nothing to that man."

"Sir, we have to corroborate your stories. If you could provide witnesses for your whereabouts this morning."

Before Cody could answer, a stranger came around the truck, peered inside and walked toward them, a kid about Cody's age dressed like a b-boy and carrying a skateboard.

"Yo. Any you guys know what happened to that dude?"

He started filming with his phone.

Incredulous, Olivia yelled, "Did you jump over my fence? This is private property."

The kid sneered, "Freedom of the press, lady. I'm checkin' out the story I heard on the scanner. I figure a murder or somethin'. For my blog. Freedomaintfree.com. You follow it?"

Richards interrupted him. "You are impeding a police investigation and if you don't get off this property you will write your blog in a jail cell."

"DV's got a jail?" He seemed truly impressed.

One of the police officers reached him and hustled him behind the crime tape. Richards snapped. "Go join the other members of the fourth estate back there."

"What you sayin' dude?" He looked around at Olivia's house and yard. "This don't look like no estate to me. No offense, lady."

Olivia got back to proving their innocence. "Cody, someone at Blackman's must have seen you. That handyman guy. Didn't he help you? And that hottie barista at Coffee and Chatter saw you on the way back. Tell him."

Cody shook his head. "Olivia, the furniture was on the back porch when I got there with a note to sign for it and just take it. They had left the screen door open."

Olivia said, "The armoire has been sitting out in the damp air? That's why the wood swelled up."

Cody gave her a thumbs up in agreement, then turned to Richards. "This is a small town and we work on the honor system."

Johnson cocked his eye toward the body in the truck and said, "Well, not everybody does." He laughed at his own joke and three rolls of chin jiggled for a moment.

Cody continued. "And Jeralyn, the barista, wasn't working today and the line was too long to wait for coffee so I drove to that new coffee drive in and it was closed. I chewed up so much time that I just came straight here without looking anyplace else for coffee. I don't think anybody's seen me this morning except you."

Richards said, "Well, that's something at least. I'll need that note for evidence." He sneezed again and backed further away from the rose bushes.

Cody said, "What? What note? I threw it away. Why would I keep a pizza flyer with some scribbles on the back? That's all it was."

Richards gave a disgusted shake of his head and turned to Olivia. "And you Miss Granville? Who can verify your whereabouts for the last, let's say, twelve hours?"

Olivia saw a look of appraisal in his eyes and immediately assumed he was judging the hook in her nose and the abysmally small breasts. She swallowed a momentary embarrassment and said, "Only Cody. He's the only person I've spoken with since I closed up shop last night, and that just on the phone."

Cody said, "What about Mrs. Harmon, O? Didn't you tell me she was going to fix supper last night?"

Olivia explained to Richards that Mrs. Harmon was her tenant. For a moment, she panicked. Irritating as he was, this Richards was the law in DV. Would he check into the zoning code on the unit?

Ignoring that worry in favor of more serious ones, she said, "Mrs. Harmon cancelled. Said her nephew was in town from Boston and was taking her out to dinner."

Oh, dear. She had forgotten all about Mrs. Harmon. What would she do when she woke up to the vision of a murder victim out her back window?

Mrs. Harmon was an unobtrusive tenant who paid her rent and utilities on time, unlike some of Olivia's more affluent clients who sat on her invoices. This town had money, all right. But it didn't like giving it to strangers. Olivia was quite surprised that her tenant had invited her for dinner in the first place. And then not surprised when no nephew showed up. When Olivia had emptied some trash at 10 pm, as she expected, she saw that her tenant's TV was still on. Nice try, Olivia thought as she realized that the timid woman had simply chickened out on opening herself up to more than a business relationship.

Richards' continued. "Maybe this Mrs. Harmon saw you or heard you moving about last night and can verify that you were here the whole time."

Olivia paused thoughtfully. "I doubt it. Her place is pretty well soundproofed, but I'll ask her." She shivered, wishing she had put on a jacket. The sun, competing with the morning fog that always hugged the coast in early summer, had yet to warm the shadows behind the house.

Richards said he had all he needed and that they should wait in the house while the crew finished securing the crime scene.

Olivia insisted, "This is NOT the crime scene. The crime scene is where he was killed."

Remaining businesslike, Richards informed her that, "The crime scene is also where we find the body, ma'am. I'll let you know when we are done. I have to ask you two not to make any plans to leave town."

Cody turned apoplectic and a flash of red crossed his cheeks, "It's not like that with O, er . . . Miss Granville and me. We don't travel together. Or anything like that."

Richards raised his hand to slow him down. "Mr. White, I wasn't assuming anything scandalous. I just meant please don't leave town. Separately or together."

Chapter Four: The Crime Scene

Olivia slumped into her chair and straightened some papers on her desk, rearranged four Hummel figures she needed to pack up and mail to a client, and opened and closed her MacBook several times like a robot. Then she started drumming her nails on the desk. "This is a disaster. What are we going to do?"

Cody dumped a stack of mail on the floor to clear the only other available seat in the tiny office, a fragile bamboo and pink linen covered slipper chair that Olivia always feared might crumble under Cody's weight. He reached across the desk and held her wrists down. "Stop. You're making me crazy, too."

Cody let go and Olivia dropped her head into her hands. He spoke to the screen of silky hair sliding over her face.

"A disaster? Copy that, Kimosabe. It's raining disaster around here. They tagged my truck as evidence, and I don't know when I'm getting it back."

Olivia sat up and flipped her hair back. The morning had turned Cody's face into a bug-eyed cartoon character scared by a monster. She was asking *him* for advice?

She could hear Richards shouting instructions to the police unit outside, and hoped Mrs. Harmon was snoring through the chaos that had become her backyard. Her backyard? How about her whole life?

"Your truck," she moaned. "Oh, god. There's that, too. Don't get me wrong and think I'm avaricious or anything, but this murder is going to wreak havoc with my sale, to say nothing of the foot traffic I depend on every day. Who's going to slip under that crime tape to come in for a pair of matching parlor chairs or a perfectly wormed oak refectory table? And with the sale of the Louis 16th bedroom set to Mrs. Gotshalk, I thought I was on my way. A word from her dropped at one of her famous parties and I could be set in this town. Now, who will want antiques tainted with a whiff of murder?"

Cody stared at her. It was hard to tell who looked more pathetic. His black tee shirt sagged at the neck and his scuffed leather jacket, torn at the pockets, looked like he had ripped it off a homeless person. Usually, he dressed up a bit more for work, in case he crossed paths with Olivia's clients. But this morning was an unusually early start for him and clearly, he hadn't given his attire a second thought. He tried to man up with a show of confidence.

"Olivia, don't get carried away. Those detectives will have this cleared up in no time. Obviously, who ever did it is connected to Blackman's shop and when they find out who, you're free and clear. You know what they say, any publicity is good publicity as long as they spell the name right."

Olivia raised her arms, a solid imitation of a mother of an adolescent down to her last nerve. "But Cody? Don't you see? He was sent special delivery to me." She thunked her chest with her index finger.

"Why me? I don't even know the man. And I hardly know Blackman's. I took a chance on them repairing the furniture because they were so highly recommended by Sunset Antiques in San Francisco. What could they have against me that they would do something so disgusting? That isn't even the word. So, so monstrous? Don't you get it?"

Cody stayed on the reassuring track. "Look, I'll give Roger at Blackman's a call when we're done here. He schedules the deliveries. He must know something."

But Olivia derailed him, shaking her head wildly. "Cody, no. He might be mixed up in it. Maybe he's the one who stuffed the man in the armoire in the first place. It could be dangerous."

Cody swatted that idea away with a wave of his hand. "That guy? Uh, not to be disrespectful, but we're not talking about Charles Manson here. Roger's good at what he does, but I've known him since high school. Not the sharpest knife in the drawer. He couldn't figure out how to zap a fly with a heat-seeking missile. I betcha by tonight we'll have this all wrapped up, Olivia."

Olivia winced. He called her by name. Not a good sign.

Detective Richards knocked on the back door. He took one look inside, but there was so little space in the office, he asked Olivia and Cody to step outside. Olivia cringed when she saw the trampled flowers and scattered garden accessories in her Garden Center. The police must have overturned every flowerpot, water feature and sculpture.

She was about to insist that Richards put them back where they belonged when he said, "I have to leave now, but it's going to take my crew most of the day to finish their work here. Expect Forensics and the coroner later. I don't have a time for you. Oh, and if you can think of anyone who can corroborate your whereabouts, I'd get on it right away. I'm going to have to ask both of you to come down to the station for your statements later today. Make it two o'clock. You can give me their names when you come in."

He eyed Olivia's outfit, jewelry and designer shoes. He gestured to his flannel jacket. "I'll dress up for the occasion if it will put you at ease Miss Granville."

The hair on her arms prickled. "Do I pay extra for the sarcasm, detective?" Olivia didn't get to be partner in one of LA's most prestigious design firms by playing Miss Mealy Mouth, but he just walked away.

She called out to his back, "Who's going to clean up this mess," but Olivia and Cody watched his car back out of the driveway and turn towards Darling Boulevard without getting an answer. She motioned Cody into the office, out of sight of Johnson and the police officers still securing the yard and the press begging for access.

"Cody, I don't trust this investigation." She nodded towards the back yard. "I mean we're not exactly in the hands of Special Ops. I'm going to have to figure out why I'm involved. Seriously. It's one thing to find out who did this to Mr. Blackman, and another to find out why he was sent to me."

By turns agitated, confused, scared and angry, she paced in front of the screen door, avoiding looking out into the truck.

"This is like something out of a Mafia novel. But I'm just an interior decorator. I know hardly anyone here. Other than pissing off all of Darling Valley by having the temerity to actually move here and set up shop when DV has two perfectly good antique stores, I have no enemies. I need some answers. Maybe it would be a good idea for you to talk to that Robert after all."

Cody turned his ball cap around, just for something to do with his hands. "You mean Roger. Okay, sure, but it's too early for him to be at the shop. If they will even open it today. I don't have a cell number for him, but I know where he usually meets the guys for breakfast before work. A diner near the lake."

Somewhere between Richards' insulting accusations and the sight of her ruined garden, Olivia slipped into action mode. "Okay. Then come back here and we'll have some breakfast ourselves and figure out what to do next."

A plan of action always gave her a sense of control, which was exactly what she needed to think clearly.

Cody gave her a quizzical shrug. "But how am I going to get there without a truck?"

Olivia rooted on her desk for her keys and tossed them to him. "Take the pickup. I parked it across the street last night, because I knew you were coming with the truck and needed access to the backyard. Go over the fence in the back alley and you can sneak around the block. The reporters won't know it's you. Make sure you answer your phone if I call. Cody. Don't freak me out by going all radio silence like you do when you don't want to talk to me, okay? And don't let the police out there see you leaving."

"Sure thing, Olivia."

He used her full name again. It brought home the seriousness of the situation and sent a chunk of ice down Olivia's spine. Through the window she watched him slink along the back of the house to a hole in the fence she hadn't known was there and disappear without anyone noticing.

Chapter Five: Tuesday's Child

"Geez, honey. I knew you wanted a MAD man, but what's up with that special delivery?"

MAD man was Tuesday's term for the ideal guy. Mature, affluent and dependent-free. A practice she preached but rarely practiced. Tuesday was like a sister to Olivia. In addition, she read tea leaves for a living in an upscale café on Melrose and was freakily accurate about her assessments and predictions. Olivia hated to admit it, but she had become a little dependent on Tuesday's advice.

"Listen," Tuesday said after Olivia finished her tale of woe. "I'm like flying up there? Even it this gets fixed this afternoon? And, I'm like sure it will? You need help with the sale."

Tuesday's valley girl lilt relaxed the tension that was making Olivia bite the inside of her cheek and twirl her hair between her fingers like a mad woman. The familiar bubble-headed dialect belied Tuesday's deep heart and soul. Olivia teased, "So is that your professional assessment, that the killer will be found quickly or are you just trying to fill dead air space?"

Tuesday said, "You're breaking up. I can't hear you. I'm looking up Virgin Atlantic flights on my iPad. I'll let you know what time to expect me. And don't worry about feeding me, I'm like on a cleanse?"

Olivia knew what that meant. Wheatgrass juice, smelly herbal concoctions and yoga in front of company, while behind the scenes when no one was looking, copious supermarket chocolate, garbage TV and champs, preferably Veuve Cliquot.

Before she hung up, Tuesday instructed, "Don't worry about picking me up. I'll rent a car."

Olivia didn't push it, though she would have loved a drive through San Francisco to the airport to get her mind off the murder and her other troubles. But Tuesday liked to go first class and would rather rent a Mercedes she couldn't really afford for the weekend than ride in Olivia's practical pickup truck. Olivia's beloved BMW M6 convertible was a distant memory. She'd had to give it up when she decided to exit LA because, as her financial advisor dryly explained, if she wanted this business venture to work, she'd have to resign herself to some unaccustomed belt tightening. Like a used Toyota 4x4 with some rust spots but, engine and transmission-wise, a heart of gold.

Olivia hung up the phone and tried to suppress the regret that dampened her excitement at seeing her friend. She had known Tuesday since they shared an ocean view apartment in Manhattan Beach with three other recent college grads when they all first arrived in LA. Tuesday's was the only friendship that took, beginning with the first night they shared a room. Tuesday had watched Olivia unpack her designer label wardrobe, turned up her nose and said, "Honeybunch. If you want me to go shopping with you next time, I know this great Goodwill shop in Hermosa Beach. We can get you some great threads and you can give this stuff like back to your grandmother?"

No one was more fun or comforting in an emotional storm than Tuesday, exactly what she needed right now. The price tag, though, would be Tuesday's insistence on bringing Brooks back from the dead. If she'd told Tuesday once that she didn't need to be reminded of what an a-hole Brooks had been, she had done it a zillion quadrillion times. Why couldn't Tuesday understand that the mere mention of Brooks' name was a rapier straight into Olivia's heart?

Olivia needed distraction and she turned to the one friend that never let her down: Facebook.

The first post, from a business acquaintance in LA, hit her between the eyes. She immediately slammed the MacBook shut. The woman, a caterer she once used, had shared a headline: *Armoires and Arsenic in Billionaire's Hollow* and the accompanying story from the Huffington Post.

How the frigging frig did it get on the Internet so fast? But of course she knew. The press posse outside her house was filing the stories from their phones as fast as they could hit the send button, even as she sat there, infuriated. But arsenic? The victim was still in her back yard. Where did the cause of death come from? She forced herself to open the computer and read the story. The reporter claimed to have a source inside the DVPD. But the medical examiner hadn't even arrived. Were they making this up?

She pondered what she knew for a moment. Poison was a reasonable assumption since Richards had said there was no blood and gore. But maybe Blackman had a heart attack and somebody panicked and stuffed him in the armoire? No, that didn't make sense. Why not call the paramedics? But it wouldn't be the first time somebody panicked and did something unnecessarily stupid. After all, why was Blackman dead in the first place? She was trying to come up with another scenario for the total disruption of her life when the jangling front door bell brought her back to the present. She looked at the computer. Who could that be this early? It was only a little after seven-thirty. Richards had wasted no time getting out of there.

The French doors were still open and she ran through the showroom calling, "I'm coming, I'm coming." When she opened the door she stared into the smiling face of George Clooney.

Chapter Six: George Clooney Arrives

At least, George Clooney if he dressed like Noel Coward. Behind him she saw a bizarre looking vintage car parked behind the press vehicles across the street. She looked from the running board on the electric blue car to the ascot around pseudo George's neck to his ornamental cane and did a double take. Had she passed through a time machine that transported her back to say, 1935? She half expected the man to break into song and start tap dancing.

But as soon as he said, "Sorry to botha you so oily but I sawr a light," she knew the New Jersey accent was more Soprano thug than elegant leading man.

Oh my god, she thought, too late. Why am I opening the door to strangers? Is he from the mob? Is that what I've gotten myself mixed up in? She asked cautiously, "How can I help you?"

How did he get past the crime scene tape?

After a courteous bow, the man said, "Charles Bacon, ma'am. I need a garage."

A garage? "But, um, I don't have one available. My tenant uses it. I have to park in back of the house myself."

Fake George pointed to the sign outside her front door. Darling Valley Design and Antiques. "Bud ahn't you an ahkateck?" It took her a second to translate. "But aren't you an architect?"

"Yes. Oh, you mean you want me to design one."

The realization all but lifted Olivia three feet off the ground. In the midst of homicidal chaos, was this a balancing act from the universe? A client? One who had braved crime scene tape? Uh oh. She saw one of the cameramen get out of his SUV and hustle up her walkway.

"Please come in," she said, pulling Imposter George into the shop before the guy reached the porch. She led him behind a large secretary, out of sight of the reporter and extended her hand.

"Forgive my manners. I'm Olivia Granville. Come in. I couldn't help noticing your, um, unusual car," she said. "I assume that's why you need a garage?"

The man's face lit up with owner's pride. "It's a Talbot Teardrop. New. That is, new to me. It was built in 1938."

Nineteen-thoity eight. She almost laughed. Did anybody really talk like this in Darling Valley, but he continued.

"They made only seventeen of the cars so it is quite unique. To answer your question, yes and no. I do need a garage for the Talbot. And my one hundred and two other cars in my collection."

Olivia could paste the most, I've-seen-everything-you-can't-surprise-me expression on her face at the mention of a celebrity name. But this news made her jaw drop. "You're serious?"

"Well, I don't want the car museum built all at once. I'd like to discuss the Talbot space wit you and see how it goes from there."

How could a guy dressed in Armani with a zillion dollar car collection get by without an education? *Wit you?* Yet Olivia found his combination of diamonds and rust charming. Despite trying to pass himself off as upper class when he was clearly South Jersey, he exuded a sincerity that warmed his smile.

And then, disheartened, Olivia realized what he meant. A beauty contest. So she'd be competing against one of DV's established shops.

"Now I'm sure I'm interrupting your breakfast and what all," he gestured to the scene outside her front door, "but you were recommended to me by Mrs. Gotshalk."

Now this was encouraging news. "Oh, yes. She's been in the shop," Olivia said casually. She hardly knew the wealthiest woman in town, but yeah, baby. She must have made an impression to get this referral. And somehow, Mr. Bacon had made an impression on her as well. Almost as hard to believe.

Bacon continued to explain his early call. "I was driving by and, as I said, saw the light. I thought you might not mind. I have a busy day and stopped on the spur of the moment like. I'm just here to make an appointment. I'd like to come back at a time when I can discuss my preliminary plans and get your ideas and what not. Do you have time this afternoon?"

No, she didn't have time, not with a date with the police, her nagging to-do list for her big sale, plus get ready for Sabrina Chase's charity auction tonight, but by crankshaft, she would make time. That Talbot car alone had to be worth a hefty slice of a million dollars. This was the client she had been praying for. This was the reason she chose Darling Valley in the first place. But first, she had to bring up the elephant, not only in the room, but crawling all over her property Sherlock Holmes-like.

"Mr. Bacon, I'm sure you've noticed the, um, police presence on my property this morning."

"I didn't pay no mind." Another small bow. "That's your business."

Was this guy for real? Was he used to a police presence?

"Okay, then. Why don't we sit down," she said, ushering him past her most expensive pieces to the red and white Toile wing chairs against the back wall. It was a tactic she used for drop-ins hoping something might catch their eye as they walked by a refectory table reputed to be from Versailles or a partner's desk that could have seen action in Scrooge's office. During the week she had been pushing the furniture in the showroom against the wall in preparation for the sale, but Olivia's eye for the exquisite detail still stood out.

Mr. Bacon stopped to admire one of the two secretaries that bookended the wing chairs, a magnificent late 18th century South German beauty, circa 1800, all parquetry, ormolu and hidden drawers. He checked the price tag, but didn't blanch at the cost, $24,000. His only complaint was that the tag didn't include the region of Germany where it was made.

Olivia said, "It came from Heidelberg."

Bacon replied, "I would have said Munich. No disrespect. Like from one of Mad King Ludvig's castles up in the Bavarian mountains. The color of the walnut and all."

Behind his back Olivia screwed her face into a who is this guy grimace. How does he know from Ludvig's castles? Wouldn't this make a great Facebook post: The time I debated German baroque details with a celebrity look alike mobster while under suspicion of murder."

Bacon said it might work in his study. "I'll think aboud it," he mused, as if making a mental note, then asked if two o'clock would work. Olivia made a show of asking him to wait while she checked her calendar in her office, then came out, assured him two o'clock was fine and walked him to the door. She could not detect a limp. Why the cane? If he's trying to pass as British aristocracy, he must have skipped the elocution lessons.

He reached into his wallet. "Two o'clock then. My card, in case there is an emergency." Emoigency.

She thanked him, and after closing the door, kissed the card and headed back upstairs to make coffee for Cody.

Chapter Seven: The Doctor Is In

A short while later Cody came in the back door beating his head and shoulders, a parody of swatting off a plague of gnats. "Those reporters were eating me alive."

The press people were edging up the driveway, but a female police officer had kept them from following Cody into the yard.

"Aren't they supposed to stay behind the yellow tape? They're getting closer and closer to the back door. Pretty soon they'll be inside."

Olivia sighed. "I know. It's like watch a river rise, waiting for it to flood your house.

He had no news. He never found Roger, so he drove by Blackman's to see what was up there. When he saw the police were all over the place, all eight of them, he didn't stop to gawk. Now he wandered around the office as Olivia plotted their next move.

Olivia saw through the showroom windows the reporters, as if hearing the blast of a starting gun, suddenly turn and run to their respective vehicles, the drivers creating gridlock and swearing at each other as they jockeyed for position to make U-turns in the narrow street and peel off towards downtown. Olivia shrugged her shoulders. "Is there a new find at Blackman's? Are they headed for the police station? Maybe they've arrested the killer."

She led Cody up the stairs to the kitchen. He dropped the Toyota's keys on the island and held up crossed fingers, "We can only hope."

After they finished up a fresh pot of Jamaican Blue Mountain and French toast, Cody cleared the dishes into the sink. Over breakfast they had tried to piece together the crime, possible suspects and motives. But the police were closed mouth and they just didn't have anything to go on. They realized they would just have to live with their impatience and anxiety until they had more information.

"I give up," Olivia said. "Let me drive you home. We're not going to get any work done this morning. She explained to the officer in charge her errand. "I'll be right back," she promised, then dropped Cody off at his parent's house.

"I'll see you at the police department," he said, waving goodbye.

Olivia leaned over to talk through the rolled down passenger window. "Are you sure you don't want me to pick you up?"

"Nah, I can walk from here." Cody set his cap and headed up the walk. "See ya."

Olivia returned home, her head roiling with questions. The first thing she noticed was the coroner's van in the driveway and an unfamiliar Mercedes sports car behind it. She checked the Toyota's clock. Eleven on the dot. Thankfully, the press had not returned. She walked up to the police officer directing traffic in the driveway and listened in on his conversation with a well-dressed man Olivia guessed was the owner of the fancy car. He looked vaguely familiar, but she couldn't place him. Probably someone she passed on Darling Boulevard, small town and all that.

"Sorry, sir. That's out of my jurisdiction. You'll have to call Detective Richards or Johnson to get permission to examine the body."

The officer recognized Olivia and said, "Please step back, ma'am. I'm conducting an interview here."

Olivia retreated several feet, but the men's voices carried. The man was objecting loudly. "But I'm Mr. Blackman's physician. He had a heart condition. From what Detective Richards told his wife, I'm sure he had a heart attack. Let me examine him so I certify that and we can move this along. Make the funeral arrangements. His wife is also my patient. She's just had a brutal shock as it is but the thought of an autopsy is well . . . I had to sedate her when she heard. I'm sure you can understand. C'mon, guys."

Olivia imagined him giving the officer a conspiratorial wink.

"Sir, this is a murder investigation. We have procedures."

"Murder? Oh my god. I wasn't told. I don't believe that." The man looked around and tugged at his hair. "Look officer, I'm a physician. I can declare Mr. Blackman dead and you can fill out your forms. Let's help the widow out here. This is bad enough without making her sit around and wait for the bureaucracy to kick in."

Armoires and Arsenic

The officer put up his hand. "I'm sorry sir. I called it in and we have to follow protocol. The coroner has to rule on suspicious deaths. I'm sure you know that."

Olivia saw the man stamp his foot like a petulant child. "What's suspicious about a heart attack?"

Olivia assumed he hadn't been given all the particulars, the armoire, the ropes. What did he think Blackman was doing at Olivia's house? The man's voice was rising.

"Well, then, I'll just call the ME who is a friend of mine and have her deputize me. You know you don't even have to be an M.D. to be a coroner, so certainly I have the credentials. I won't stand for my patient having to bear any more stress than is necessary when we can settle this right now, right here."

He stepped away and pulled out his cell phone, punched in a number. A moment later he left a message saying, "Amelia, call me as soon as you get this. It's about the Blackman case. I need you to step in. It's urgent. Call me." He gave his number and stuck the phone back in his pocket.

Just then two men came down the driveway steering a gurney with a body bag riding on top. The doctor tried to stop them, then watched, spluttering expletives as they secured Blackman's corpse inside the van and handed a clipboard to the police officer for a signature.

The doctor made one more try. "Stop, stop. I'm a doctor and I'm giving you orders to stay right here until Dr. Hardy calls me."

He pulled out his phone and held it up as if the EMT's didn't know what a call meant. The officer gave the clipboard back to the van driver then turned to the man. "Doctor, you'll have to move your car so the van can get out."

"And if I refuse?"

The officer spread his hands. "Up to you. Obstruction of justice. I'd have to take you in." He rattled his handcuffs hanging from a loop on the side of his pants.

The doctor brushed past Olivia without looking at her, got in his car , backed out of the drive way and drove off in a squeal of rubber. Olivia wasn't sure, but she thought she heard the officer call the man an asshole to his partner. Then he informed Olivia that the victim was being transported to the coroner's office and they would all be leaving.

"Can you take the crime tape with you?"

"No, ma'am. We can't have anyone messing around here. This is still an active crime scene."

Olivia watched the last car drive off and returned to her loft to collect her thoughts. First up, a run to clear her head.

She followed her usual route through the flat streets behind Darling Boulevard, past the smallish Tudors and Victorians, homes on property too small to allow teardowns, unless the buyers bought two homes and rebuilt on double lots. In some cases they'd need three to compete with the larger mansions up in the hills, but so far Darling Valley hadn't approved the zoning for that kind of land grab. She had mixed feelings about that development practice. On one hand it was good for her business if she could snag one of the renovations. On the other, she hated to see historic homes demolished. Some of these buildings dated back to the late 19th century. Not her problem today she decided half an hour later as she rounded the corner and headed for her driveway.

She entered her house by the back door sweaty and red-faced, her phone buzzing with news alerts. The press had identified the victim, variously speculated on the cause of death, positing everything but drowning and disembowelment and listed the location where the body was found. One website confused the name of her shop with Blackman's, calling it Darling Valley Antique Restoration. For once she didn't mind a publicity miscue. Maybe it would tone down unwanted attention. The next alert squashed that when she saw a dated picture of herself with Brooks at an opening in Beverly Hills. For the first time, she had top billing: *Noted Designer Fingered In Billionaire's Death*. Blackman a billionaire? Then why was he running a cabinetry shop? And she'd been fingered? Whatever happened to checking your sources? She stuck her phone deep in her purse as though that would silence it and stripped off her running jersey as she headed for the shower.

She zipped up the Tory Burch tunic and smoothed it over her knife-creased pants just as the shop phone began ringing. By now, the whole town must have read the Internet reports of a murder in Billionaires' Hollow, Wall Street's nickname for the town favored as a retreat for the world's wealthiest. Some called it

Newport West, but that was stretching it. The boutiques on Darling Boulevard rivaled Beverly Hills' finest, but thanks to the Alaska current running down the Pacific west coast, the nearest beach required down jackets and fur-lined boots suitable for the arctic.

Olivia picked up the extension phone. The janitorial company had to cancel their appointment to clean the shop prior to the sale. Something about staff catching a virus. Within fifteen minutes, three of the personal assistants for her best clients called to cancel orders. Best clients meaning the ones who only bought knickknacks and inexpensive occasional pieces. But, somehow, the chairs and tables that had been perfect finds last week would no longer work. Each assistant gave a version of, "So sorry, Olivia. I'm sure you understand."

Oh she understood, all right. The few people who had taken a chance on the newcomer regretted their decisions now that they were doing business with a possible murderer. That brought up another issue. Was Sabrina Chase going to proceed with her charity auction on the heels of losing her business partner? And, if yes, did she still want a donation from Olivia? She dialed her number, but it went into voice mail, so she left a message. Mentally crossing off that task, she turned her attention to her tenant.

Mrs. Harmon would be up by now and Olivia needed to find out if she had heard her knocking about last night or this morning. She locked the French doors into the showroom, a habit to keep customers from wandering into her office, and put a "Back in 10" sign on the front door. But now she could see through the pane windows that CNN and FOX News trucks were setting up their Star Wars equipment across the street. Where had they come from? Were they Johnny come latelys who had gotten stuck in traffic on the narrow mountain road from Highway 101 while the local outlets were nailing down the story, or was something new about to break?

As soon as she opened the door to walk around to the side, two reporters raced up and jammed microphones in her face.

"Is Brooks here, Olivia? Can we have a picture of you two together?"

Olivia slammed the door, locked it from the inside and ran back to her office. Even here in Darling Valley everything was about Brooks. She expected the paparazzi to follow them on their dates in LA when she was his current eye candy. By herself, though, even as a murder suspect, by comparison she was as interesting as a chain link fence. They only saw her as an opportunity to get a shot of Brooks, find out something sleazy about him and do an exclusive. But if they could tie the sensational Brooks Baker, boy wonder, to a murder case, that could make careers. She looked down at her hands. They were shaking. Would she ever get that man out of her life?

She took the inside stairs down to the tiny sliver of basement left after the Cooks had carved out Mrs. Harmon's apartment. Mrs. Harmon's living room door opened onto the driveway, giving her a private entrance and easy access to the garage, another contingency Olivia had to swallow. It was a one car garage with no room on her property to add a space for her truck. However, Mrs. Harmon's kitchen door opened onto the laundry area they both shared, plus a few shelves holding flashlights, Olivia's household supplies and a toolbox. At the end of the narrow corridor, there was a door that led up a few steps to the outside that Mrs. Harmon could use to get to the trash and her corner of the garden out of sight of customers in the Garden Center. Olivia complained about that perk to the Cooks. "I have no private space in my own garden." They suggested she give up her Garden Center, part of her livelihood.

As yet, the press didn't seem aware of Mrs. Harmon's existence. What would the poor woman do when they parked outside her door, forcing her to fight her way to the garage? Olivia tried to be sympathetic to that one.

In answer to Olivia's knock, Mrs. Harmon cracked open her door in a matching peach Charmeuse and lace peignoir and negligee elegant enough for an opera opening. She gave Olivia a cool greeting. Olivia did not assume her tenant hid behind her door because she was embarrassed about her attire; the reclusive Mrs. Harmon always acted as though she were hiding something or someone in her apartment. Olivia could not see much beyond the woman's perfectly coiffed silver hair and that she had yet to apply her signature pale lipstick and navy mascara. Her stately looks always took Olivia's breath away. If Olivia was a Botticelli, Mrs. Harmon was a John Singer Sergeant.

Mrs. Harmon waited for Olivia to announce her intentions. "Mrs. Harmon. I'm sorry to bother you but I'm sure you've seen the commotion in the back drive."

Armoires and Arsenic

The small apartment was half below ground but with many high windows that afforded brilliant morning light and a view of the rear Garden Center and yard.

"I could hardly avoid seeing the police." She spit out this observation as though she were being taxed for each syllable.

At least their feet Olivia thought but didn't say.

"Is there a problem, Miss Granville?" She had so far refused all of Olivia's entreaties to call her by her first name."

"Well, yes, you could say that. It seems a body was crammed into an armoire of mine." Olivia all but gagged on the word body.

"Oh dear. Who is it and how did it get in there?"

"Well, that's part of the problem. I took delivery of a shipment from Blackman's shop. Well, when Cody and I opened the armoire, well . . . " Olivia shuddered. "There he was. Mr. Blackman is the victim. But why and who did it? That's the puzzle."

Was it just Olivia, or wouldn't it have been nicer for Mrs. Harmon to invite her in to sit down for a moment?

Mrs. Harmon fairly sneered at the name Blackman. Her aging vocal chords rasped, "I didn't know you dealt with those unsavory people."

"Unsavory? Why they came very highly recommended," Olivia said, surprise all over her face. Mrs. Harmon had spoken little to her in the few months they had lived in the same building, but she had never said anything negative or backstabbing.

Yet, she certainly wasn't shedding any tears over Mr. Blackman's demise.

"Recommended? Not by anyone I know." The haughty response was a side of Mrs. Harmon Olivia had not seen before. Maybe this little old lady wasn't all sweetness and tea in English china cups after all, as Olivia had assumed from her stately demeanor.

"And who would that be, Mrs. Harmon? The people you know?"

Mrs. Harmon smiled blankly as though she hadn't heard the question, but Olivia didn't believe that for a minute. She knew she was pushing the bounds of privacy in asking who her tenant socialized with, but Olivia's timeline didn't allow for the niceties of waiting until they were BFFs to reveal details of their personal lives. She was on a mission and her own safety was in jeopardy. Someone in town had something on Blackman's. Was her own life in jeopardy? She had to find out who was behind this murder.

Who could have a grudge against Olivia and implicate her in a deadly plot? In her experience, DV didn't like newcomers, though the realtor never told her that as she extolled the virtues of the town when Olivia was on the hunt for property. Would someone do this just for spite?

"Mrs. Harmon, I'll get to the point. The police have asked that I provide a witness to my whereabouts last night and this morning . . . "

Now it was Mrs. Harmon's turn to show surprise. "Did you have something to do with it . . .the murder?"

"Well, of course not. It's merely a formality since the body appeared on my property." Olivia noted how quickly Mrs. Harmon put two and two together and got murder. No slouch she. But why wasn't she shocked or upset? This seemed to merely be an inconvenience for her. An occasion for Olivia to bother her by knocking on her door.

Olivia heard the phone ring in her office upstairs. "Mrs. Harmon, I'll get to the point. Did you by any chance hear anything coming from the showroom or my office or even my loft last night or this morning?"

"No, I can't say that I did. You know my apartment is soundproofed. I can only hear noise coming from upstairs if I am out in the hall, as you are now."

"Yes, that's what I thought. Well, I won't bother you any more. Thank you, but if you think of something, would you let me know?" Olivia gave a little laugh. "My don't I sound like a TV crime show?"

Mrs. Harmon looked puzzled and started to close her door. Olivia said, "Oh, by the way, how was your dinner with your nephew?"

She knew it was a mean shot. She had been downstairs working in her office and showroom last night and would have heard the nephew's car drive up and the brass knocker on Mrs. Nichol's front door announce his arrival.

Mrs. Harmon gave her a cool smile. "We had a lovely time, thank you for asking."

Olivia excused herself and ran back upstairs, but the caller had hung up. She was amused by Mrs. Harmon's answer. Of course she would hide the fact that she had been here by herself last night after lying about meeting her nephew. People, Olivia thought wryly. Would she ever figure them out?

She checked her messages and saw that Detective Richards had called. "Miss Granville," he said curtly on the voicemail, "would you please bring with you a pair of shoes when you come in this afternoon? We are interested in a specific brand, Jimmy Choo. They style number is," and Olivia's mouth dropped when he described the treat she bought for herself upon arriving from LA and suffering her first pangs of homesickness, her last dose of retail therapy. Sling back pumps in a red and yellow striped silk with a two-inch platform. He left no explanation. How he could sound so certain that she owned a pair? Was he stalking her closet?

Olivia stared at the cradle as if it might give a reason for the odd request, or an explanation for Richards' continuing rudeness. He hadn't even said goodbye.

Chapter Eight: Gimme Jimmy Choos

Olivia edged her pickup into one of the three parking spaces in front of the Darling Valley Police Department, located at the unfashionable end of Darling Boulevard, a short strip mall with a dry cleaner, pharmacy and ATM for the bank she used. A moment later, Cody steered a Harley Davidson into the space next to her. She greeted Cody and cocked an eye the machine.

"My brother's," he explained. "But only for the afternoon." He pointed to the Jimmy Choo box under her arm. "What's with the dogs?"

Olivia held the shoes up like a trophy and said, "Got me." She explained that Richards had requested them.

Cody winked at her and said, "Bet he learned the Cinderella move at Scotland Yard. If you don't fess up," now he slipped into Al Pacino in Sea of Love, "you're never gonna see these babies again."

Olivia grinned, gave him a two-fingered upside down V salute with a hip-hop dip, then nodded toward the small parking lot. "They don't do a lot of business, do they? I didn't realize I had something in common with DVPD."

Inside, a chunky female officer in a midnight blue police uniform with a visible fresh coffee stain down her front sat at a desk. On it, an old console computer, a desk phone with a few buttons along the bottom, vintage 1970, and a Coffee and Chatter cup smudged with lipstick were lined up to form a barrier between her and the criminal element of Darling Valley that might burst in through the front door.

Like most businesses in DV, the police did their sleuthing in a renovated and repurposed old home, this one a vintage Edwardian with the original pine floors and small rooms made into offices. Olivia had changed into a sedate LBD and ankle boots that thudded across the wood planks. Before she had time to announce her name, Richards emerged from an office behind the woman's desk.

Olivia couldn't hide her amazement when she saw that he had changed into a tailored suit and tie, probably with Milan labels. He was serious about dressing up for the occasion. His shoes needed a shine, however, but she chalked that up to the hazards of stumbling around crime scenes.

He nodded to each of them. "Miss Granville. Mr. White. Thanks for being on time. Miss Granville, if you'd like to come into my office," he gestured to the open door behind him, "And Mr. White, Detective Johnson will see you."

Cody joked, "Uh oh, O. They're separating us to see if our alibis match," but Richards didn't crack a smile. Instead, he pointed to the shoebox.

"I see you brought your shoes, Miss Granville. Would you mind leaving them with Officer Ridley?" He indicated the woman in the badly fitting uniform at the desk.

Olivia stared at him horrified. He answered the question on her face. "Don't worry, you'll get a receipt if we need to retain them."

"Retain my shoes? What is this, the Keystone Kops?" She meant it as a joke to break the ice, but Richards scowled.

"I assure you, Miss Granville. There is a reason for everything we do. Just part of our investigation."

Olivia put the box on the officer's desk and raised her hands in a show of peace. "Whatever you say, detective." Did he have magnetic fields in those dark eyes? She couldn't stop staring at them.

Richards, however, had no trouble breaking his gaze. He walked over to a closed door adjacent to his office, knocked, opened it and in a low voice said, "They're here."

Detective Johnson came out with one arm trying to find the opening to his suit jacket sleeve and the other sleeve flapping behind him. Without much chat, he nodded to Olivia, finished dressing himself, hiked his slacks under his belly, and ushered Cody into his office.

Richards led Olivia into what she guessed was once an old English-style snug gone horribly wrong. The coal fireplace hadn't produced any warmth in probably half a century, and instead of the porcelain dogs that were fashionable when the house was built, files and books teetered on the mantel. The designer in Olivia cringed at the white Formica IKEA desk taking up most of the small room. She wondered if she should suggest that the Darling Valley Police Department invest in the Tudor settee she acquired just before she left LA. And then she had that cherry partners desk that was a little large for the room, but if she moved the file cabinet . . .

Richards interrupted her design reverie and offered her one of the two swivel chairs in front of the desk, also vintage IKEA. Then he closed the blinds on the window that had been carved into the wall between his office and the anteroom where Ridley sat. This gave him a view of the front door. She settled herself and started to drop her purse onto the floor next to her, but one look at the grit and another at her $2,500 Prada bag and she plopped it onto the vacant chair. Richards didn't so much as dispense with pleasantries as completely ignore them.

"Miss Granville, tell me about your relationship with Mr. Blackman, the deceased." He sat ramrod straight, making no attempt to lean in and warm up the space between them.

"I didn't know him." Since that was the way he wanted it, Olivia leaned back, creating even more distance, marking her territory with a disinterested smirk.

Richards snapped, "How can that be? You did business with him."

Her cell phone rang. She ignored Richards' dark look and reached into her bag. It was Tuesday. Considering the seriousness of the meeting, she should let it go into voicemail, but instead, she held up her finger for Richards to give her a minute and said effusively, "Tuesday! Babe! Don't tell me you're here already. Oh, you're on the runway about to take off."

She enjoyed the annoyance on Richards' face.

"Three-forty five? Perfect. The Veuve Cliquot is chilling, girlfriend. What are you wearing? Oh, I've got to see that! I'm rocking Tory Burch. I was going with Stella first, what? Oh you don't want to hear about Stella. You've got to get over that, girlfriend."

She decided she had pushed Richards' buttons enough, said, "See ya! Safe trip, doll," hung up and without turning off her phone, dropped it back into her purse.

It wasn't hard to figure out that Richards was biting his tongue and forcing himself to be polite. "Perhaps you'd like to turn off your phone for a few minutes, Miss Granville?" He clipped his words like they were ice chips.

"Am I under arrest?" Olivia was not usually combative, but she wanted Richards to know she had done nothing wrong and was not intimidated by him.

"Of course you're not," he answered impatiently.

"Well then, I have a business to run, and my phone is my lifeline. Especially since your, um, people have made a mess of my grounds and scared off customers with that ugly tape."

She didn't add that there was slim chance any customers would be calling with new business, anyway, but he didn't need to know that.

Richards gave her a longsuffering sigh. "Very well. Miss Granville, can you explain how you can do business with someone in this small town and not know them?"

"Mr. Blackman? I knew of him, certainly, but he was always out of town or otherwise unavailable the few times I visited the shop, so I never actually met him. I communicated with Sabrina Chance, his partner. I'd only begun dealing with Blackman's on this order."

Richards looked thoughtful. "This order. Yes. Tell me about this order. What was the nature of the transaction?"

Olivia loved talking about her business even, it seemed, under these circumstances. "Well, my business is selling antiques and doing renovations and interiors for my clients. I have an inventory of furniture that I brought up with me from LA."

Richards interrupted. "And what exactly brought you to Darling?"

His question sounded like an accusation rather than the standard icebreaker Olivia was used to hearing from shopkeepers, new clients, attendees at the few charity events she to which she had been invited since her arrival. The occasional neighbor who condescended to speak to her.

"I, I, . . ." Olivia was a master at small talk, a requirement in her business. But suddenly this detective was turning her brain into jelly. The grim atmosphere and the officer sitting at the front desk hammered home the reality that she was being interrogated about a murder. Was she really discussing murder? That was one of the things she assumed she had said goodbye to when she left LA for bucolic Darling Valley. Somebody in this town was guilty of false advertising.

She took a breath and composed herself, yet she was evasive, not wanting to mention being left at the altar by Brooks.

"I worked in a similar business in LA for a number of years. Actually, I was a partner at my firm. But LA is very cut throat. I felt it was time for a change. I wanted a slower pace. You live here; surely you understand the appeal."

To herself, Olivia snarled, LA is a meditation center compared to what you have going on in Darling.

Richards ramped up the hostility. "I don't live in Darling, Miss Granville. My job doesn't call for gazing out over the lake."

Olivia didn't know how to respond. Was that somehow her fault? Was he referring to having to live in Marin City, the working class community just north of the Golden Gate Bridge? Most of the people who worked in DV couldn't afford to live there and Marin City still had reasonable rents and housing prices. It wasn't so much what he said but the way he said it that sounded like she should apologize for the opportunity to reside and pay impossibly high property taxes in this idyllic town. She bristled at the suggestion that she was somehow privileged. She had invested her life savings into establishing herself here, a boon to Darling's economy. And so far, Darling wasn't showing her any love.

"Anyway, I moved to DV several months ago and I'm just getting established. I acquired some new pieces recently at an estate auction in Seacliff in San Francisco and they needed some restoration work. I had a team to do this for me in LA, but up here I needed to find a new shop. A friend in the city recommended Blackman's to me. There were four pieces, no five, that we, Cody and I dropped off two weeks ago. The doors on the armoire needed fixing, the side tables needed refinishing and the bergère chairs needed upholstering. I supplied the fabric, a heavy damask that matched the period perfectly."

"The what chairs?" Richards said, raising his eyebrows in a question.

Instantly, Olivia realized she was giving him TMI, a habit of hers whenever interiors were involved.

"Bergère, Detective. It's a wood and fabric chair and the legs were also nicked. Actually, I've been on pins and needles waiting to see the quality of the work. Sometimes the shops with the best reputations can make a mess of things. I still haven't had a chance to inspect the rest of the order. And as for the armoire, that's going to need more work after struggling with those doors."

Richards was unsympathetic. "How well do you know the people at Blackman's," he asked with an edge in his voice. "Apart from Mr. Blackman."

"Well, I've spoken with Sabrina Chance a few times. She invited me to a fundraiser soon after I moved here. As if her exorbitant prices weren't enough. It was for a fund to repair the grounds around the lake."

"I remember," Richards said. "My department provided security."

"Did that include keeping an eye on the gropers going after the cute servers?"

If Olivia had had any illusions about the propriety of the philanthropists and venture capitalists of Darling, she saw they had just as much trouble keeping their hands in their pockets as did the movie moguls in LA.

Richards didn't reply. Was this a test of some sort, or was there a virus in Darling Valley that made people hostile and antagonistic to newcomers?

"You were telling me about Ms. Chance.

A vision of Sabrina came back to her. The little Chloe number that was sumptuous even by LA standards, the House of Graff baubles hanging from her ears. Olivia had assumed the furniture refinishing was a hobby. The shop, even with its astronomical prices, wouldn't keep her in Christian Louboutins for very long. She didn't wear a wedding ring, so Olivia guessed there was a nice alimony settlement in her past.

"Sabrina introduced me to a number of her clients and we had a drink together at the party but that was it. I was left on my own after that. I chatted with a few people . . . in fact I met Mrs. Blackman there and we said little more than hello. It was so fleeting, I doubt she'd even remember me."

Olivia paused to reflect on the widow.

"Poor woman. Anyway, I told her that I knew her by reputation and that Sunset Antiques in the city had referred me to her. Mr. Blackman wasn't there. I think she introduced me to a doctor or somebody."

She paused. That was who showed up at the house wanting to examine the body. The doctor at the auction.

"Then I found Sabrina and thanked her for the invitation before I left. She thanked me back for coming and made sure I had filled out my pledge card. Since then, Sabrina and I have had a few business chats, run into each other at some local events. In fact, I'm supposed to deliver a donation for an auction she's running tomorrow night. Though I bet, after all this, she'll cancel, or have someone take her place. I certainly would."

Olivia shuddered at the thought of having to put on a brave face after a death, something she had to do when her grandmother died.

"And Mr. White? Tell me about your relationship with him."

Olivia could not repress a smile. "Cody is my life saver."

"Oh, how so?" Richards made a note on a pad at his elbow.

"He showed up on my doorstep the weekend I moved my inventory into the showroom. The movers had dumped everything in the middle of the floor or out back. It was threatening to rain. I knew very few people and didn't know where to get help in a hurry. I had assumed the movers would do more or I would have arranged helpers beforehand. They had to get the truck back or something."

Olivia could tell Richards wanted to give her the wrap it up sign. She didn't care and gave as much useless detail as she could, just because she could.

"Cody said he had been watching the renovation of the house and word was out that I was putting in a shop. He asked if I needed help. He needed a job. He's worked for me ever since. I couldn't do without him."

"I see. And what do you know about his personal life. What does he do when he isn't moving armories for you?"

She repeated, "Armoires, detective. Well, I know he has lived here most of his life. Went to high school in Darling and Junior College in San Rafael. What is it they say these days, he's considering his options. He likes to party like anyone his age, but he comes through on every project I give him."

"Like picking up dead bodies."

Olivia bristled. "Detective Richards, we had nothing to do with what happened to that man."

"Miss Granville, run through your morning for me, up to the time the body was discovered. Just one more time."

Olivia rolled her eyes, deliberately sending a signal of annoyance across the desk. "Well, like I told you this morning. I got up about five, showered, made coffee and went downstairs to my office to get a head start on the mountain of paper on my desk before I got dressed for the day. That is my usual routine. I stayed busy with paperwork until Cody arrived. It never ends, paperwork."

She noticed a slight tightening around Richards' mouth, as if acknowledging that he, too, was intimate with the scourge of paperwork. Then an image of the armoire crossed Olivia's field of vision. How could she possibly stand to have that in the shop again, tainted as it was with death? In a snap, what little patience she had reached its expiration date. "Detective, your investigation is having a negative impact on my life."

"If you'll excuse me, Miss Granville, but I think the person who experienced the negative impact was Mr. Blackman."

Olivia blushed, realizing how bratty she sounded. "Yes, I understand that. And I'm terribly sorry about that. Especially when I think about his poor widow. How is she, do you know? Oh, we both know how she is. Devastated. But nevertheless, I think I am owed some answers. You have taken over my property so that I can't conduct business. I have advertised a sale this weekend for which I must get back to my shop and organize. Plus, you have a $30,000 piece of furniture that belongs to me."

It was Richards' turn to drop his jaw. "Are you kidding me?"

"I have valuable inventory, Detective. You know the people who live here. They want the best. I am able to give it to them. That is, if you would let me conduct my business."

Richards threw his Bic on top of his yellow pad. "I'm sorry, but we can't release the chest until the crime lab is finished with it. And probably not even then. It is evidence in a murder case."

He looked at Olivia's shocked face and apologized. "I'm sorry but that's the way it is. It's out of my hands. Let's move on, shall we? Now what was Mr. White's relationship with the deceased?"

"Well, it was not something we ever discussed. I know he went to school with Mr. Blackman's children, though I'm not sure if they were in the same year. Cody is very sociable. He knows everyone in town."

"And what time did you first see him this morning?"

"About ten minutes after seven. He was supposed to show up at six. In fact, I never asked him why he was late, but that's Cody. Gets the job done, but on his schedule sometimes. He drove up, I helped him unload the truck, and we found, well, you know what we found."

Armoires and Arsenic

Richards made another note then scowled at her. "You're sure you didn't make an early morning trip to Blackman's to help him load that chest in the truck? Or help Cody stuff it with Mr. Blackman's body?"

Olivia all but levitated out of her seat. "Are you kidding me? You're accusing Cody and me? Detective, I'm going to sue you for defamation of character. I've never heard of such a thing. Why would I load a dead man into an armoire and drive him back to my place. Wouldn't I dump him in the lake or something if I did it?"

"Good story to take suspicion off you. Why would you have done it and then put the body in your own furniture? A ruse? Unless something happened on the way to the lake and you had to improvise? You'd be surprised at the stories guilty people come up with to avoid suspicion."

Olivia just stared at Richards, not knowing how to answer. How could eyes that sexy turn so hard? Finally she said, "But I'm not guilty."

Richards persisted. "Who was with Mr. White? How do we know he didn't act alone, put the body into your chest and deliver it and act all innocent and I don't know how it got there?"

If the situation were not so dire, Olivia would have laughed at Richards' tuneless imitation of a young, clueless kid.

"Okay, Miss Granville. I think I have enough for now. I can let you get back to work with the caveat that you not leave town, at least not without letting me know."

"Yes, you've already told me that."

Richards nodded and gave her a cold smile. "Call any time if you think of anything that might help us. Oh, and by the way. Was your tenant any help in giving you an alibi for your whereabouts last night and this morning?"

Olivia had an odd feeling of dread at the mention of Mrs. Harmon that she couldn't identify. "No, as I said, her unit is soundproofed. She heard nothing." A body in her armoire, a liar in her house. What was next?

"Well, that will be all. Thanks for your time, Miss Granville. You can go now."

"Um, my Jimmy Choos?"

"Your what?"

Didn't this guy know anything? After all, there was a Shoe Candy on Darling Boulevard. "My shoes. And how did you know I owned a pair? Or are they part of the Darling Valley uniform? Jimmy Choos and prison blues?"

Richards didn't respond, just said, "I'll call you later and give you the status."

Olivia grabbed her purse and stood up. "What do you mean by the status? What could you possibly want with my shoes?"

She thought she saw a faint smile crack through his police demeanor, but he didn't answer.

"And one more thing. How come," she held up her fingers for an air quote, "armoires and arsenic is all over the internet? With the name of my shop attached? While the body is still in my back yard?"

Richards scratched his stubble and Olivia wondered what he had been doing last night that he hadn't shaved this morning. "First of all," he explained, "the case is still under investigation. We are pursuing several leads.

"Second of all, as I'm sure you know, the press will print anything that will attract readers, whether or not it has any bearing on the facts. That guy that showed up when we were investigating had a lookiloo into the truck and put up a post that said it was arsenic because there was no blood. A fair guess, but only a guess."

Olivia said, "Oh, so it wasn't arsenic that poisoned Mr. Blackman, is that what you're saying?"

Richards answered, "I'm not saying anything. We don't have the autopsy and tox reports back from the coroner yet. Let me walk you out," he said, standing up and pushing his chair back with his legs, abruptly ending the interview.

"I think I'll wait here until Cody is finished if you don't mind."

"Hmmm. Not a good idea. Mr. White is going to be awhile."

Olivia looked up at the ceiling in disgust before she leveled a steely gaze at Richards. "Surely you don't really think Cody had anything to do with this. What possible reason could he have for killing anybody, much less one of my vendors?"

"Miss Granville, would it surprise you to know that the DVPD responded to a call at Blackman's about six months ago? Mr. Blackman called because Mr. White was threatening him. Then he decided not to file charges. Do you know anything about that?"

Olivia had to sit back down in her chair. "I beg your pardon? No. I find that hard to believe. Cody is a very peace-loving guy. He crumbles if I have to call him on anything. He hates conflict. And sometimes when things get rushed in my shop, I can provoke conflict."

Richards said, "Yeah, I bet you can."

Olivia ignored him. "He always backs down and apologizes even when I'm being unreasonable. I find that hard to believe. That he would threaten anyone."

"Blackman claimed he was harassing his daughter, Jessica."

Olivia immediately jumped to Cody's defense. "How do you know Blackman was telling the truth? It doesn't sound like the Cody I know."

Richards was obviously a master at deflecting questions he had no intention of answering. He walked around his desk and extended his hand. She was still sitting trying to absorb the news about Cody.

"Thanks for your time, Miss Granville. Once we get all the forensics, we may need to talk to you again. I'll let you know. You can get back to work now."

He snapped his fingers, remembering something, then went back to his desk, opened the middle drawer and shuffled things around. "I know I have a card in here someplace. Oh here." He handed Olivia a dog-eared business card.

"Call any time if you think of anything that might help us."

Almost the exact same words she had said to Mrs. Harmon. Olivia took the card and stuck it in her purse in a daze. The news about Cody had her heart racing. But she was not so out of it that she didn't notice that when Richards shook her hand, he held on to it for a beat, and then let it go slowly. When she stood up again, he walked her out to the waiting room. She felt Officer Ridley's eyes on her back.

"Thank you, Detective," she said, then opened the door and walked into the bright morning sunshine, though there was nothing that transpired in his office for which she was grateful.

Chapter Nine: Paymoors

On the way home, Olivia stopped at Graymoor's market, which locals called Paymoor's because of the high prices for its organic, free range, artisan and imported foodstuffs. Olivia knew the markup on many of these items. In LA, she had pushed a line of caviar, imported olive oil and fruit vinegars from France. Tuesday'd said she could retire on the profits as long as people equated imported and expensive with will this make my butt look important.

Olivia paused at the display of oysters and prawns in the seafood department, trying to decide if she wanted to bother shucking oysters after the agony of this day. Tuesday may say she's on a cleanse, but if Olivia didn't stock up on their favorite goodies, she'd have a grumpy friend to take care of in addition to everything else she had going on.

Behind her, Olivia heard, "Having a party, Olivia?"

She turned around and almost ran down Marcia Smart with her shopping cart. Marcia was Mrs. Blackman's personal assistant.

Olivia could hardly speak. What was the protocol? Should she offer condolences? Marcia was not related to the deceased. Should she apologize for Mr. Blackman showing up dead in her armoire? Olivia hadn't done anything wrong. In fact, it seemed to her, as she struggled to answer Marcia's question, that nobody realized that she, Olivia, was due an apology. How had the restoration business allowed this to happen, and why had they involved her?

She knew why Marcia was ridiculing her. Buying luxury food while she was suspected of murdering her employer's husband? Should she apologize to Marcia? She didn't really know the woman. She had come in once when Olivia first opened her shop to check out the new girl in town. Olivia had neutral feelings about her, other than she had abysmal taste in clothes. Who under seventy wore polyester pants with an elastic waistband these days? Apparently 40-somethings in Darling. Personal assistants in LA were chosen because their drab looks made their employers look good. But if they dressed the way Marcia did, they'd get fired. There were standards, after all.

Marcia worked for Mrs. Blackman, though the widow was not connected to the shop. Cody had explained that the business belonged to her husband and Sabrina Chance. Could Marcia be mixed up in this, maybe have some grudge against her employer's husband? She made a note to ask Cody about her. If she ever got to see him again. Olivia stared around the store, feeling as though she were being stalked. The killer could be anywhere. Was he also shopping for upscale foodstuffs?

Marcia took the lead in breaking the awkward silence. "I ran into Mrs. Harmon at dinner last night and we chatted a bit. Little did we know what would turn up on her doorstep in just a few hours."

Olivia spluttered. "At dinner? Oh, so she did go out with her nephew, after all. Usually I can hear her leaving and entering her apartment. Not that I snoop, it's just we live in such close proximity. I thought she had stayed home."

Olivia felt relieved. An unexpected visit from a relative was a perfectly good excuse for cancelling a dinner date. Far better than being snubbed, as she had assumed.

Marcia pushed her glasses up on her nose and said, "Nephew? How could Mrs. Harmon have a nephew? She has no siblings."

Olivia was not only flustered, she was embarrassed. She hated to look stupid and this mix-up made her look decidedly stupid. Mrs. Harmon was her tenant after all. How could she not know some basic details about her life? To close the awkward silence, Olivia said, "I must have misunderstood."

Marcia said, "Hmmm," in a highly suspicious tone.

But Olivia had not misunderstood. There was nothing wrong with her hearing or her memory. Mrs. Harmon had knocked on the back door yesterday afternoon where Olivia was toiling in her office and said, "I'm so sorry. My nephew is in town from Boston and has invited me for dinner."

What could be clearer than that? And it couldn't be that Mrs. Harmon was dotty. Yes, she was seventy-four, which Olivia learned from the previous owner of the house by way of explaining why they insisted her tenancy not be changed. "At her age, where would she go? She's a dear to us and we can't have her uprooted."

But Mrs. Harmon was an example of seventy being the new twenty-five. She never stumbled over her words or repeated herself and on sunny days she did yoga in the back garden with an agility that made Olivia jealous. And elastic waistbands? Never. One reason Olivia was eager to get to know her was to perhaps get a look into her closet, which had to rival her own.

No, Mrs. Harmon had been clear about why she was asking Olivia for a rain check.

Marcia said, "I'll be curious, of course, to find out who did this. Mrs. Blackman is beyond consoling. Her physician has her medicated."

"Well, of course, she was the first person I thought of when I discovered who it was. The body I mean. Please give her my condolences, if that's all right. I mean she may not want to be reminded of me, and the place . . . er the circumstances." This conversation was getting very hard to navigate.

Marcia said, "I'll tell her if it seems appropriate," and then wheeled her cart towards the meat department.

Then, unexpectedly, Marcia turned to her and said, "Oh, by the way. Mrs. Harmon was having dinner with the Blackmans' daughter. Maybe they were talking about her divorce," and then Marcia pushed off leaving Olivia open-mouthed and still undecided about the oysters. Jessica was getting a divorce? Jessica was married?

By the time Olivia made it to the checkout counter with enough high priced convenience foods, take out and champagne to last through the weekend, no less than six DV residents had stopped to chat with her. Women who openly snubbed her were suddenly intensely interested in how the business was going, how the renovations were coming along or suggested that they were way overdue for lunch or tea at the

Redmond, the inn that boasted an afternoon tea service to rival the Ritz in San Francisco.

Two men openly hit on her, but she tossed their business cards in the trashcan in the produce department. As she waited in line with her debit card in her hand, she said under her breath that if all it took was a murder to warm DV up to her, she would have knocked off that icy neighbor across the street when she first unpacked.

Before pulling out of the parking lot, she checked her phone. The New York Times texted an update that odds were that strychnine had killed Blackman and Tuesday texted *Chill the champs!!!!!!* She had landed and was heading to Hertz to pick up her Mercedes.

A slight smile broke the grim line of Olivia's mouth. There was nothing more appealing right now than a glass of champagne with Tuesday, especially when she got home and found the card of Mr. Black, the garage man, stuck in her front door. "Did I make a mistake? 2 pm, right?"

She looked at her watch and let loose with many expletives. Three-thirty. How could she have forgotten their appointment? Inside, she checked her office voicemail. Sabrina called back to say that, of course, she wanted a donation and reminded Olivia that the auction was tomorrow night, not tonight. She wasn't going to penalize her charity over this tragedy. And did Olivia know why Detective Richards wanted her Jimmy Choo shoes? Olivia apologized into the phone for messing up the date. Her excuse-- too much fareekin crime news for one day.

Chapter Ten: A Vision of Tuesday

Tuesday was a vision in black and white. Stripes, polka dots, zebras, plaids and a 1968 hallucinogenic geometric nightmare adorned her blouse, sweater, skirt, petticoat, scarves, shawls and Paris-themed apron. Each floaty and fighting for attention.

"Apron?" Olivia said when she ran down the walk to jump on her friend. "Who wears aprons anymore? Even to cook?"

Tuesday howled. "You know me. I love Paris," she sang, twirling like a whirling dervish as she showed off her outfit.

It wasn't until after the marathon hug and many cheek and air kisses that Olivia noticed the pink hair. But that wasn't a surprise. Tuesday rainbowed her locks regularly. It had been a purple Mohawk when they'd kissed goodbye.

"Come in, come in," Olivia said, grabbing some of Tuesday's luggage, enough for a six-month getaway to Europe.

Tuesday made the appropriate cooing noises about the beautiful space and extravagant pieces for sale. Her first act was to head to the kitchen with a carryon and line up a new age pharmacy worth of herbs, teas, plus various remedies and cleanses. She said what Olivia already knew, "I can't go anywhere without my stash."

Later, on the white couch that Tuesday claimed because it was the perfect backdrop for her two-toned look, she drained her first glass of champs, held it out to Olivia for a refill and said, "So? Details please?"

Olivia obliged her with the Veuve Cliquot and said, "Tues, if I knew the answer to your questions, I'd take over Detective Richards' job. I don't know, I don't know, and, let's see. There's one more thing. Oh, yes. I don't know."

That took care of Tuesday's bugging her about who killed Mr. Blackman, why and what on earth was he doing in your armoire, girl child?

Olivia leaned back in her leather club chair and shrugged her shoulders. "Can I make you some tea so you'll tell me?"

"I'm off duty, Devil Diva, at least for today." Olivia grinned and cut a diva-ish pose. She loved the affectionate names Tuesday called her. Once she accused her, "You call me sweet buns and babykins because you can't remember my name."

Right now, Tuesday had her attention no matter what she called her.

"You don't have to be clairvoyant to know you had better do some sleuthing of your own to find out why this detective dude is after your hide. And what does he have on Cody? An argument six months ago? What's that about? Does he think Cody is carrying a grudge? And what do the Blackman's have against you?"

Olivia put up her hand to stop the rush of Tuesday's questions. "If I knew, don't you think I'd give you an exclusive?"

Armoires and Arsenic

Tuesday frowned, her pink Afro dipping over her forehead. "What I don't understand is why poison the guy? I mean, if they were trying to cover it up to make it look like a death from natural causes? I mean, why else would you use poison? And like, with forensics these days? Don't they like watch CSI? Who even does poison anymore? So why stuff him in the armoire and tie it up so it is obviously a murder? I mean, what's up with that, Ollie Mollie?"

Olivia gave her a wide-eyed are you kidding me look. "You're asking me to get into the mind of a killer? I don't even step on ants."

Tuesday gave her a two thumbs up. "And that's why you're my girl."

Olivia bowed her head in thanks, then continued. "And another thing. Strychnine? Isn't that easily detectable? I know arsenic is cumulative. You have to give many doses over time, right Tues?"

Tuesday guffawed. "Like I should know? Do I look like Lucretia Borgia? Hmm, come to think of it, I wouldn't mind glamming it up with some jewels and velvet. But later for that. Seriously, why are you under suspicion? I don't get it."

Olivia threw up her hands in frustration. "Tuesday, come on. That's why I need you. Can't you give me a hint? Can't you feel some vibrations or what ever it is you feel? Seriously. I'll make some tea. We have to figure this out and get Cody out of jail and . . . ."

Olivia leaned over and picked up the tray of triple crème cheeses and seed crackers to tempt her friend. With a mouthful of St. Andre, Tuesday said, "Wait a minute. I thought he was just being questioned."

She leaned over to let the cracker crumbs fall from her mouth to her plate before continuing. "That's not the same thing as being in jail." She wiped her mouth with an ivory cocktail napkin that had DVD&A in a circle around Olivia's logo, an ornate Greek plinth.

Olivia still couldn't eat, though Tuesday's arrival both calmed her anxieties and lifted her spirits. She hadn't mentioned Brooks yet. But a hole had opened up in her center that wouldn't close and wouldn't accept food. In this abyss, all the unknowns of life yawned before her. Life, death, the misery of uncertainty and insecurity. What had happened to the sense of adventure and freedom, of limitless possibility that had swept her from LA to Darling Valley? It wasn't just to get away from Brooks. She'd also been exhilarated at the prospect of a new life, new challenges. Now it all seemed like a huge mistake. She punched the pillows on her couch and fussed with them until they looked camera ready. The futzing calmed her a bit, as it always did. She was born to make spaces beautiful. Her grandmother said so. The bit of pillow primping helped her climb back into herself, up from that ugly pit of despair. She answered Tuesday.

"Jail. Questioning. Whatever. He's still in the hands of the police department and I've got to get my life back on track. If I don't sell enough pieces over the weekend, I'm in serious trouble with the bank or whoever really owns this place. I can't afford to have crime tape on my front lawn and suspicions floating around that I am involved in a murder. I'm so rattled, I can't think. Help me out, here."

Olivia got up and turned on the gas fireplace to take the chill off the evening wind whipping around the windows and seeping into the room. In an instant, blue and purple flames threw warmth across the room. Olivia emptied the last of the champagne into their glasses. As was their habit, the hostess kissed the bottle goodbye. Olivia upended it into the ice bucket and said, "I have a buttery Chardonnay for dinner." Then she hinted, "But I can always make tea."

Tuesday put her glass down on the coffee table. "Sweetie, if you want to know if your man is cheating on you, well I'm your fortune teller . . . and don't forget, I told you not to go to that dinner party."

"Tuesday! It was a week after the breakup! How did I know he'd be there with a new girlfriend? After a friggin WEEK?"

She slumped back. This always happened with Tuesday. The pain she had worked so hard to deaden with a new business and new life came flooding back as soon as she hinted at his name. "After what happened?" she said into her hands.

Tuesday waved her arms. "Back on topic. Back on topic. This is about me, remember?"

Olivia lifted her head and Tuesday said, "I don't do crime. It gives me the willies. I don't even want to know the answers. What we do know is that you didn't do anything wrong and this town has what, twelve people tops? How hard can it be to figure out who did this?

She unwrapped a zebra print scarf from her waist and tied it around her hair. Up on her haunches, she checked herself in the gilt mirror over the mantel. She looked at Olivia. "The world is watching. African princess with a bad hair day?"

Olivia gave her the once over and laughed, ready for some comic relief. "Hmm. Could be early Diana Ross. Nah, you've nailed it."

Tuesday sank back down on the cushy sofa and grinned, "Exactly the look I was after," then turned serious. "Give me a list of the suspects."

"Suspects? How would I know? Well, of course, as far as Richards is concerned, there's me. And Cody."

Tuesday stretched out and put her feet up on the coffee table. "No, seriously. Who do you know connected to Blackman's business and why would they want to kill him? Let's look at Cody. I know you think he's a sweetie, but what do you really know about him? You've told me yourself that he can be unreliable and now we know he lies. He never told you about the police call."

Olivia came to his defense. "That wasn't a lie. He just didn't reveal some personal information."

"I'll say. Nor that he was into Blackman's daughter."

"Well, he's private. In a funny way."

She and Cody had a lot in common. They both had a past that was still very present. Cody had never come straight out and admitted it, but whenever he referred to his friend, Jessica – were all females born in the 1990's named Jessica—she recognized the signs of a torch carried too long, the singeing around the eyes that usually shone like the sun, the faint sigh and quick turn away to finish a chore, or take a swig of coffee to avoid explaining what happened to them. After one or two tries to get him to open up, she let the subject of Jessica go until Cody brought it up, which he probably did more than he realized.

She looked over at Tuesday. "You can't get real serious with Cody. He makes a joke out of everything. Wait till you meet him. You'll know in a minute he couldn't have done this."

Tuesday was hesitant with her next question. But after a pause, asked, "So why was he an hour late?"

"Tues, he's twenty, twenty-one soon. You remember what that age is like. Your mission in life is to sleep as late in the morning as possible."

Olivia telegraphed her discomfort with Tuesday's grilling. She kept her arms in a death grip across her chest, and that tight line for a mouth was back. But none of it stopped Tuesday. "A tendency to violence is no joke, hon. An hour is plenty of time to send someone to the great beyond and tie him up in a chest."

This made Olivia so uncomfortable she had to stand up and walk around the room. "I don't believe he did it. I swear, Cody is pumped up with muscles, but it's amazing how well he can stand without a backbone. If there was an altercation, my money is on Blackman starting it."

Tuesday took over. "I've never met the guy, but how well can you know him in four months? I'd sure love to see that police report. Is that in the public record?"

"I don't need to read a police report. I just know when somebody is being straight with me. And I don't need tea leaves to tell me." Olivia took the last sip of her champagne. It wasn't having its usual calming effect.

"Oh. Like with Brooks? You had his number all right, didn't you?"

"Tuesday, that's cruel."

The conversation was becoming a drag on her heart, pulling her back to the past, to all the things she was trying to forget, her partnership in a prestigious firm, her open-ended bank account, her engagement to Brooks, all the things that once said the world was her oyster.

Tuesday sat forward and put her hand on Olivia's knee. "I'm just sayin, sweetie. Love is blind. Even the platonic kind. And I know how hard this has to be on you. You feel things deeply. After all, you're a Cancer." She threw out her arms. "That explains the decorating, the domesticity. You need home. It's why Brooks is so hard for you."

Olivia signaled stop. "Please. Don't go there."

Tuesday backed down. "Okay, okay."

There was a pause while they both took a breath, then Tuesday said, "Um, I know it isn't my business, but it is platonic, isn't it? I mean if you two have a situation going, more power to you, but if you do the down and dirty . . . ."

Olivia did an exaggerated cringe. "With Cody? Ugh. We don't. He's like my little brother. Even the thought of it gives me the creeps."

"I'm just saying, you don't want to give Richards anything that smells like a conspiracy. Cougar covering up for her boy toy. Or, could you be in it together? Revenge for Blackman killing the relationship with his daughter and you coming to his defense?"

Olivia pulled herself back from Tuesday's comforting touch. "Tuesday! Whose side are you on? You're reading too many crime novels."

"I know honey. Humor me. It makes for a good story line. Maybe I could pitch it to this new studio guy I just met. Seriously, you've been getting some funny stories today. Mrs. Dimwiddy downstairs having a clandestine dinner with the deceased's about-to-be divorced minor daughter who once hooked up with one of the suspects."

"We don't know she's a minor."

"Humor me. Who else could be in on it? Sounds like the wife is genuinely snockered with grief, so we can eliminate her. There's the business partner. From what you've told me she's the creative and he's the deal guy. But if Blackman is, er was, her meal ticket, hmm, maybe there was business insurance or something. You know, like sometimes partners insure one another's lives kind of thing?"

Tuesday put her speculating on pause to smear some more St. Andre's on a cracker and sprinkle it with caviar. She wiped her mouth on a cocktail napkin, looked thoughtfully at Olivia and said, "Well, I'm fresh out of suspects. How about you?"

Just then, they heard Cody's brother's Harley roar into the driveway.

Tuesday said, "Speak of the devil."

Chapter Eleven: Speak of the Devil

Olivia gathered up the glasses and stuck them on the kitchen counter. Tuesday followed with the cheese plates just as the doorbell rang.

Olivia turned to Tuesday and said, "Do you mind if I speak to Cody on my own? He might not open up to a stranger."

So after the introductions, Tuesday claimed she needed to do some Internet research. "I wonder if someone slipped some oleander into his scotch."

Cody said, "How do you know he drank scotch?"

"Cody," she said, displaying abundant annoyance. "It's just an expression. Oleander is a poisonous plant." Then she disappeared into the guest bedroom in a cloud of black and white second hand chiffon.

Olivia called out, "Dinner in an hour," while Cody helped himself to a beer in Olivia's refrigerator and carried it back to the living room. He was too antsy to sit on the camelback sofa, so he stood at the mantle with his back to the fire.

Olivia noted his beard was a three day now, signaling that he had not showered or shaved yet today. She waited for him to take a few swigs, then said "So tell me, Cody, why did they keep you so long? I've been tearing my hair out."

He shook his head in disgust. "That Johnson had it in for me. I had a little run in with Blackman last year. It was nothing. A simple disagreement and he calls the cops."

Olivia played dumb. "What was it about?"

She unbuckled her boots, slipped them off, and tucked her feet under her legs.

Cody's voice rose, beseeching her to believe him. "Nothing. Nothing serious. I wasn't threatening him or anything. He's a very touchy guy. Was a touchy guy. And not very well liked around here."

"Why would that be?"

In just a few minutes Cody had drained his beer. He opened his mouth to say something, but before he could stop himself, he belched. His cheeks bloomed with embarrassment. For all the kidding he did with Olivia, he was never crude. But she had turned mellow from the wine and laughed, surprising Cody and embarrassing him even more.

His unease showed when he continued. "His um, whaddyacallit, um, reputation preceded him. Word was, he was involved in a business deal that went very sour before he moved here. Somewhere down in Silicon Valley. That was about three years ago. You know how it is with the rumor mill. It goes viral before you know it. Mrs. Blackman made it her business to get connected socially, but they were only included on the fringes. You know, fundraisers where they had to pay a hefty price for tickets. But they never like, got invited to Mrs. Gotrocks' private dinner parties."

He looked at his beer bottle as if it would tell him whether to have another. He placed it on the mantle and continued. "Then someone asked him to appraise a very expensive pair of lamps. He took them to his shop and the owners claimed that he returned reproductions."

Olivia let out a moan. "Oh no. Cody, why didn't you tell me this before I did business with him?"

"You didn't ask me, O. And nothing was ever proved. It just became some buzz around town. And my friend Carrie, you know, from A Salted Caramel? The pastry shop?"

Olivia nodded. "Of course I know Carrie. Go on."

"Well she moonlights for a caterer and hears things while she's passing hors d'oeuvres. The Blackmans were looked down on."

A light bulb went on for Olivia. "That explains why Mrs. Harmon trashed him this morning. But listen, weren't you afraid you had a conflict of interest?"

"What do you mean?"

Suddenly, Olivia felt motherly towards Cody. Not exactly a nurturing mother, but a calling you to task for your own good mother. "Cody, Detective Richards told me about the altercation and about Jessica. Shouldn't you have told me?"

Cody rolled his eyes and put his head down on the mantle.

"Tell me about Jessica."

He raised his head and pleaded to the ceiling. "There's nothing to tell. There is no Jessica. Not in the sense you mean."

"Why did Blackman refuse to let you see her? Was she underage?"

"No. Not by then. We met senior year in high school, right after they moved here. By the time things got serious she was already nineteen. Her old man didn't want her hanging with somebody from the wrong side of the tracks. My family was here before there was a wrong side of the tracks. Before Darling Valley was on the map. Just a little town like Marin City. Working class. Hard to get to from Highway 101 so it was cheap. My family fit in back then, been here for generations working in the quarry. My dad was an extra in the Dirty Harry movie. You know the one where Clint Eastwood is standing in the quarry, near the Larkspur trestle, but I can't remember if that is in the movie, and he says, 'Do you feel lucky?' That's our claim to fame. By the time the money found DV, we were being pushed out. Probably will be soon. That's what the Blackmans had against me, I guess. There was nothing else I could put my finger on, other than he had plans for her. Or, Mrs. Blackman did. And they didn't include me."

Olivia didn't know how to ask the burning question. They both were quiet for a moment, lost in the complexities of the day. Then she just came out with it. "Did Jessica have a big wedding?"

Cody stared at her in shock. "What? What wedding? Jessica's married?"

"Well, not for long. I assumed you'd know about this. She's getting a divorce." Olivia could have kicked herself for delivering this heartbreaking news.

"You're kidding me. Who did she marry? I never heard about that. I haven't seen her since that night with her father, but I'm sure somebody would have told me. People knew we had a thing."

Cody's face crumbled. Olivia thought she detected a tremble in his voice and hoped she hadn't brought him to tears. How could he not have known?

"Mrs. Harmon had dinner with her last night. I ran into Mrs. Blackman's assistant at Paymoor and she told me. I was surprised because, you know, I told you, Mrs. Harmon was supposed to be with her nephew, who apparently doesn't exist, and then she told me that dinner was cancelled and turned out she hangs out with Jessica pretty regularly."

Cody looked truly puzzled. "Jessica can't stand Mrs. Harmon."

"Well, according to Marcia, she is a mother figure to her now, especially during this divorce. She saw them together. She told me."

Cody became quiet, and Olivia's heart ached for him as she saw him locked in shock and hurt. An image of Brooks at that hideous dinner party crossed her mind. She knew what it was like to be reminded of the lost love.

"I'm sorry, Cody. I just assumed you knew. After all, this is such a small town and all."

Cody pulled himself together. "I gotta go, Olivia. I'm beat and I need some dinner. This is all too much. I'll see you in the morning."

Before she could stop him or ask him about his interview with Richards, he was down the stairs and out the back door.

Chapter Twelve: The Darling Valley Bills

In the morning, Tuesday burst into the kitchen, a vision in swirling purple and orange.

"A Pucci knockoff?" Olivia asked as she stood back, coffee pot in hand to admire the maxi dress. Tuesday preened, proud of the dress. "Not this time. This is the real deal," she said, not the least bit squeamish from the clash of colors. She reached for a tangerine in the fruit bowl. "A consignment shop off Melrose that nobody has discovered yet."

She draped herself across the island and stared mysteriously off into the distance. Olivia said, "A black and white Calvin Klein ad for Vogue?"

Tuesday straightened up, a smile of victory across her face. "None other."

Olivia couldn't tell if the feathers were hanging from her ears or the tiny braids in her hair. She stopped herself from pointing out that feathers were circa 1985, but she did lean forward and whisper as though she were revealing a state secret, "I've heard from my spies in New York that long dresses are so last month. Not kidding."

Tuesday rolled her eyes. "Ollie, I've only had it a month. Who's going to know in this burg?"

Olivia surprised herself by bristling at the remark. "Tuesday, we are a picturesque twenty minute drive from San Francisco. There is more money and style in Darling Valley than all of Beverly Hills."

Where did this sudden loyalty to Darling Valley come from? "Don't you know where you are?"

Tuesday gave her a blank look.

"There are two thousand billionaires in the world, give or take a few hundred. Twenty-three of them have homes here. In the barely three square miles of Darling Valley. That is an unprecedented billionaire density. Now they don't live in their houses the way we do, set up housekeeping and have the mail delivered every day. They are more like honey bees, flitting around the world, going from beautiful residence to unbelievable residence as the mood or business deal moves them. Their houses have everything but throne rooms.

"About eight years ago, Grace Petri, who started an oil refinery empire, stumbled on Darling Valley. Back then it was still a sleepy little village close to San Francisco, but secluded enough that almost no one knew it was here. It has very little incorporated land and it is surrounded by government property or conservation land trusts. Grace immediately knew what that meant. Nothing left to develop. She and her friends could buy up the few available lots and homesteads, tear down the houses and have their own private universe. The rest of the world wouldn't be able to follow them like in Silicon Valley and Atherton because once they got started, in the space of less than a year there was no more available land to build on or little bungalow to tear down and turn into a turbo mansion.

Olivia thought she might have lost Tuesday, but she pushed on. "Plus, they don't need the likes of Detective Richards and his DVPD. Unlike the Silicon Bills . . . "

Tuesday interrupted. "They have their own football team?"

"Silicon Bills, Tuesday. What I call the billionaires who live in Silicon Valley. Those guys have a much harder time keeping their abodes and whereabouts secret. But here, they have their own private security details. Nobody can get close to them because Darling isn't near anything that attracts the great unwashed. But they are still close enough to the action so that their helicopters can drop them at SFO in ten minutes to board their private jets, or half an hour down the peninsula to meet with Larry Ellison or Bill Gates if he's in town. That's why Blackman's death has the press in a media frenzy. He's not that important as far as I can tell. I mean, a furniture renovation shop? But his proximity to power has them going wild. He was killed in their back yard. There has to be a story there."

Tuesday gave a so what shrug of her shoulders. Outside of Hollywood it took a lot to impress her.

"You scoff at this place, Tuesday, but up in the foothills where you can't see them are homes with art collections the Met in New York and the Tate in London would kill to get their hands on. Why do you think I picked this place to set up shop? I'll be lucky if I can get close to one of the bills. But millionaires? That's my feeding grounds. The Mills are much more visible—you'll see them at an auction we'll go to tomorrow night. It's all new tech money. They like to show it off. I'll take you for a drive and show you the pile of sticks one of my clients, Mrs. Gotshalk, calls home. And wait till you see the boutiques on the upper end of Darling Boulevard. Compared to the Bills, whom nobody has access to unless you're sleeping with one of their PA's, the Mills are low hanging fruit."

Tuesday helped herself to some coffee. "Well why aren't they throwing any of their ill gotten gains your way?"

"That's what I'd like to know," Olivia said with a mournful droop of her mouth. She pushed a plate of croissants toward Tuesday.

Tuesday grabbed it and said, "Hon, why are we here in the servant's quarters? Let's go downstairs and sit on that gorgeous furniture you have and act like we own the joint."

"And spill coffee and crumbs on my period brocade chairs?"

Heading for the stairs, Tuesday chirped, "You just said yourself, nobody's buying, so what does it matter? Besides, I'm a grownup. I know how to put a napkin on my lap."

Olivia sighed and followed her with her own cup and the container of half and half.

Olivia directed Tuesday to the two wing chairs in the back that gave them a view of the traffic on the street. She didn't turn on any of the lights, letting the early sun send a warm glow over the gleaming wood and gilt that filled the showroom. In the dim light, passersby could not see them, however, the two friends had a clear view of two voyeurs pressing their faces against the window, trying to catch a glimpse of the murderer of Angel Row.

Olivia blew on her coffee to cool it and mused, "I haven't had this many people interested in my shop since it opened."

"All publicity is good publicity."

"I know. Cody reminded me of that last night. So why did the janitorial service call yesterday with some lame excuse that they couldn't come until next week? And the spring water company, ditto. My neighbors aren't interested in patronizing my business, but they sure are interested in the gossip about me. Later we'll cruise Darling Boulevard and I'll introduce you to the locals and pick up some cleaning products and bottled water."

Tuesday pointed to two more women mounting the porch and shading their eyes to get a better view of the interior. They shrugged their shoulders at each other and turned away, clearly disappointed. She said, "Too bad we couldn't drag out another dead body for them. You could charge a viewing fee."

Olivia shook her head. "Don't Tues, I'm still in a state of shock."

Tuesday finished her coffee and gave a dainty swipe of her mouth with her paper napkin and brushed non-existent crumbs from her palm and swept them onto the plate for Olivia's benefit. "Let's not be all gloomy and gloppy. Give me a tour of this place. Let me see what you've acquired since you left LA."

Olivia started with a Louie XIV chest, dripping with carved wood and inlaid ivory. Even Tuesday, who didn't know an end table from a worktable and cleverly decorated her studio with vintage Goodwill, fairly swooned.

"This is my prize, my baby. I will hate to see it go, but I'll be sure it finds a good home." Olivia's sadness cracked through her bravado.

Tuesday gave it a once over. "And how much do you want for it?"

"Twenty-nine."

Tuesday did a double take. "Twenty nine hundred? That's a nice piece of change. What's that, 50% markup?"

Olivia scoffed. "Nooooo, my dear. That's twenty-nine thousand." She canted her head forward and drew out the thouuuusand for emphasis.

Tuesday let loose with some purple language, then said. "Holy coffee table, girlfriend. I knew you dealt in pricey goods when you worked for Griffiths and Graham, but you never told me you were this upscale."

Olivia rested her head against the secretaire, remembering the scary days after she quit her job and had made an offer on the house. "I was afraid to. If I crashed it would be more humiliating. What kind of a decorator can't sell the best to the people who want the best and have the money to pay for it? But now that seems to be the position I'm in. I've had a few low-end projects, but seriously? I haven't been able to get these people to budge. And now? With a murder in my shop? I don't see how I can come back from this. It kept me awake all night."

Armoires and Arsenic

Tuesday wrapped her Pucci-draped arms around Olivia. "Look sweetie, you're not there yet. Finish the tour and let's get out of here for a bit until you open the door for your non-existent business."

So Olivia showed her the Napoleon chest that the seller swore had actually been in the Emperor's camp tent. And the handmade leather club chair that Clark Gable had once owned—verified by a photo of the actor sitting in it staring lovingly at Carole Lombard. Next the twin lamps made from ebony and a pair of beautifully twisted antelope horns that rumor had it, Hemingway himself had shot.

"Olivia! You have some serious goods here."

"I know. And if this sale doesn't pull me out of the hole this weekend, they will end up on the auction block."

Tuesday slammed her fist into her palm. "We're going to do something about that. And I'm not going home until we do!"

"Okay," said Olivia. "I like the sound of that. I don't know what we can do, but you're right. Let's get out of here for a bit. So what if there is dust on the library stairs. Who's going to see it? Let's go. Oh, but first I want to show you the little treasures that arrived yesterday. My netsuke."

They threaded their way around the silk-shaded floor lamps and carved dining chairs to the Duchess's table. "They aren't worth that much," Olivia explained over her shoulder, "but sometimes a little gem of an accessory can attract a customer to the expensive table it sits on. Over here."

When they got to the table, Olivia's eyes widened. "Where are they?"

Tuesday drew her Cleopatra eyebrows together. "What do you mean?"

"I set these on the table yesterday morning before Cody arrived. Now they're gone."

Tuesday tried to be helpful. "Maybe they got swept onto the floor. You know how people are when they browse through a shop. They can be so careless with things that don't belong to them."

"I didn't have any customers yesterday. Well," she said, remembering Charles Bacon. "One, but he didn't come back this far."

She hoped. The table stood next to the French doors, far from the chairs where Olivia and the car collector had sat. He would never have seen them.

"Unless," she said, remembering that she had left him alone while she ran to check her calendar. "Nah," she answered to herself. "How would he have known they were there? And I saw them after he left, didn't I? Or did I?"

Tuesday wasn't putting her mind at ease. "Could someone have come in the day before and cased the joint."

"Tuesday, really? Cased the joint? You have to get your head out of film noir."

"Well, excuse me. Perhaps someone came in and surveyed the premises and conveyed the information to a colleague who returned the next day and surreptitiously removed the items from said premises. Madam."

They laughed, but Olivia dismissed that possibility because she had only unwrapped them yesterday morning. She ran through the rest of the day.

"Nobody else was in here except for the police. They came in to talk to me in the afternoon for a few minutes before they took off and walked through the front door into my office. But I can't imagine a cop recognizing potentially valuable netsuke."

Olivia remembered the crew of officers and detectives eying the shop and checking price tags when they thought she wasn't looking, nudging each other with raised eyebrows.

"And I locked up after they left so no one else was in here."

"What about Mrs. Dimwit downstairs."

"Tuesday! Be nice. She'd need a key to get in and I had the locks changed during the renovation. And she never comes up here."

"Olivia, yesterday was a crazy day. You probably moved them without realizing it. You can get a little spaced out when you're stressed."

"Oh, look who's talking. You, who had the key to the Tea Room on opening day and left it at Starbucks, then tried to open the shop with their restroom key."

"Mistakes happen. I'm just saying. If nobody was in here, they have to be someplace. Let's get a pendulum."

Olivia waved her hands in front of her face. "No, I can't do that right now, Tues." The suggestion hit a nerve. Tuesday reading tea leaves was one thing. She always got a positive hit. But these other things

Tuesday was into spooked her. Probably because sometimes they hit the mark.

"Look, babe, this is just to find a lost object. The most common use for a pendulum. We won't go near your love life. It won't be like last time. Come on, this is harmless."

Olivia was caving, but reluctantly. "None of your stuff is harmless, Tues. Remember the time you read the Tarot for me and my cat died?"

Tuesday rolled her eyes. "How many times do I have to tell you? The cards didn't kill your cat. They just foresaw a loss and helped you prepare for it."

"Yeah. For three weeks I was walking on eggshells waiting for something awful to happen."

"If you'd followed my advice, you would have let go of the reading, but instead you obsessed on it. It was a lesson in detachment. Look at all the stuff you have." Tuesday swept her arms around to include the showroom and the rest of the house. "Possess it. Don't let it possess you."

"Like you let go of your 20,000 thrift store scarves." But then, Olivia's last objection faded. Sometimes it was easier to give in to Tuesday than to fight her. "I'll get my locket."

Tuesday went over the rules for divination with a pendulum, even though Olivia had done this with her dozens of times.

"Okay. Nobody has touched this locket in the past 24 hours, right?"

"Check."

"Good. We don't want anyone else's energy contaminating the answers. Now remember, ask only yes or no questions. If it swings left to right that's a no answer. Backwards and forwards is a yes. Circular moves mean your higher self knows the answer but won't reveal it."

Olivia never admitted to her friends that she believed in Tuesday's shenanigans, just that she liked to humor her. Tuesday was her best friend, yet no one else in her circle accepted her. She hadn't gone to the right school. And those hideous clothes. But Olivia and Tuesday cemented their bond the night they had too much champagne and shared their mother stories. Olivia's was typical. Her mother was a gold digger and social climber and groomed Olivia to find a rich husband. She insisted her future home contain a separate residence for her in her old age. She saw Olivia's career leading her to the rich and famous, or at best, the cover of Architectural Digest. She never appreciated her daughter's talent. Her grandmother was almost as cold but recognized Olivia's true gifts. Her encouragement balanced the insecurities borne of her mother's criticism of her looks. *Why won't you do something about that nose? Get a boob job. You make enough money for plastic surgery. Just your luck that men like short girls.* Her grandmother, however, preached that *there's only one thing we owe to the world, dear, and that's the fruit of our gifts. And you have them in abundance.*

By comparison, Tuesday's mother kept herself blissfully medicated and determinedly unwed. When she asked her mother at a young age about her father, the answer shocked her so much Tuesday never asked again. *Well, he could have been one of three jerks. Maybe five. Whoever he was, you don't want anything to do with him.* They subsisted alternately on food stamps and mysterious infusions of cash that her mother never explained, but Tuesday came to believe were from drug deals. Her goal in life was to rise above all that and saw the occult as a spiritual path. The idea of unseen spirits watching over her got her through the day.

"Okay," Olivia asked. "But what's a yes or no question this time? I want it to tell me where the netsuke are."

Tuesday hovered the locket. "Hold it between your thumb and index finger. Be very still. Don't try to influence its movements and don't visualize it moving. Let your higher self take over."

"Okay, okay. But how do I ask where the things are."

Tuesday made soothing motions with her hands, a symphony conductor slowing the tempo. "Ask if the netsukes are close by."

Olivia corrected her. "Netsuke. No "s" for plural in Japanese." Then she obeyed. "Are they close by?"

"No, Ollie. Name them. You have lots of stuff close by. How is it going to know which you mean?"

"Well if it can read my mind, wouldn't it know?"

Tuesday ignored her. "Do it again."

Olivia, despite herself, moved into a zone. She stood very still until the locket hung over her feet still as a stone. Very quietly, she said, "Are my netsuke close by?"

The two friends studied the locket as if waiting for a genie to appear. It began to make minute movements. They became stronger and in a few seconds indicated yes.

A big smile erupted on Olivia's face. "Am I standing next to them? Uh, the netsuke? Am I standing next to the netsuke?"

The answer was no this time.

"Am I standing near the netsuke."

The pendulum answered with a resounding yes."

Excited, now, the friends searched the room, but saw nothing on the tables or the floor near where they stood.

Tuesday pointed to a clump of furniture by the wall. Olivia protested, "I wasn't over here yesterday," but did as she was told. Still nothing.

Tuesday insisted they do it again. "But remember. Ask about them by name. That's important."

Once more, Olivia stood riveted in place until the locket was still. "Am I near the netsuke?" she asked

This time the locket took off like a firecracker, giving an affirmative answer. Again, they scoured the floor and the furniture, two tables, a sideboard and pie chest, but found nothing. Olivia continued moving around the showroom and the pendulum continued to answer that she was near her valuables. The only spot that gave a negative swing was by the front door.

Tuesday saw that as a triumph. "It's telling you they didn't walk out of the showroom."

Olivia stuffed the locket into her pocket. "Enough. We've been over the whole showroom and it tells me it's here. But where? Come on. We've got errands to do."

Tuesday frowned. "It isn't going to work if you don't cooperate and believe."

Olivia retorted, "If it's dependent on my believing it's telling me the truth, then it doesn't have any power of its own."

"That's not what I meant."

Olivia headed up stairs for her purse and jacket. "Come on. I need to make a call to a client, then let's get out of here."

She meant Mr. Bacon, who hadn't returned the message of apology she'd left yesterday. He didn't answer his phone this time either, so she left another message suggesting a meeting time later that day. Before they left, she stopped Tuesday.

"This isn't hot LA summer, Tues, it's northern California freeze-your-bohonkus-off-in-the-summer summer. You'll need a cover-up."

When Tuesday returned with a turquoise faux monkey fur wrap, Olivia wished she had kept the weather report to herself.

Chapter Thirteen: Downtown DV

They stopped first at The Fresh Fishery that stocked the morning's catch. Jesse, the owner, trucked it over from Bodega Bay every day, along with a crate of Hog Island oysters. Jesse, a twenty-six year old Harvard biz grad, once explained to Olivia that he ran a computer model of his business and used focus groups to test everything down to the exact faded blue color paint that would lure customers nostalgic for Nantucket Island. It worked. Even at 9:00 am the line for his homemade chowder, which he sold by the quart, was down the street. Rather than waste the morning in line, Olivia suggested they get an early start the next day for chowder, and settle for a dozen oysters for lunch, which Jesse's assistant shucked and packed in seaweed and lemon quarters and tied up in a plastic bag.

Jesse emerged from the back office as they were leaving and threaded though the crowd leaning into the counter trying to decide between ocean-caught salmon and halibut. He called loudly enough so that Olivia heard him over the din and pulled on Tuesday's arm to wait. He shouted into Olivia's ear over the crush of customers. "So sorry, Olivia. I heard about that tragedy at your place."

Jesse wasn't a friend, exactly, but part of his business model was to be nice to everyone, because, he once told her, you never knew who would turn out to be a valuable contact and that included Olivia. She wasn't sure that was a compliment, but chalked up his tactless observation to youth. When the shop was slow, he'd pass a little time of day with her while she picked up a slice of the day's catch.

Olivia mouthed, "It's a nightmare," so as not to attract any more attention than she already was. Several of the locals were nudging each other and nodding knowingly in her direction. She wasn't sure if Tuesday with her gaudy dress and jacket or herself with her mantel of scandal attracted the looks this morning.

Jesse leaned over again and in a stage whisper said, "I guess you couldn't avoid the newcomer's curse after all."

Olivia did a double take, not sure she heard correctly.

"What newcomer's curse?"

But Jesse's assistant motioned to him that he was needed behind the counter. "Have a good day, ladies," he said, and pushed through the line of regulars to tend to business.

"Did you hear that," Olivia said as she signed her credit card receipt and stuck the oysters into her market bag.

Tuesday said, "No, what? I was checking out the cutie deveining prawns. Did you see that butt?"

Olivia said, "You're unbelievable," then outside in the gray morning, Olivia told her what Jesse had said. She pointed to a hardware shop across the street. "Next stop," and they dodged the lazy morning traffic to get to the Darling Hardware's front door.

Tuesday shook her head, sending her feathers swinging violently. "You had to have misheard him. That's just too daytime soap opera."

Olivia reiterated. "I did NOT mishear him."

Tuesday said, "It probably means to be accepted in this town you have to walk on fire."

"Uh, I think that's what I've been doing, sista. But what would that have to do with murder?"

Darling's sold high-end kitchen equipment, expensive Japanese cutlery and displayed wine glasses on glass shelves that gleamed like crystal. It was the only hardware store that Olivia knew of that advertized in The New Yorker. The routine nuts and bolts were hidden somewhere in the back.

Greg Regan, the owner, knew Olivia because of her renovation and had supplied her crew with rented floor sanders and dozens of cans of paint over the last several months. Of all the shops on Darling Boulevard, this was most familiar to her.

"High, Greg," she said. "I need to stock up on spring water for my dispenser today. If I come by later with my truck, can you help me load it up?"

"Sure thing, Olivia. If I'm busy, just ask for Jake." Olivia knew Jake. He was a friend of Cody's.

"Heard what happened over at your place. Sure was a shocker."

"You can say that again. I don't know when I'll get over being stunned."

Greg was grinning at Tuesday like a cat eying a mouse, so Olivia introduced them. He shook her hand and said. "Is that pink hair found in nature?"

Tuesday smiled at his lame attempt to put the make on her. Olivia reached into her purse for her wallet so she could pay for the water delivery and get them out of there.

Greg, oblivious to the thud with which his pickup line landed, continued to grin at Tuesday. Then he said to Olivia, "I guess you just can't skirt that newcomer curse."

Olivia jerked her head up. "What do you mean, newcomer's curse? That's the second time I've heard about it this morning. What is the newcomer's curse, Greg?"

Just then the phone rang and someone in the back asked Greg a question about a stock item. He gave Olivia her receipt and excused himself.

On the way out into the street again, Tuesday said, "They are just trying to spook you, honeybun. Don't pay attention."

"But I do feel cursed, Tues. I mean, sending a dead body to me? It almost sounds like voodoo."

Tuesday changed the subject by mocking Greg and his laugh. "Duh, that color pink found in nature? Ahuh ahuh."

Olivia apologized for him. "He's a nice guy. Just trying to be friendly. Greg grew up here before DV made the map. He doesn't have the polish of those that rushed in to capitalize on wealth and privilege. But he has the savvy. He's done all right for himself considering his grandfather started the store to cater to oystermen, back when it was Regan's Hardware and Dry Goods. I mean, this place is a little conservative compared to what you're used to in LA. We don't get many pink heads."

"No kidding, Marian the Librarian," she said, giving Olivia's cashmere twin set and pencil skirt a disapproving once over.

"Tuesday, this outfit cost . . . "

Tuesday stopped her. "Don't give me that fancy label gar-baj. When are you going to learn that high-end stores sell conformity, not style? You gotta let me dress you, my gorgeous but so out of touch baby girl."

Olivia stopped in her tracks and turned to Tuesday. "If I let you dress me I'd get arrested for badly impersonating Lady Gaga."

"Yes, sweetheart. My point exactly. You'd have that one in your inside pocket."

They linked arms after that and window-shopped their way down the street, admiring diamond rings and other goodies in Xavier's, designer purses and boots in Shoe Candy. They stopped to ogle wedding dresses in a small boutique, which was so exclusive, celebrity brides were known to come from Paris and New York to have the designer create a one of a kind gown. Olivia momentarily forgot about the rumored curse when Brooks appeared in front of her, the night before she was supposed to wear her own white confection and walk down the aisle. Brooks telling her he needed space. Space for crying out loud. Couldn't he have come up with something original? She shivered as if to throw off the memory and rushed into a brief history of Darling Valley. Tuesday gave her a where did this come from look, but listened anyway.

"It was named after Captain Darling, over a hundred and fifty years ago," she explained. "He made a killing selling eggs from the Farrallon Islands during the gold rush."

In fact, the canon Darling had set up on one of the bird rookeries he raided, and which he used to repel poachers on his unofficial claim, accounted eventually for the extinction of several species of sea birds. Today it stood in the middle of the park in the center of town.

Tuesday scrunched up her face. "Eggs? Canon? What?"

Olivia explained that eggs provided the main source of protein to the influx of actual gold diggers after nuggets were found at Sutter's Mill. Before 1850 San Francisco was a barren outpost ill prepared to feed the thousands who came searching for instant wealth. Darling was a sea captain, distantly related to his namesake in South Africa, but one of the first to capitalize on the free protein sitting twenty miles off shore on the Farrallon Islands, rocky outcrops where millions of birds nested year round. He sold the eggs to the bar keeps and hotels for $.50 each and the buyers sold them to the hungry miners for a buck, beginning the tradition of entrepreneurship that continued today, peopling Darling now with tech titans and venture capital giants that Olivia targeted when she came up with her plan to place her interior design business smack in the middle of the wealthiest town in the country. Mostly philanthropists now, they and their wives, and in increasing numbers, husbands, competed with each other to see who could build the grandest palace to show off their wealth, much like the robber barons of Newport in the 1800's. It was Olivia's plan to decorate these shacks.

At the end of the history lesson they found themselves standing in front of a display window full of Chanel bags, Gucci shoes and Tiffany lookalikes made of chocolate, marzipan and royal icing. Tuesday stretched her neck and saw the sign overhead, The Salted Caramel.

"Heavenly cream puff, Olivia. Look at those cakes and cookies. This is better than the Cooking Channel. I thought pastries were extravagant in Beverly Hills. This is unbelievable. I could take that Chanel bag home and put it on the table in the Tea Room and somebody would steal it thinking it was the real thing."

"So there are a few commercial items you covet."

"Accessories, girlfriend," she said, hiking up her rented Hermes Birkin. The right bag or shoe will make any old rag look good."

Tuesday had a friend who brokered expensive handbags for rent so the owners could afford to pay for their indulgences.

I know," Olivia said, biting her tongue to stop one more whine about how edible accessories would be all she could afford if her fortunes didn't change. She feared she was becoming a broken record. "Would you believe one of my clients, Mrs. Gotshalk, has a Chanel diamond encrusted evening bag worth a quarter of a mill?"

Tuesday did a double take.

"That's nothing. Listen to this. An oil sheik has a house up there." Olivia tilted her head toward the surrounding hills that masked the truly outrageous mansions. "He bought his wife a handbag from The House of Mouawad in Dubai. Two and half million."

"No!"

"That's what money will buy. Off topic. It's early for me. I usually don't indulge in chocolate before noon, but the baker here trained in Paris with Pierre Hermes. Dodie Greenspan orders from here. No kidding. Let's treat ourselves."

"You don't have to twist my arm, girlfriend. And it's Dorie Greenspan. I thought you knew chocolate, Ollie."

"Whatever. I can't be the world's foremost authority on everything, you know." Olivia pushed open the glass door and Tuesday's good cheer mingled with the intoxicating scents of chocolate, coffee and cinnamon.

"Oh good," Olivia said, pointing to a petite blond behind the counter, a porcelain doll of a girl except for cruelly bad skin. "Carrie is working today. She actually speaks to me like a real person and not an alien from space. She's a sweetie. She has it bad for Cody, but he doesn't even know she exists. Poor thing."

While they waited on a short line, Olivia told Tuesday that, after Carrie found out she was from Hollywood, she asked Olivia if she knew anyone famous. Olivia revealed that she had decorated a bathroom for one of the Twilight stars. Carrie had faked a swoon, then became a fan of Olivia's from that moment on.

Tuesday said, "But if this is such a hot place to live, doesn't she get to see famous people all the time?"

"I don't think teenagers are turned on by venture capitalists."

Soon Carrie batted her glorious long-lashed eyes at them. "Hey, girl," she drawled seductively at Olivia. "How ya doin'? Gonna get down and dirty with something gooey and gorgeous today?" She beamed a crooked-toothed smile at them, sweeping her hand over the counter as though she were a QVC presenter showing off Joan River's jewelry.

Olivia laughed, her first genuine guffaw since the discovery of the body. She silently thanked Carrie, a nineteen year old too impressed with Olivia's familiarity with Hollywood stars to snub her, and plagued with bad skin and teeth that unfairly prevented her own celebrity.

Tuesday said, "I'll have that chocolate bomb," and pointed to a heart-shaped confection of chocolate, mousse, whipped cream and raspberries.

Olivia ordered her favorite macaroons, which were said to be identical to Ladoure's in Paris. "And we'll have two coffees, Carrie. Thanks."

Olivia and Tuesday settled themselves at a table back from the window to avoid the gawkers they had passed on the sidewalk. Carrie brought their order. Before she could walk away, Olivia tugged on her sleeve.

"Carrie, can I ask you something personal, well, not really personal, but something that seems to be a secret in town?"

Carrie looked over her shoulder at the crowded shop filled with customers clattering their forks and spoons and licking up crumbs off The Salted Caramel's pink plates. "Yeah," she said tentatively. "What?"

She leaned forward conspiratorially. "Is it about the murder? If you don't mind me asking? I mean like everybody's heard about it." She kinked her eyebrows up. "Armoires and arsenic? Who doesn't want to talk about that?"

"Tell me about it," Olivia said returning a valley girl eye roll. "I've been hearing about something called the newcomer's curse. Do you know what that is?"

Carrie shook her head. "No, no, no. Olivia, you don't want to go there. Ugh. Nobody talks about that."

But Olivia insisted. "Carrie, something terrible has happened to me. Well, it's worse for Mr. Blackman, of course, and his wife. I can't stop thinking about what she's going through. But it's coming down on my head, too. Please. Tell me."

Carrie put her hands on the table to be able to lean over and speak low. "It seems like whenever somebody new comes to Darling Valley, somebody else gets killed."

Olivia and Tuesday looked at each other, too shocked to respond.

Carrie continued. "Everybody tries to keep it quiet. I mean nothing has ever been proved. It's just, like. Okay, so the first one was this girl who moved to Darling Valley, actually over by what we call meth park now. By the back entrance to the yacht harbor where you yousta could live cheap. But probably not any more. The town is trying to get rid of meth park and build," she drew air quotes around "expensive houses." Olivia hid her impatience with information

Armoires and Arsenic

she already knew by taking a bite of her pink macaroon.

"Yeah. I knew DV was trying to stamp out the beginning of a drug trade, but what does that have to do with murders?"

Carrie settled into her tale. "Well, you didn't hear it from me, but this girl came from someplace back east. Nobody knew much about her and she never came into the shops here. Probably too pricey for her. Anyway, she'd go to the clubs." She looked at Tuesday to educate her as well.

"We got a lot of rich kids who need to play. We have three clubs and get good bands coming through. So she'd show up and the guys would buy her drinks. She was a guy magnet, let me tell you. I couldn't see it myself, but," and Carrie nodded to Olivia, "ask Cody. He'll tell you. The guys were all over her. Anyway, before long she made a connection and got a job at Mrs. Gotshalk's as a housekeeper or something."

That name brought Mr. Bacon to mind and while Carrie described the girl's fate, Olivia surreptitiously opened her purse and took a peek at her phone to see if he had texted or left a voicemail. A news alert from the Marin IJ profiled the widow, calling her a competitive sailor, but nothing from the garage guy. She looked up at Carrie with a smile of recognition. "Mrs. Gotshalk! Yes, I know her. She's been in my shop."

Olivia remembered Cody's story about driving to her house. "She has peacocks."

"That's the one. Well, after a few months a story went around that something was going on between Mr.

Gotshalk and the hot housekeeper and one day there was an accident. She somehow fell down the stairs and broke her neck. Well, you can imagine, lots of talk, but the police said it was an accident and that was that."

Olivia said, "You mean there were suspicions that Mrs. Gotshalk pushed her? Killed her?"

"She's a customer here, Olivia. I'm not saying anything more. The police said accident, so accident it was."

"And that's it? I mean that's terrible, but it hardly sounds like curse material."

Carrie made a show of wiping the table to avoid suspicions of fraternizing with the customers. "Oh that's not all. There were two more."

Olivia shook her head like she hadn't heard. "Two more murders?"

"Judge for yourself." Carrie rearranged the friends' silverware while she spoke. "A couple moved in to a shop down the street. Great location, fancy up your pants. They were from England and they made tailored shirts for men. Charged $1,200 a shirt. Can you imagine?"

Olivia and Tuesday looked at each other and nodded their heads. "We're from LA, Carrie. We can imagine. So what happened?"

"Well, they were making a delivery to Mr. Gotshalk. If you don't know him . . ."

"Yes," said Olivia. And to Tuesday, "My client's husband. Not a billionaire but close."

Carrie's nodded. "Yeah, well, they never arrived."

Tuesday said, "The shirts?"

Carrie said, "Not the shirts. Not the couple. Their car was found by the lake with the grass all trampled like there had been a scuffle. Nobody could find them. They had a son in college who reported them missing, so they dragged the lake and sure enough, they popped up. I mean literally. Like dead fish. Pardon me. But not even where the police were looking."

Tuesday leaned in. "What happened to them?"

Carrie shrugged. "Nobody knows. Couldn't find any cause of death. Maybe they had a fight and pushed each other into the lake. The son said they couldn't swim. Maybe they made somebody mad. Who knows? But how do two people end up in a lake? It was all over the Internet. Being Darling Valley and all. Eventually it was chalked up to drug violence. They were either innocent victims or making a buy."

Tuesday said, "Are you counting them as two deaths or is there a third?"

"Yeah. Mrs. Harmon."

"Wait a minute," Olivia said. "She's not dead. She's living in my house. I saw her yesterday."

"No, her husband. Mr. Harmon. But Mrs. Harmon has never let anyone forget about him."

Olivia was puzzled. "But I thought he died of a heart attack. That's what the previous owners of my house told me."

"The Cooks. Yeah. They were friends with him. Except he was young and healthy. Well, younger than his wife by maybe ten years. You'd see him jogging all over town. He'd go for his runs late at night after work, sometimes. He was supposed to be retired, but he was one of those men who could never stop working. Anyway, he was found in the park one night, dead. They did an autopsy but it didn't show anything. No heart attack or stroke or anything. No marks of violence, though that would be odd because we don't have any violent types."

"Ask Mr. Blackman about that," Tuesday said.

"I mean we don't have police out on calls, you know. I happen to know the guy who picks up the trash at the funeral home and he told me that he knew someone at the coroner's office who said they called it a heart attack because they couldn't find a COD." She gave a little laugh at showing off her crime show savvy. "You know, cause of death. It was a cover up. But you didn't hear it from me. So people started talking about a curse. Somebody new comes to town, goes to work or starts a business and bingo. They end up dead. Now you, Olivia."

Olivia quickly corrected her. "I'm still very much alive, Carrie."

"Yeah, but Mr. Blackman isn't. And he ended up on your doorstep, so to speak. And he hasn't been here that long."

A light bulb went on for Olivia. "So that's the reason everybody in Darling Valley keeps their distance from me? They think I'll end up dead? Or someone close to me will?"

Carrie kept looking over her shoulder and sped up her story. "Well, Mrs. Harmon lives in your house. And the Harmons were associated with the Blackmans."

"How were they associated? Mrs. Harmon doesn't have anything good to say about Mr. Blackman." Olivia looked at Tuesday. "I told you what she said about him."

Carrie got ready to leave. "Well, she wouldn't."

"Why is that?"

"Mr. Blackman and Mr. Harmon were in business together once. There was some funny business. You know, double dealing."

"Oh whose part?"

"Not sure. I hear a lot in here. This is one of the most popular spots in town. You know the drill. Because I wait on them I don't have ears. So people say anything. But mostly I just hear snatches and have to put two and two together. And my boss? She's terrified of losing a customer and won't hear of any gossip by the employees about the customers. And outside nobody's talking. So I told you all I know. But I'll tell you one thing. Your Mr. Blackman is the only death that is a clear cut murder."

Olivia interrupted. "But he's not MY Mr. Blackman."

Carrie stretched her back. "Whatever. No mystery about this one. Course we don't know how he died, but somebody stuffed him in that chest of yours, Olivia, and it wasn't no accident, if you get my drift."

Olivia laughed. "Yeah, I think the police have figured that out.

"That's a surprise. I don't think they can figure out how to put cream in their coffee without help. Talk to me when they finger his partner."

Olivia cocked her head as though she hadn't heard correctly. "You mean Sabrina Chase?"

"That's the one. She's one cold cookie. She worked here we wouldn't need a freezer."

"Carrie, what do you know? Tell me. I'm in trouble here."

Carrie looked over her shoulder and then hunkered down on her knees. "It didn't come from me, you swear?"

Olivia held up her pinkie. "Pinkie swear."

Carrie looked at her like she was kidding. "Um, this isn't high school. Pardon my saying."

"Carrie, whatever. It stays between us."

Carrie looked at Tuesday. Olivia said, "If you can tell me, you can tell Tuesday. And she'd know anyway. She's a fortune teller."

Carrie looked at Tuesday with new respect. "No kidding. Well, then, she should know, right? If she can read my mind and all?"

Tuesday said, "Crime isn't my specialty."

Carrie seemed to forget about the urgency of getting back to work. "Psychics specialize? I never heard of that."

Tuesday adjusted her bracelets. "Everybody specializes, honey. I do the heart. Breakups, trouble with the kids, is he the right guy for you? That kind of thing."

"Oh, yeah. Can you do something for me?" She gave a little dismissive laugh to mask her interest.

Tuesday closed her eyes and held her temples. "Let's see. I'm getting a shape. Tall. Would fill a barn door. Brownish hair. No, more sandy. No strawberry blond. Green eyes. Sound like anybody you know?"

"Yeah, but could be a few guys."

"Let's see if I can get a name. He's a sweetie. Matt. No. Mark, that's it. Mark. Umm, no, here it is. Cody. That's it Cody. I never get last names, only initials."

"Yeah, yeah . . . I know a Cody W." Carrie's eyes lit up. "You do too, Olivia. What do you see?"

Tuesday closed her eyes and sank her forehead into her hands in a pose of concentration. "Well, he's in some kind of trouble. I don't see his aura around you. I see somebody else. Not yet, but he's coming."

Carrie said, "Really? Somebody new? Boy I could use a dose of that."

Olivia broke up the charade. "Okay, Carrie, so what about Sabrina Chase."

"Well, you didn't hear it from me. She's having financial troubles and she blames Mr. Blackman for it. She was in here last week with a friend blabbing about it. Wants him to buy out her share of the business because she needs the cash and he wouldn't do it. That's all I heard. But if I were you, I'd keep my eye on her."

Olivia looked disbelieving. "Really?"

"You'll see. Well, the shop is filling up. Gotta go. Can I get you girls something else? Heat up your coffee. Here let me get the pot."

But Olivia stopped her. "We have to go, Carrie. Thanks for all this . . . information."

Carrie hustled off, thanking Tuesday profusely. "You've saved my life."

Olivia scowled at Tuesday as she drained her coffee cup. "That was mean to give Carrie all that gobbledygook about Cody. You just told her what I told you."

Tuesday gathered up her purse and adjusted her various scarves, necklaces, belts and, this morning, pink hair extensions. "Yeah, and you don't have be a psychic to know how it's going to turn out with Cody or that someone else will come into her life. Eventually. Because that is what always happens. To everybody." She said the last quite pointedly to Olivia.

Olivia put up her hand. "Don't bring up Brooks. Puleeze."

Tuesday sent her a longsuffering sigh. "At least Carrie'll stop looking in the wrong drawer."

Olivia looked at her watch and shook her head, more teasing than disapproving. "Whatever. We have some time before I have to open the shop. I'm going to stop by the police department and file a complaint about my missing netsuke."

On the walk to the police station, Tuesday brought up Carrie's information. "So it looks like that business partner has more at stake here than we figured. Wouldn't you love to know what their business deal was?"

That gave Olivia an idea.

Chapter Fourteen: The Widow and the Doctor

Like a bee swarm, the reporters that had buzzed off from Olivia's house had resettled along the front of the police station. Several recognized Olivia and poked their microphones at her as she passed. When she replied no comment, they turned to Tuesday to ask about her role in the case. Olivia pulled Tuesday inside before she could say more than her name and reply that she was Miss Granville's tasseomancer. The reporters asked her to spell that as the door closed on them.

Safely inside, Olivia scolded her friend. "Tuesday!!!!! That's all I need to have the word out that I have my own tea leaf reader when this town barely listens to weather predictions."

"Listen, Miss Worry Wart, by the time they look up tasseomancer on Google, this case will be solved."

Not convinced, Olivia dragged Tuesday across the pine floorboards to find the same officer sitting at the desk in her same ill-fitting uniform. Olivia knew it was the same uniform because the same coffee spot covered the same middle button of her shirt. This time, though, the officer was chewing gum.

"I want to file a complaint . . ." Olivia remembered her name. "Officer Ridley."

Detective Richards must have heard her, because, before Ridley could respond, he opened door the door to his office wearing the same woodsman plaid flannel jacket and jeans he wore the day of the murder. Didn't he have a middle ground? He was either dressed inappropriately down or inappropriately up. "Miss Blackman," he said. "What can we do for you?"

"It's Miss Granville. You can return my netsuke."

"Of course, I'm sorry. Miss Granville. But I don't understand your problem. Did you leave something here yesterday? A jet ski?"

Olivia busily hiked her purse up over her shoulder to avoid looking into his eyes. She enunciated, "NET-SKI. No, I didn't leave anything, but I believe one of your men may have walked out of my shop with something. These little ivory trinkets. Japanese. Very valuable." Well, she told herself, maybe not to me but to a police officer $1,500 would be a downright windfall.

Then, as if he had just noticed Tuesday, he gave her a brief handshake. "I'm detective Richards. And you are Miss. . .?"

"Tuesday," she said.

He looked puzzled. "Miss Tuesday?"

Tuesday smiled coquettishly. "No, just Tuesday."

"Okay. Why don't you come into my office and explain the problem to me."

They each found a chair in the cramped space. Olivia explained that she believed someone had stolen the small ivory charms the day before while they were busy investigating the murder.

"The shop was closed for business yesterday." She added archly, "As you know," as if it were Richards' fault. "The only people who entered the shop were you, Detective Johnson and the police officers. No one else could have taken them." She crossed her fingers under her purse. She was not going to bring Mr. Bacon into this.

Richards leaned forward on his desk and gave her a friendly scowl. "I assure you, Miss Granville. No one took your netskies or anything from your shop without giving you a signed receipt. You received one, I believe, for the chest containing the victim. I don't recall that we took anything else."

"You're forgetting my Jimmy Choos. When am I going to see them again?"

"Ah, yes, your shoes. As soon as we have finished our investigation we'll release them."

Hmm. He said release them, not return them. Before Olivia could respond, Tuesday leaned forward, creating a cacophony of jangling jewelry and rustling skirts and shawls.

"Detective, you're a nine. Has that been a problem for you? I should think it would be in your line of work." She crossed her legs and planted her elbow on her knee, her chin on her fist.

Richards actually reared back a bit. "I beg your pardon Miss Tuesday?"

She winked at him. "Just Tuesday. I did a quick reading of your name. A secret numerology system I learned in Tibet. You have a high curiosity quotient so I get the sleuthing bit, but you need more space. You should be traveling. It would help your chakras breathe. Just saying."

Olivia couldn't help herself. "Tuesday! Can it or your chakras will need some breathing room."

Tuesday laughed. "You're a witness, detective. That was a threat. If I end up in the emergency room with suffocating chakras, you know who's responsible." And to Olivia, "I can't help what I see. He should get out more."

Olivia whispered under her breath, "When were you in Tibet," then stared at Richards, apologizing with her eyes. He smiled a little. "I think my chakras are in good shape, but thank you for your concern, Miss Tuesday." To Olivia he said, "Suppose you tell me what I can do for you."

Tuesday stage whispered, "It's just Tuesday."

Olivia acted as though she hadn't heard her. "Well, I want to report a theft. Someone came into my shop and stole my netsuke. Three of them."

"Well, I don't know what netsukes are, but that is your right. Officer Ridley outside will help you with that."

"It's netsuke whether it's one or a hundred and one."

Richards said, "Netsuke. Whatever. Just fill out the form."

Olivia didn't expect to be dismissed so quickly. She hemmed and hawed and finally said, "As long as I'm here, can you tell me how this case is proceeding? Do you have any leads? You certainly kept my assistant a long time. I'm sure you're satisfied that he had nothing to do with it."

Richards stared up at the ceiling before answering. "I'm not at liberty to say."

Olivia pressed him. "Well, has Mrs. Blackman given you any information? Surely she would know if someone had a grudge against her husband."

"Miss Granville, I just told you . . . "

Olivia thumped her hand on the edge of his desk. "Detective Richards, my business, my livelihood is at stake here. If this case doesn't get solved like yesterday, I'm liable to lose everything I've got. People are suspicious of me, they are too freaked out by all this to come into my shop. There are . . . and . . . and . . . and nothing is being done. Have you been questioning Sabrina Chase? From what I've heard, she certainly has a motive. Mr. Blackman seems to have made more enemies than friends. Surely, you can put two and two . . . "

"What do you mean Sabrina Chase has a motive?"

"You mean you haven't heard? She and Mr. Blackman had some dicey financial deal that has put her in jeopardy. Sounds like a motive to me."

Olivia couldn't believe what came out of her mouth next. "And what about Mrs. Harmon and the other suspicious deaths in Darling Valley? What are you doing to solve those crimes? I'm being shunned, it turns out, because of all these homicides that I had nothing to do with."

Richards spoke to her as he would indulging a child. "Miss Granville, I think I know the cases you are referring to and I assure you, we have done everything possible to explain those deaths. There is no credible evidence to prove that, with the exception of Mr. Blackman, there have not been any homicides in Darling Valley."

"It seems to me you are having an epidemic of murder, Detective Richards, and people are looking at me as though I'm Typhoid Mary."

Tuesday burst out laughing, then covered her mouth, faking a cough.

"We have investigated those incidents and I assure you we have found no evidence of foul play."

Just then, the front door opened and all three turned to watch a man and woman, both in their forties, enter the waiting area. The drably but expensively dressed woman leaned into the man for support and he led her to a chair. Olivia recognized her floor length Missoni cardigan that hung on her like tent. He helped her remove a bulky knit shawl and placed her purse on the chair next to her. She immediately retrieved a tissue she had tucked under the sleeve of her sweater and dabbed at her eyes. The man made his way to Officer Ridley's desk.

Olivia froze as she watched the scene, growing a little pale. "Oh, dear. This is awkward. That's Mrs. Blackman." She turned to Tuesday to explain. "The widow. What do I do? Apologize for her husband showing up dead on my doorstep? Offer my condolences?"

Richards said, "I'll take care of this. She's here to pick up Mr. Blackman's effects and sign some papers. Stay here." He walked out and closed the door behind him, but not before Mrs. Blackman looked up and saw Olivia

The widow began screaming. "There she is. Murderer! Are you arresting her? And that, that boy she was conniving with." She broke down sobbing into her tissue that began to shred under the pressure of too many tears, and too much folding and refolding. Her companion turned from Officer Ridley's desk and ran to her side. The widow collapsed into his shoulder, weeping into his sport coat.

"Murderer! Murderer! Get her out of my sight. She's so heartless she's out buying oysters and champagne to celebrate."

Chapter Fifteen: She Did It

Tuesday said, "He knows him," when she saw Richards begin speaking to the man without bothering with introductions.

Olivia, in shock at the woman's accusations, said, "Yeah, and I think that's the guy who showed up and wanted to examine the body. And it looks like her assistant, Marcia, is her spy. She didn't keep her mouth shut about seeing me at Paymoor's."

They listened to the conversation through the two-inch gap between the door and the threshold. The man was speaking.

"Detective, can't you put her in a cell or something and get her out of the way until we are finished here? This day is stressful enough. How could you even think of having her on display while my patient is here." Mrs. Blackman sat with her head in her hands.

Richards tried to calm the situation. "Doctor, Miss Granville is not under arrest nor has she been accused of anything. I have no reason to put her in a cell. She is here on legitimate business, just as you both are. It is an awkward coincidence that you are all here at the same time. I will find someone to escort you to a room where you can have some privacy and then I will join you in a few minutes. I do apologize. It is understandable that Mrs. Blackman is so distraught under the circumstances, but please, you must explain to her that she cannot go about accusing anyone without just cause."

Mrs. Blackman came to life and swept her highlighted hair out of her eyes. The stress of the past days cast a gray pallor over her slender face, rendering it drawn and severe, rather than soft and heartbroken. She leveled steely eyes at Richards.

"Without just cause did you say? What do you mean without just cause? Surely you don't believe that claptrap about finding my husband's body in her armoire? How convenient for her. My husband told me about her. She was trying to ruin him. Now he is dead and she can move her LA celebrity designers in here to take over the business and . . . "

Richards tried to put a comforting hand on her shoulder, but she brushed it away. "You outsiders are all alike. Coming into Darling Valley and disrupting what we built here . . . "

Richards visibly bristled. He turned to the desk. "Officer Ridley, will you escort Mrs. Blackman and Dr. Chandler to the conference room and make them comfortable." He turned to the couple. "Can we get you some coffee or tea?"

Mrs. Blackman snapped, "I want nothing from you but the killer brought to justice. Oh dear. I feel faint again."

She began fanning her face with the tissue. The doctor leaned over. "Please, Greta, don't upset yourself any more than necessary. Did you take your blood pressure medication this morning?"

Mrs. Blackman waved him away. "Oh, I can't remember. I can't think anymore. What that woman has done . . . she has ruined my life. I will never be the same. My dear John. How can I go on without him? How could she have been so brutal? He was the sweetest, gentlest man. You know that, Ross. Wasn't he?"

She became incoherent after than, sobbing uncontrollably.

The doctor put his arm around her. "Of course he was. Everyone knows that. But you must collect yourself, or I'll have to give you another sedative. Here, let me help you up. We'll go into another room until Detective Richards is ready for us. "

He looked at Richards and gave him a pleading look. Olivia caught the doctor's profile and thought of Swiss ski instructors in 1940's films, impossibly blond and competent.

Richards and the doctor each took an arm and eased Mrs. Blackman up and out of her seat. Officer Ridley came over and took her handbag. She braced the grief-stricken widow around the waist when she threatened to sag. Then Mrs. Blackman gathered herself and the trio limped and shuffled down the hall, in time to Mrs. Blackman's heart-rending moans. Richards returned to his office and addressed Olivia.

"I'm sorry you had to witness that." He sat down at his desk. "Did you hear Mrs. Blackman?"

Olivia nodded that she had.

"Do you have any idea what she meant by accusing you of trying to ruin her husband?"

Olivia spluttered, "I couldn't believe my ears. I've told you. I didn't actually know him. Why would I try to ruin him? We weren't in competition with each other. He provided a valuable service. Antique dealers depend on crafts people to repair and restore their valuable pieces. I don't even know anyone who is interested in leaving LA for, for, . . ." She looked incredulous. "Darling Valley?"

Richards said gently, "But you did."

"Yes, but I had personal reasons. I gave up a lot to come here, Detective, I assure you. I left my family, friends, business connections to start over. I don't know anyone who would leave the excitement of the LA scene for the country. I assure you, LA has its share of multimillionaires and billionaires."

Tuesday broke in. "And far better restaurants."

Olivia kicked Tuesday under the chair.

Richards settled into questioning Olivia again. "But you haven't explained to me why you did that, gave up a successful life to go it on your own in out of the way Darling Valley."

Olivia looked at her watch. "Is this part of your interrogation, Detective? Am I required to answer that? I'm beginning to feel like I should have a lawyer with me?"

"Oh, do you need a lawyer?"

"No, of course not. I haven't done anything wrong. Except maybe pick Darling Valley in the first place."

"Miss Granville. It's my job to find out everything I can that will help me solve this case. Naturally, you are a person of interest because of the circumstances of Mr. Blackman's death. So, yes, I do need to know why you picked Darling Valley. It would seem to be an unusual choice for someone of your interests. This is a town where people of means come to live out of the limelight. It is a bit of a closed community in that sense. People have the luxury here of living a lifestyle that is comfortable and private. Very private. How did you find us?"

Olivia stopped to think for a moment and answered literally. "Well, as I recall, I took a wrong turn coming back from Mendocino. I had driven down the coast and was looking for the road to Highway 101. I turned too soon and found myself winding my way through Darling Valley. I'd heard of it of course. Wall Street calls it, what? Billionaire Hollow? Hard to keep that under wraps. And then I saw the lake, the hills shielding it from the ocean fog, the perfect weather and the most scenic town outside of the south of France. I had a personal situation in LA that I needed to remove myself from and the timing coincided with my long range plans to start my own business. I stood on Mountain Road overlooking the lake and the town and knew this was it."

"Was that personal situation named Brooks Baker by any chance?"

Olivia's looked at Tuesday and spoke through clenched teeth. "Have you been talking . . . how could you? You haven't been out of my sight since you got here."

Richards interrupted her. "Miss Granville. Mr. Baker is the most famous architect working in America. The boy wonder. Commissioned to do his first museum at age 19. He has looks, money, prestige. The paparazzi are all over him. I just did a Google search for your name and according to some pictures on E TV News, you two were apparently an item up until four months ago. He's down there, you're up here. What kind of detective would I be if I couldn't put two and two together and come up with celebrity break up?"

"Well, then," said Olivia, fussing with a button on her jacket to cover her embarrassment, "there you have it. But you have the time wrong. It's been almost seven months since we broke up. If you can't trust Wikipedia who can you trust? Any more questions? Can I file my theft complaint and go? I have to deliver an Imari bowl to Sabrina Chase for a charity auction tonight."

Richards gave her an appraising look and said, "Certainly. If I have anymore questions I know where to find you."

"Yes you do."

Richards escorted Olivia and Tuesday to Officer Ridley's desk. He asked her if Mrs. Blackman was okay, and she shook her head up and down, intent on chewing her gum.

To Olivia, "Now if you'll excuse me, ..." and he took off down the hall in the direction of the conference room where Mrs. Blackman waited.

Olivia filled out a form and then she and Tuesday pushed their way past the wall of microphones outside the police station, and, as it was past eleven now, they half jogged back to the house. Tuesday said she wished she had the widow's shoes.

"Why's that," Olivia wheezed.

"Didn't you see the outfit she was wearing? English housekeeper chic, circa 1920. She was a vision in sensible shoes. Hashtag bor-ing! But they'd be comfy on this hike. Slow down for a minute. I can't breathe."

Chapter Sixteen: Reading Tea Leaves

Tuesday ran ahead of Olivia up the walk to the house, her colorful long dress fanning out behind her like a kite.

"Tues?" Olivia waved the keys in front of her. "Hold your horses. Do you have to pee?"

"I'm getting a hit," she said impatiently while Olivia found the right key from the dozen or so on her key chain and wrestled the ancient lock open. "Tea time."

Tuesday rushed upstairs and into the kitchen. She searched through the cupboards and whined, "Ollie, where are your real china cups?"

Olivia dumped her purse and keys on the counter and slumped onto the stool. "Finally, but we have to make this fast. I have to open the shop. You never know. Someone with a taste for the macabre might walk in."

Tuesday was at work opening and closing cabinet doors. "Surely with all the treasures in this place you have a china cup. Real china. And your good pot."

Olivia opened a cupboard under the center island and retrieved a bubble-wrapped blob, unpeeled the plastic and handed a Wedgewood cup and saucer to Tuesday. The matching pot was featured on the lower shelf of her china closet, just below eye level rather than dead on, the better for people to find it in the natural downward sweep of their eyes as they sought out the various treasures on display. Everything was for sale at Olivia's, even some of her personal belongings.

She retrieved the teapot and handed it to Tuesday with a warning. "Rinse them out. I haven't used my good stuff since I arrived."

Tuesday pointed to the shelves displaying the yellow and black Villeroy and Boch pottery that Olivia used for everyday meals. "What are they, plastic plates?"

But she knew what Olivia meant. In LA Olivia threw weekly, sought after dinner parties. Gourmet had featured her in a spread when the magazine was still alive and well. Just before she pulled up stakes and slipped out of Montrose, she was starting to trend on Twitter. When she and Brooks became an item, there was talk of her joining the Real Housewives of Los Angeles. After the sudden breakup, however, Bravo stopped taking her calls. So Olivia had the dining room bling and she knew how to show it off. But she needed a social network to do the kind of entertaining her possessions deserved and that was not happening in Darling Valley.

Tuesday poured water from the boiling tap, swirled it in the cup, then emptied it. "What's your poison? Darjeeling, smoky Lapsang Suchong? Orange Crescent?"

Olivia handed her a black tin of Mariage Freres.

Tuesday examined the label. "Ah. Wedding Imperial. A good omen."

Tuesday prepared the tea and while it steeped, Olivia set a placemat on the table. "You having tea?"

"Not while I work."

Olivia knew the drill from the hundreds of times she had sat at a table while Tuesday pored over the meaning of the scattered fragments of leaves and stems in the bottom of a cup. But the habit of hospitality was too hard to break and she always asked.

Tuesday would only use china cups for her readings. Mugs did not have the sloping bottom that allowed the bits to drift and slide and form the messages. She did not believe in drinking tea while she did a reading. "It dilutes the information." Though it was essential for the questioner to drink the tea they wished to query.

The two made themselves comfortable in the cane chairs at the wrought iron table topped with an old slab of zinc from a bar in Paris. The window overlooked the back garden. To the left was the parking area still held off limits by yellow crime scene tape. Olivia adjusted her chair to block that view. Now she could admire the fuchsia Bougainvillea beginning to climb the back fence.

"I wonder if it will make it through the cold winters here," she mused while Tuesday poured her tea.

"What?" Tuesday looked up to see what Olivia meant. "Oh, yeah. It wouldn't be your house if it didn't have a wall of Bougainvillea."

Olivia's mission in life, one of them anyway, was to recreate a swag of Bougainvillea she once saw on the balcony of a house in Monaco, a trip she made when she did her gap year in Paris. That balcony encouraged her to work harder at her French so she could track down gardeners who could tell her how they managed to drape the lush pink vine all over Provence and the Riviera. Her gardener in LA, whose efforts came close to the Monaco prize, warned her that the winters in Northern California were too cold for Bougainvillea. She must make sure to wrap them in plastic when the temperatures dropped.

"Small price," Olivia had said at the time, though the thin strands of green leaves had few blossoms. She wasn't sure they would make it to November. Unwittingly, she had planted them directly in the path of a sharp wind that came off the Pacific and whistled through her yard.

Olivia blew on her tea to cool it, musing over her garden to take her mind off less pleasant and more immediate subjects, such as murder and theft. Finally, she said, "Done," and placed the cup in its saucer.

Tuesday asked, "Did you leave a little for me?"

Like a little girl at show and tell, Olivia pushed the cup in front of Tuesday, who peered into the cup. "Perfecto."

She pulled her chair closer to the table and began her ritual, which started with a worn silk scarf that she withdrew from her purse. She carried it with her at all times, claiming it kept the spirit energy flowing. Olivia almost caused their first fight by curling her lip and asking, *what energy.* Now she knew better.

Tuesday noted where Olivia had left the spoon, which was critical to her interpretation of the leaves. Then she took the cup and turned the handle towards Olivia, swirled the cup several times to distribute the tea leaves evenly and upended the cup. Each of them watched transfixed as the last spoonful of tea dribbled out, completing the pattern of leaves in the bottom and along the sides of the Wedgewood. Last, she replaced the cup in the saucer and encircled the pale blue silk around it.

Olivia's pulse raced and her heart thrummed in her ears, but she knew better than to rush Tuesday, so she quashed her impatience and waited for Tuesday to begin.

It was the differences between the two friends that made the friendship work. Olivia needed Tuesday's free spirit to loosen her up. In fact, she suspected that one of the reasons Brooks departed so abruptly was that she was too straight-laced, too business focused. Olivia was talented and creative and in the beginning that drew them together. And the sex, of course. But he was the consummate artist and needed someone who would encourage his free-ranging imagination. Olivia claimed he was too impractical. Not in his vision of buildings, but in their day to day life. She once found him trying to create a sculpture out of garbage scraps, and when he saw the disgust on her face. stormed out of the room, snarling, "You never let me see where things will go. You live in a box. I live on the wind."

But Tuesday was the right blend of ingénue and explorer for Olivia. Her friends, struggling under the weight of professional pressures and the need for social dominance, couldn't see the flow between them. They thought Tuesday's cockamamie wardrobe and absorption with the occult too scary oddball. *Tres unprofessional,* one of the partners at her firm observed when Olivia invited Tuesday to a groundbreaking ceremony for a building she had helped design. Brooks questioned the friendship outright. *How can you link yourself with someone who will do NOTHING for your career?* But, despite their fashion disputes, it was Tuesday's unconditional acceptance of Olivia that cemented her loyalty to her madcap friend. In turn, over time, Olivia anchored Tuesday. She believed her when Tuesday first offered to do a reading, admitting that her grandmother had been a sensitive. And despite her strong pragmatic bent, Olivia believed it as well when Tuesday said that she, like her grandmother, also could sense things others could not. You didn't always have to understand something to believe in it.

Whether or not she took the readings seriously, Olivia pressed Tuesday to perfect 'her knowledge of her calling. Recognizing that Tuesday would always color outside the lines, she said, "If you're going to be a tasseomancer, whatever that is, be the best blinking one on the planet."

So, with Olivia's encouragement and United miles, Tuesday studied with a British reader in London who boasted a long list of celebrity clients. The next year she even wrote a book on the subject. Sales tanked, despite her marketing efforts, but the book landed her the gig at the pricey café where she now earned a satisfying living and ballooned her Facebook page to 1,673 followers. In addition, Olivia convinced her that the fact that she could sit still long enough to produce a book was proof she was evolving. That was the magic word. Tuesday wanted to evolve. So it was a serious Tuesday that pondered the spray of leaves across Olivia's cup, looking for symbols that would help Tuesday guide Olivia's own evolution.

"Okay, c'MON. What do you see?" As much as Olivia needed to get downstairs and set up the showroom for customers, should an unsuspecting stray appear, she could not resist the lure of the tea leaves. As far as Olivia was concerned, Tuesday's accuracy was greater than fifty percent and that was good enough for her. Why resist a reading that invariably told her she was on the right path, which was how Tuesday ended their sessions, with probably the same prescience that allowed her to tell Carrie a new man was on the horizon. Everybody's on the right path, whether they know it or not.

Tuesday studied the cup and without looking up, asked, "Are you expecting company?"

Oh no, was it going to be one of those readings? "Tuesday. You're here already."

Tuesday pointed to the leaves. "Someone's coming to see you."

"Duh. I run a business that's open to the public. People are always coming to see me. Well, sometimes they do. On a good day. Are they going to give me money, that's what I want to know?"

Tuesday shook her head, her hair accessories floating from side to side. "No, I think this is personal. A man. And he has dark skin."

"So Detective Richards is coming back? I should hope so. To return my armoire and shoes."

Tuesday spoke in a caricature of a fortuneteller, assuming a trance-like voice and a fake Transylvanian accent. "You will disappoint him. And there is a problem on the horizon of your own making."

Just because she was doing a reading didn't mean she couldn't laugh. It was her sense of humor that made her readings so popular.

"What kind of problem?"

"I can only tell you what I see, sweet pea. A clump of leaves at the bottom near the handle."

Olivia threw up her hands. "Stop. I can't listen any more. I'm too nervous. I don't want to know bad things. And don't give me your spiel about bad things are opportunities. I've had all the opportunities I can stand since I moved here. A failing business, a tenant who hates me, a town that won't accept me, a murder in my armoire and a thief in my showroom. Give me some good news or let me get on with my day."

"Well, you'll like this. You're going to get a nice surprise."

Olivia brightened.

Tuesday scrutinized the bottom of the cup again. "Hmm. Or is it a disappointment?"

"Oh Tues! Enough. Where is the instruction that I'm on the right path and doing what I was born to do?"

Tuesday sat back and folded her arms. "If you're going to insult me, I can't concentrate."

Olivia stood up, ending the session. "I'm washing up the china and going about my business. If I have any, that is."

She air kissed Tuesday as she scooped up the Wedgewood. "Not a good time, Tues. Truce?"

Tuesday air kissed back. "Whatever. Truce."

An hour later, Olivia put the Closed for Lunch sign on the front door and went upstairs to confirm to Tuesday that, as she herself had predicted, no one was coming in to buy Olivia's gorgeous antiques.

She found Tuesday sitting at the counter, green from the clay mask plastered all over her face.

"Listen. I forgot about the oysters. Let's make a salad and my special champagne mignonette and put our feet up. Sabrina left a message while we were out this morning. She's miffed that I didn't make my contribution to the auction sooner, but I've had other things on my mind. It only occurred to me two days ago to donate something as good PR. She's up to her ears in planning the auction, though I don't know how she can cope after what happened. Wants me to come early and drop off my donation tonight before the affair gets started. She is really pissed that she has to give her shoes to Detective Richards. What is that all about? Does he have a shoe fetish?"

While she fixed the salad, she opened up a new line of conversation. "I have a decision to make, Tues."

"I'll say you do." Tuesday's face was still rigid from the mask and she spoke as though she had dental instruments in her mouth. "Should you 'ake a 'ove on 'ichards 'fore or after 'is case is settled. Tell you what I'd do."

"Tuesday! What a disgusting thing to say. I don't have designs on that guy. He's got ice in his veins and he's terribly rude."

"Oh 'at's not what I saw flowing when he looked at you. He is all over you like butter on toast, girl."

"That's not what the tea leaves said."

"You didn't let me finish. But my eyes saw what my eyes saw at the police station. I'm just saying, he's there for the picking if you ask me." *Ee's air for the icking ih you ask ee.*

"And just how does he fit the definition of a MAD man? He's mature, I'll give you that. He does seem to take control of things. But a cop who's affluent? And he's probably got a whole family in the Punjab that he's supporting. Course I do get lost in those eyes, but no. What are we doing? Tuesday, what I'm talking about is, do I go ahead with the sale knowing that if this murder is not solved no one will come, and I will look even more foolish with my prize possessions on the lawn and no buyers? Or do I throw in the towel and just pack up and go back to LA. Maybe Griffiths and Graham will take me back. I know my clients would love to see me. I made good contacts there."

Tuesday pointed to her face and said, "Ee ri ack." She took off for the bathroom and came back a few minutes later rubbing a fragrant cream into her clean face. "Now what was I saying?" She gave an approving look at the salad Olivia was piling on to plates.

"Look honey, it's the beginning of the week. You have until Saturday. Let's get busy and see what we can find out to move things along. Do we have a cause of death yet? What's with that business partner? Sabrina? Remember what Carrie said about her? Seems to me she should be too broken up about losing her business partner to carry on with a society function? Right?"

Olivia served lunch, but before she sat down, checked her phone for news updates. The doctor who wanted to certify the cause of death must have pull. The San Francisco Herald was pushing a theory that it was an illicit sex game gone very wrong and the Hollywood Times ID'd the location where the body was found as the Darling Valley home Olivia shared with Brooks. That made Olivia so mad she started to throw her phone across the room until Tuesday snatched it out of her hands.

After their first bites, Olivia told Tuesday all she knew about Sabrina Chase. "I swear, there must not be a charity event that she doesn't run. Rumor has it that she raises more money in Darling Valley than anyone in Hollywood. She knows how to reach into those deep pockets. I'm curious to see what she'll get for my Imari bowl. Probably more than I would selling it in the shop. I wish I had her touch.

Olivia stopped to slurp the last oyster and lick her lips. "But other than that, I don't know much about her. Could she have a motive for killing her partner? I wish I knew. But I don't know their relationship. Did they have an argument? Does she have a financial stake in his death? I'm handicapped here. I don't know enough about the players without a scorecard. But now that you've made me think of her, she's on my mind. And speaking of which, I should wrap up the bowl for tonight." She made a wry face. "To protect it from the wild hordes lining the driveway wanting to snap it up. I'll go get it."

Tuesday pushed her plate away and said she'd come with her.

Olivia described the piece with her hands as they descended the stairs into the showroom. "It's not the most valuable thing in the shop, but it is beautiful. An onion neck vase. It's only late 19th century, but the gold work is exquisite. Wait till you see it. Probably worth $1,200 or so. I have a piece that is from the Topkapi Palace, but I wouldn't give that away to auction. I have it on consignment from a collector. He wants $8,000 and I think just on its reputation, I'll get it. Early 18th century. Japanese not Chinese. You know the difference?"

They had reached the French doors. Olivia didn't turn around to see Tuesday shrug her shoulders in a gesture of, what do I know or care about Imari bowls?

"The bowl is over there on the tray table." Olivia walked towards the outside wall where she had arranged under the window a duck egg blue klismos chair and small mahogany tea table and porcelain reading lamp. "It won't take a minute to get this ready. I have some bubble wrap in the office."

But as she got closer to the wall, circling around an English table with barley twist legs and a pair of Chippendale bedside tables, she saw a circle in the light film of dust where the bowl should have been.

"Wait a minute. Where's the bowl? It's been in the same spot for two weeks. Where did it go?"

Tuesday came up behind her to look, though she had no idea what she was looking for. She asked the most obvious question, "When did you see it last?"

Olivia put her hands on her head and looked from side to side. "Well, I'm not sure. It's been there so long it's like a fixture. But I would have noticed if it were gone. I come through each day to get the showroom shipshape before I open the doors for business. I know everything in this shop. I'm sure I saw it yesterday. You know how I am."

Tuesday shook her head acknowledging her friend's compulsiveness when it came to her business. "Do I ever. But, it has been a crazy time. I believe you, but I'm just saying. Things get away from us when we're stressed."

Olivia walked over to the table that, until this morning, held the netsuke. She pointed to the empty spot and called to Tuesday, who was searching tabletops for the bowl. "Tuesday, someone is stalking me. Mr. Blackman's body, the netsuke, and now the bowl. I'm being targeted. I know I am, and I don't know why."

Olivia narrowed her eyes, a signal for anyone in close range to watch out. "But I'm going to find out. Now I have to find something else to give to Sabrina. And call Detective Richards to report this."

The DVPD arrived within fifteen minutes of Olivia dialing 911. They scoured the shop and Olivia's living quarters, but found nothing that would lead them to the bowl.

Two hours later Sabrina Chase called to say she was behind schedule. Would Olivia mind coming even earlier to the auction to drop off the bowl. Say 6:30 instead of seven?

"Of course not," Olivia assured her, a plan that began to form in Detective Richards' office now presenting itself to her full blown.

Olivia told Tuesday she had to run an errand. "You don't mind watching the shop, do you? I'll be gone a half hour, tops. The only people I think would come by are the gawkers we saw this morning. If they ask about prices add a zero to the number on the tag or tell them to come back on Saturday when everything will be on sale."

Olivia searched her bag and withdrew her keys, climbed into the truck and was gone, making a beeline for Darling Boulevard again. Without Tuesday for distraction, she obsessed on the scene at the police station and Mrs. Blackman's allegations. She could imagine what the pedestrians were saying, especially if they were friends with Mrs. Blackman. Imagine, accusing her of trying to ruin her husband. Olivia tried to talk herself out of her anger. The woman is in shock, she told herself. Needs to blame somebody. Clearly her husband meant the world to her and she was desperate. But accusing Olivia of murder? She was mid-thought when she arrived at the bank and, with a squeal of tires, pulled into one of the parking spaces reserved for customers.

Olivia nodded at Darlene, The Darling Valley Bank greeter, when the girl opened the door for her and offered a silver tray with an actual linen doily upon which rested assorted cookies from The Salted Caramel Bakery. Darlene knew her by name from the frequent trips Olivia had made to the bank negotiating a loan.

Olivia waved away the tray. "No thanks, Darlene. Not hungry today. Is Mr. Fastner in? I need to see him."

Without waiting for an answer, Olivia headed for the loan manager's office, a glassed in cubicle distinguished by a cheap, spiky plant standing guard outside his door. Olivia hated it. Fastner looked up from his computer to see Olivia marching toward him.

Instead of leaping across the desk like an Olympic hurdler as he usually did, he flustered about for a moment with papers before finally getting up to open the door. The Ichabod Crane lookalike gave her a tenuous hello, as if Olivia might be carrying a flesh-eating virus. A sign that he had been reading the news and listening to the gossip. How could he not know what had been going on at Darling Valley Design and Antiques? Why would he not want to distance himself from her?

During their loan negotiations for her house, Fastner had made it clear that he would do everything possible to help Olivia secure her financing. When she signed the final papers and their business was done, he had all but kissed her hand as she left his office and said, "Olivia, call on me for anything. ANYthing." She had giggled at his fawning all the way to the car. But now she would take him up on that offer.

Olivia helped herself to the seat across from Fastner. It struck her that this was the second time that day she had sat in a man's office pleading her case. "Mr. Fastner . . . "

Fastner had turned down the heat on his usual greeting, but remained courteous. "Please. Olivia," he said, leaning back in his chair instead of salivating across the desk. Call me Elgin." She gave him props for that.

"Yes, well, Elgin." She beamed a buttery smile at him, and he returned a slight upturn at the corners of his mouth. "I'm sure you've heard about the difficulty I'm in."

"You mean because of John Blackman. Yes. I can't imagine what it has been like for you."

But he was not showing all of his cards. He had yet to offer to help her, which was what she was hoping for. She hated groveling. But business was business she reminded herself as she began her speech.

"Well, as you can imagine, there are rumors going around town that instead of being victimized by this crime myself--my business has absolutely dried up--I am being implicated in it. Can you imagine?" She allowed her lower lip to quiver.

She fussed with the top button of her shirt as if to get some air, pleased when Fastner glued his eyes to her bosom, small though it was. She heaved a big breath, holding her chest taut for just a moment, until she was sure she had his full attention. Then she relaxed into a desolate sigh. "I need to do everything I can to find out who did this hideous thing and exonerate myself." Eyes up high now, Elgin. Look at me, she instructed silently. Time to look at my eyes.

As though he had heard her, he looked into her eyes, momentarily lost in the shimmering green pools. "Yes, of course. But how can I help?"

"Elgin." she drawled his name shamelessly. "I have heard some, shall we say nasty rumors about one of the bank's clients. And I fully understand confidentiality and all that. But I thought perhaps under the circumstances, and because we are such good friends . . ." She leaned forward, almost laughing at her ridiculous performance, but Fastner seemed rapt.

"Yes, and who might that be, Olivia?"

"Mr. Blackman's partner. Sabrina Chase."

"Why yes, she's a client of ours. I'm not revealing anything out of school. She did a public promotion on the local cable station for the bank."

Olivia leaned over the desk and extended her hand, all but inviting Fastner to stroke it. "Well, I have heard that Ms. Chase is in financial difficulties. Quite extreme, I understand. The awful suggestion is that she might have had a motive for, for. Oh, I can't even say the word. For harming Mr. Blackman. I don't know the details. There might have been business insurance or a buyout or some such issue. I thought perhaps you could tell me about it."

Fastner sat back in his chair immediately and vigorously shaking his head. "Oh, no, Olivia. No, please don't go there. You're a businesswoman, after all. You know how important confidentiality is between banker and client. Why, the bank would suffer terribly if I were to reveal anything about our customers' affairs. I'm sorry. You know I'd do anything to help you, really I would. But there is a line I cannot cross. I'm sure you understand."

Olivia scoffed to herself, Hm. So he has a backbone, after all. She realized she was barking up the wrong tree and mentally kicked herself, realizing that this might have been a very bad move. In fact, she hoped she had not lost Fastner's interest in her. Why had she acted so impulsively? She hoped this wasn't going to backfire. After all, she needed to call in some chits if she couldn't meet her mortgage payment this month. Fastner was not somebody she wanted to alienate.

She stood up and extended her hand. "Of course, I understand. What was I thinking? I'm just so, so desperate." And that was the truth, and heartfelt.

Fastner came around his desk and took her hand in both of his. "Don't think about it any more, Olivia. We'll just forget this discussion ever took place. Should anyone ask what you were doing in my office, well, I'll plead client confidentiality."

He gave her a smirk, clearly pleased with his own joke.

"Thank you so much," genuine notes of sadness notes coloring her voice.

He walked her to his door, but did not accompany her through the lobby. Covering his bases, she thought, in case one of Mrs. Blackman's peeps should see him.

Chapter Seventeen: The Auction

Tuesday sashayed into Olivia's bedroom drenched in feathers and beads. She did a coy shuffle off to Buffalo and asked, "How do I look? Boring? Brilliant? Off the charts?"

Between trying to convince Tuesday to tone down her jewelry and explaining the pecking order to expect at the auction, Olivia saw the time slipping away. In less than an hour she had to deliver the replacement bowl to Sabrina. She hoped Sabrina wouldn't know there'd been a switch, she'd said it was already on the program. Before they left for the country club, she also had to track down Mr. Bacon. She missed his call again when she ran down to the laundry room for a moment to put a load of towels in the washing machine. When she called him back, he had not picked up. She'd give him one more try tonight. Her mood was not conducive to socializing, but she had to put on her game face. And do something about Tuesday's outfit.

"Tuesday, I think the feathers and beads, well, they compete. And when you wear them, they are so, well, unique. No, that's not the word I want. You want them to stand out as individual pieces and not, you know, well, like compete."

Tuesday shot her a get over yourself look. "Miss Priss? How long have we known each other? You think I don't get the code for over the top and I'm embarrassing you in public?

In LA, Tuesday's rainbow combinations found in thrift shops and last call sales blended in with her crowd. All her Melrose Avenue friends had multi-colored hair. They tried to outdo one another to see who could come up with the most outlandish outfits and show off the most cleavage without getting picked up for public nudity. Olivia was the one who got called to task for her conservative wardrobe. Tuesday would harangue her: *Show your individuality. Why do you always have to look so Rodeo Drive? People will think you have no imagination.*

Even though Olivia would remind her that just one of her outfits cost more than Tuesday's whole closet, Tuesday scoffed. "You're just lucky I can overlook things. I don't know why you're so afraid of the fashion police."

But tonight Olivia needed Tuesday to tone it down. She dropped the mask of fashion consultant and laid it on the line.

"Tues. I can't give these people any more ammunition. Even if Detective Richards," at the name Tuesday pantomimed fluttering eyes and pressed the back of her hand to her forehead in a swoon.

Olivia shot her a look. "Even if he takes the spotlight off me, this is ultra conservative USA. I need to blend in, not stand out. Now if we were socializing with the billionaires it wouldn't matter. They have made it. They are so high on the pile that they regard bohemianism as fun. They don't have to please or answer to anyone. But the mere multi-millionaires? Watch out. They don't want to be thrown out of the club for wearing the wrong designer frock or sporting diamonds at breakfast. Even if they once belonged to Catherine the Great."

Tuesday cocked her head in surprise.

"True story."

Olivia could do nothing about her friend's tri-tone pink hair, but she did get rid of the feathers and convinced her to wear one of her dresses instead of a Bollywood costume she got in a trade with a prop girl she knew at Warner Bros. That Olivia's dress was covered in sequins helped seal the deal, along with a promise of a mouthwatering halibut dinner at Hugo's, the best restaurant in Darling Valley.

Olivia had already schooled Tuesday in the guest list, explaining that the first tier, the true billionaires never attended these charity events. They gave endowed chairs to universities, not trinkets like early 18th century porcelain just to wring some dollars for the town's historical museum. Those hotshots had suffered through the boring dinners and auctions on their way up the ladder and now they could stay home and watch basketball, probably a team that they owned. Any excuse to behave like the little boys they all were at heart.

Tuesday didn't recognize any of the names on the list, anyway. She wasn't connected to the world of finance, cutting edge biotech innovations or venture capitalists. In Tuesday's world, if you weren't a rock star or movie mogul, you weren't anybody.

They took the Mercedes for the dress up occasion and Tuesday pulled into the country club valet parking lane, making their way to the ballroom just as the caterers were setting up the champagne and caviar bar. Olivia asked an officious server where she could find Sabrina. "You mean the bitch with the frozen hair who thinks she's Empress of Darling Valley?"

"That would be our Sabrina," said Olivia.

The guy pointed to an archway near the bandstand. "Down that hallway. You'll come to an office at the end. She's in there still swearing over seating charts. At this hour." He shook his head in disgust and returned to stacking flutes next to the champagne fountain.

Sabrina said, "Tuesday, see if you can grab yourself a glass of champs. I'll hand this off to Sabrina and join you. We'll only stay a few minutes."

Halfway down the long corridor she heard voices coming from the office at the end of the hall. Male and female. The man's voice sounded familiar, but she couldn't place it. Oh, yes. It was Elgin Fastner, the banker. Olivia was tempted to back away and return to the ballroom, but realized that having Sabrina there would smooth over any awkwardness from their chat this afternoon. He certainly wouldn't reprimand her again in front of Sabrina for her tasteless request. Would he?

Closer to the office, she could make out two figures behind the open door. She was about to call *Hello* when she heard Sabrina say, "Elgin! Take your hands off me. How many ways are there to say no? Why don't you find someone in your own zip code, like in Marin City."

What came next was just a muffled low exchange and then footsteps stomping toward the door. Olivia slipped into a musty closet and tried to melt into the woodwork while she suppressed a sneeze. Footsteps continued past the closet and in the distance she heard Elgin say hello, and a female gush back that she was so happy to see him, then the click of heels down towards Olivia. They continued on into Sabrina's office and she heard two women chatter about details of the auction. Olivia thought it safe to slink out of the closet and present herself to Sabrina, her opinion of Elgin changed from a numbers nerd to a garden-variety sleaze ball, hitting on every woman with whom he had veto power over business loans.

Olivia peeked her head around the door, spotting Sabrina leaning over a chart of some kind discussing names with the woman. Olivia knocked lightly. Sabrina looked up, clearly surprised at the interruption. It was obvious to Olivia that Sabrina did not realize she had overheard her conversation with Elgin.

Rushed, Sabrina said, "A moment please, Olivia," and turned her attention back to the volunteer. The hand done calligraphy on her nametag was a nice touch, Olivia thought, expensive but showing the patrons that their money was going to a class act. No *Hello my name is* . . . for Sabrina.

Sabrina dismissed the woman, then gestured for Olivia to come to her desk. And hurry. "Finally you're here. Is that the bowl? Give me a minute and we'll find a place for it on the display table in the ballroom." Then she turned her attention to the chart again.

Olivia held the bowl to her bosom like it was a fragile newborn. Though no one would know or care that she had made a substitution in place of the stolen one, she would feel an ache each time she saw the empty spot on the book case, long time home of the bowl. She had a special fondness for Imari. Not because she thought it was particularly beautiful. She admired the craftsmanship of the gaudy blue and red pieces threaded with gold, but she preferred Meissen. The bowl she was about to give away had belonged to her grandmother, from whom her grandfather insisted Olivia inherited her good taste. Though she was prickly in her relationships, Nan had insisted from the beginning that Olivia had talent and subsidized her education when student loans and grants dried up.

Sabrina tossed her Mont Blanc onto the chart in disgust. "These people who don't respect RSVP dates. They've had six weeks to decide if they are coming and then they accept two hours before the event. If they weren't paying for a premium table, I'd tell them where to go."

Olivia thought, I bet you just would, but nodded with a commiserating smile. Sabrina led her back down the hall and out into the ballroom to the linen-draped table with the pieces for the silent auction. Olivia handed the bowl to her and said a silent, "I'm so sorry, Nan," when she set it down.

Olivia made her apologies. "You know I have a guest, Sabrina. I can't stay too long. I've promised my friend Tuesday one of Hugo's famous dinners."

Sabrina blew her off. "Just chat up a few people during the cocktail hour to get them interested in your piece. Then consider the handcuffs off." Within a nanosecond, she was heading back to her office.

Olivia called to her. "Oh, by the way. If it doesn't sell, when can I pick it up?"

Sabrina turned and replied, her voice dripping with ice, "If it doesn't sell? Everything sells at my auctions." Olivia felt the temperature in the room drop at least twenty degrees as Sabrina continued to her office. Olivia regretted giving her grandmother's bowl away. Sabrina wouldn't have noticed if she'd given her an old motel ash tray.

Gradually the room filled with partygoers and the wait staff faded into the crowd. A few jewels glittered, but this was an after work party and the guests strutted in Italian business suits and designer daywear. The bling was on their feet. Women in Christian Louboutain, Manolo Blahnik and Jimmy Choo, the men in handcrafted English leather laceups. Olivia nodded to a few familiar faces and introduced Tuesday to the few who stopped to chat. A server came by and offered a tray of caviar toast. Tuesday refused, but Olivia took one to take her mind off what might be happening at home. She all but heard stealthy footsteps creeping through the showroom, her valuables clinking into someone's pockets. She mentally kicked herself again for passing on the high tech alarm system Elgin had suggested she include in the original loan. Olivia heard a friendly voice. "Olivia? Why am I not surprised to see you here?"

Olivia turned into the face of Carrie wearing too much makeup and juggling a tray of champagne flutes.

"Carrie! Thank you, I will." Olivia took a glass and gestured for Tuesday to help herself.

Tuesday replaced her glass and said brightly, "Ready for Mr. Right?"

Carrie whispered, "I been walking on air since you told me that stuff. And until he shows up, I'm here serving up your poison. We were told to keep the booze coming so's it will open up the checkbooks."

Olivia laughed. "Well I'm a donor so you don't have to waste the good stuff on me."

"You a donor!" Carrie laughed.

Olivia pointed to the Imari bowl that now sat next to a pair of wedding champagne flutes, the stems tied with white satin ribbon.

"That's mine. Next to the Baccarat." She recognized the pattern. "Let's see which cheapskate donated them. You can get those at Bloomingdales for a hundred dollars."

Carrie shot a you're kidding me scowl at her. "A hundred bux for a set of glasses?"

Olivia returned a hapless grin. "Each, my dear. A hundred bux each."

Tuesday giggled and finished off her champagne and replaced her empty glass with a full one before Carrie said bye and offered her wares to a couple behind Olivia.

"What's the matter with you, Ollie. You passed up a golden opportunity."

Olivia wiped the corners of her mouth with her cocktail napkin, mainly for something to do while she smiled inanely at the incoming partygoers who looked at her like she carried the plague. "What do you mean?"

"Carrie. She's a gold mine of information and you natter on about cheapo wine glasses?"

Olivia tipped her glass to Jesse the fishmonger who squeezed his way to the oyster bar. "Got to see how

Sabrina's displaying the wares," he said, his excuse for not stopping to chat. Olivia mouthed, "Yours?" to a set of Japanese carving knives and Jesse nodded and mouthed back, "Diamonds," and Olivia noticed the little studs in the handles. To no one she said, "This place is too over the top even for me."

Tuesday nudged Olivia and in a stage whisper complained, "And you let Mr. Gorgeous 2013 go by without snagging him for a little tête-à-tête?"

"Tuesday. I told you this afternoon, Jesse's young enough to be my little brother."

"Um, girlfriend. You're not the only one at this party that could use an infusion of testosterone."

"But Tues, you're only going to be here a few days."

"Like, my point exactly? And who's going to entertain me while you're locked up in the pokey?"

Olivia shook her head in a vehement no. "You'll move on and I'll have to face my neighbors with their heads spinning from a slam bam with my friend Tuesday. This isn't LA where you can disappear into the crowd if your sleep over doesn't turn out to be love everlasting."

"What do you think is going to happen, you'll get picked up for pandering?"

"In this conservative town I wouldn't be surprised. Behave. And what about the script guy you were telling me about."

Tuesday turned up her nose. "He's not a script guy. He's in turnaround."

Olivia took another sip of her champagne and said, "Whatever," into the glass, and when she looked up it was into the velvety eyes of Detective Richards.

"Miss Granville, this is unexpected."

He turned his attention to Tuesday. "And Miss, Miss"

Olivia said, "Tuesday."

"Yes, of course. Miss uh Tuesday."

Olivia's surprised gaze whipsawed from his eyes to the equally beautiful orbs of the brunette beauty holding his arm. The air went out of what little bit of party ebullience Olivia had managed to resurrect for this event. Richards turned to his companion to introduce her, but a man next to him backed up without looking and when he gestured to apologize, sprayed his champagne down the front of Richards' lapel and shirtfront. While the detective was busy brushing away the man's cocktail napkin and offer of help, the girl introduced herself. Olivia heard Tasmania, but the last name got lost in the buzz of the growing crowd and the swish of her jet-black waves cascading down her back.

Olivia gave Tasmania a weak smile, fighting a surge of disappointment that dampened any last enthusiasm she had for the fundraiser as surely as the stranger's champagne had soaked Richards' shirt.

She had a sudden desire to get out of that ballroom in a hurry. If she mentioned to Richards that, once again, the police had been singularly ineffectual in tracking down her stolen Imari bowl, she wasn't sure how she would camouflage her rage. She didn't know what else they would talk about.

To fill in the awkward silence as the foursome smiled blankly at each other, Olivia raised her glass in a wordless toast, downed her champagne and said, "Well, Tuesday, time for us to mosey."

She turned to Richard's companion. "The Imari bowl is mine. See if you can bid up the price," and both Richards and the woman gave Olivia a puzzled look.

Olivia reached past Tasmania to plant her empty glass on a passing server's tray, motioned to Tuesday to do the same, took her friend's arm and marched her through the crowd to the exit.

Outside, while they waited for the valet to bring Tuesday's rented Mercedes around, they heard a commotion in the bushes on the side of the colonnaded entrance.

Angry male voices cut the air and the two women strained to look.

"You pay up or else."

"Don't you threaten me, you . . . "

The parking attendants rushed to break up the fight, too late to stop the first blow. The four attendants outnumbered the combatants and quickly subdued the two men. But they couldn't stop the swearing and threats. They pushed them back from each other, further out of the lights in the entranceway, making it even harder for Olivia to see what was going on. A manager of some kind came running out and pressed the arriving guests back, trying to block their view of the fray. One of the men was ordered to leave and Olivia could see a short, stocky figure in work clothes retreating to the parking lot. He made a final assault, turning to yell, "We're not done here."

The other man shouted back, "Don't you threaten me. I know what you did the other night." By now the attendants had pushed him further back towards the bushes. He insisted he had an invitation to the party and searched through his pockets until he retrieved a square envelope.

Olivia saw the attendant read the name and, satisfied, allowed him to pass, saying, "But no more trouble, okay Mr. Gotshalk?"

Olivia whispered in Tuesday's ear. "Gotshalk? That's my customer's name. Must be her son."

The Mercedes arrived. Tuesday wound around the parking lot to the exit. Olivia shouted, "Tuesday, look!"

Tuesday stopped the car and they watched the pugilist getting in to his truck. He gunned the Toyota and backed out of his parking space, giving Olivia and Tuesday a clear view of him raising his fist to his passenger, and pounding on the steering wheel. Tuesday followed him slowly. He pulled under a street lamp and Olivia gasped. The driver was raising his fist to Cody.

Chapter Eighteen: Dinner at Hugos

At Hugo's, the server cleared the ratatouille and goat cheese tart crumbs from the table and signaled to her assistant to serve the halibut while she refilled Olivia and Tuesday's wine glasses with another two fingers of Pinot Grigio. Olivia assured the woman that the start to their meal was all they had hoped for and, yes, they couldn't wait for the halibut in cream and champagne but, they would try to leave room for the queen of desserts, Grand Marnier Soufflé.

Tuesday remarked that judging by the menu, it must be retro night at Hugo's, but otherwise, the scene outside the country club had subdued the two friends. They'd said little after they got onto the road and left Cody and his contentious friend behind. Now, half an hour later, the wine began to work its magic, relaxing them and opening them up.

Olivia said, "I have more questions than there are answers in the universe. Why didn't Mrs. Gotshalk's son take off his Ermengildo Zegna sports coat before pounding the other guy into the boxwood topiary?"

Tuesday said, "My list has," she pretended to read a piece of paper, "who is Mrs. Gotshalk? Why was the poundee giving Cody what all in his 4x4? And if I'm allowed one more, how can that dreamy detective afford to pony up $2,500 a plate for himself and his plus one?"

She looked at Olivia's face. "Gotcha. You winced when I mentioned the girlfriend. Don't tell me he's just an annoying gumshoe."

Distractedly, Olivia drew a circle in the condensation on her wine glass. "You didn't see anything of the kind on my face. This has been a dreadful day. I'm just tired, that's all."

Then it was Tuesday's turn to jaw drop. Olivia said, "What?" and turned in the direction of Tuesday's wide-eyed gawp. She quickly whipped her head around.

"Don't stare, Tues. Don't let him know we've seen him."

Tuesday said, "So maybe he was there to check on security, but if I paid cash money for those tickets I'd sure want my rubber chicken. What does Detective McDreamy want with dinner here?"

Olivia tasted her halibut, scraped some of the cream sauce away, then squeezed a few more drops of lemon over it. "He probably doesn't want to conduct his affairs in front of all of Darling Valley. There's a little more privacy in that dark corner over there, since this is a slow night at Hugo's."

"Yeah, or maybe he's running a protection racket in DV and Hugo lets him order in his pricy restaurant without worrying about paying a tab. Or maybe . . . "

"Stop Tuesday, I don't care what he's doing here, why he's here and who he's with. Let's eat, go home and get some sleep.

Tuesday adjusted her sequined shift to show a little more of her muffin tops. "Well, okay. All I have to say is, did you see the mouth on that girlfriend? Those lips would rival an Orangutan in the zoo. I didn't know there was that much Botox outside of Hollywood. New topic, what do you think young Master Gotshalk meant when he said he knew what that guy was doing the other night. Too sinister for me. I mean the whole scene was creepy, but what else could he mean but some involvement with Blackman's death. I don't think anybody on the planet is talking about anything else."

Olivia nodded. "Yeah, I'm thinking the same thing. And there's something else that happened tonight that I haven't had a chance to tell you about."

She recounted the scene between Sabrina and Elgin Fastner. "I just can't get over it, Tues. He's pimping himself for bank loans. After giving me that speech about the moral compass of the banking industry wouldn't allow him to help me out with info about Sabrina when I've got a life and death situation on my hands."

Tuesday fiddled with her fork. "What I don't understand, Olivia, is why you've been telling me since you moved up here that Darling Valley is the next best thing to Nirvana? So far I haven't met anyone who isn't under suspicion for murder, unfriendly to the point of rudeness or convinced you are the devil's spawn. What, exactly, is so great about this place? And this is okay halibut, but compared to Spago's in LA? Are you kidding me? Surely you didn't have to come all this way to avoid running into Brooks."

Olivia threw down her fork, paying no attention to the clattering that registered at least three tables away when it bounced off her water glass. "I've asked you, Tues. Brooks is off limits. I don't want to discuss him. You keep asking me about him, telling me what he's up to and I've told you I'm not interested and he can fly to the moon on Pegasus for all I care. Subject closed."

Tuesday said, "I've been doing all that? Seems like our conversations have revolved around your lack of money and the town's epidemic of murder. I don't recall mentioning Brooks that much." She rolled her eyes. "But that's just me."

Olivia sank her head into her hands. When she looked up, she laughed. "Have I been borrowing a jack? Yeah, maybe I have."

She meant the story of the man out in the country with a flat tire and no jack. He sees the light of a farmhouse off in the distance but by the time he gets there, he has convinced himself that the farmer won't let him borrow a jack. He knocks, the farmer opens the door and the salesman has worked himself into such a fit of anger, he punches the guy in the nose. Borrowing a jack became their code for stupidly obsessing over something, usually a man.

"Listen," Tuesday said, "I'm picking up the check on this one. Let's go back to the house, have a small brandy and call it a night. But just so you know, the reason I got no love from these people tonight is this granny dress you made me wear."

Olivia laughed, carefully avoiding casting her eyes in the direction of Detective Richards and his gorgeous date.

Tuesday eased the Mercedes into the driveway and Olivia took a flashlight out of her purse.

"What's that for?"

"Just in case we catch the robber red-handed."

"And what, you're going to deck him with your purse light? Let me get my phone if you're afraid. I have 911 on speed dial."

Olivia stumbled a bit. Even though Sabrina ordered good champagne for the event, Olivia had more than she realized. She righted herself and said, "Okay, Tues. Let's secure the perimeter."

They crept up to the porch, looked through the paned windows. Olivia cautiously opened the front door and called out, "It's the police. Show yourself now."

Tuesday sighed. "Please, baby girl. Let there be light," and reached in front of Olivia for the switch next to the door. The crystal chandeliers came to life and flooded the showroom. She gave Olivia a *what did I tell you* glare. Olivia dropped her purse, flashlight and keys on the nearest table and took off her shoes, Morse code for why do I torture myself with these stilettos. Then she grabbed the shoes with one hand and her purse and keys with the other and led the way to the back staircase.

Chapter Nineteen: Sons of Anarchy

Olivia called Cody as soon as she poured her first cup of coffee the next morning. Half a second later when Tuesday staggered into the kitchen squeezing sleep from the corner of her eyes and yawning so wide Olivia saw the gap in her back teeth, she held up the phone and pointed to the pot. Tuesday said something but Olivia turned her attention to Cody, who answered with a groggy, "Yeah?"

"Cody? You have some explaining to do. What were you doing with that thug who was fighting with Mrs. Gotshalk's son last night?"

A silence during which Olivia slugged down a big gulp of coffee and Cody played innocent.

Olivia wasn't having it. She glared at her phone as if to send the evil eye through cyberspace. "Yes, today is a work day. And what do you mean, what thug? I was at the country club last night and saw the whole thing. The fight, one of the guys peeling out of there in a pickup shaking his fist at you."

More silence and another sip of coffee. "That was Roger? Roger from Blackman's? Come over here now. We have to talk." Then she noticed her sweats-for-pj's and Tuesday's bedroom hair and skin tight T-shirt and thong that she slept in and changed her mind. "No, make it an hour. We need to get decent."

She hung up. "Want some eggs, Tues?"

Tuesday answered, "Does a drowning man want a lifeline?" sounding like she had been at the same all night kegger with Cody.

"But after breakfast I'm going to start my cleanse and give up sugar and alcohol."

Olivia drained her coffee. "Why don't you shower while I cook?"

Tuesday nodded sleepily, looking like she was suffering an attack of morning sickness.

Olivia pointed to the colorful array of alternative treatments Tuesday had unpacked, but never looked at. "Tues? Do you think maybe you need one of your potions?"

Tuesday looked at the corner of the counter cluttered with her stash and shook her head. "I need to neutralize my body. I'll start taking them this afternoon."

She headed back towards the bathroom just as the front door bell rang. "Holy wake up call, is this Granville Central Station?"

She looked at the rooster clock over the stove and grumbled to Olivia, "Why are we up so early? Did our mothers arrive while we were sleeping?"

Olivia scowled. "I told you to go easy on the brandy last night. We've got work to do today. Everything in that showroom needs a new tag with the sale price on it. Now let me get rid of who ever is bothering me again at seven a.m. Probably the reporters are back."

Olivia plodded downstairs and opened the French doors into the showroom. What was it with seven a.m. callers? This was the same time Cody showed up with the body and almost the time that George Clooney appeared on her doorstop. Tomorrow, she promised herself, she was going to sleep until eight and avoid what was becoming a seven a.m. curse. Not that she could call Mr. Clooney, er Bacon, a curse, but the timing of this visitor certainly threw her off guard.

Closer to the door, she could see her caller through the paned windows. Her heart revved up a few beats. Detective Richards stood on the porch flipping through his note pad. Quickly threading her fingers through her hair and making a futile attempt to arrange the sweats into some kind of fashion statement, she opened the door.

"Detective Richards?" She fumbled lamely for a greeting. "Um, have you found my Imari bowl and netsuke?"

Richards stuck the note pad in his pocket, his expression as grim as ever. Did he look particularly appealing this morning because she knew for certain that he wasn't available? She wouldn't put it past her cockeyed psychology when it came to men.

He shook his head. "No, afraid not. But that is what I want to talk to you about."

She opened the door wider and invited him in with a sweep of her arm. "Please."

The press trucks were still across the street, but apparently no one had ordered a wake up call.

So Richards entered without being seen, looking around, taking everything in. Olivia recognized it now as an occupational tic.

"So I take it from your question," he said, not yet looking at her, "your valuables have not appeared?"

"Haven't seen gum nor tooth of them."

Richards squinted his confusion.

"My grandmother's expression." Olivia was acutely aware of her grungy appearance, but always rejected the coy tactic of apologizing for the way she looked, thereby inviting a forced disclaimer and compliment. "Gran hated clichés and wouldn't say hide nor hair."

The detective's expression never lost its half-grimace. Olivia considered whether he was suppressing a smile or indigestion. She'd put her money on a sour stomach, probably part of the hangover syndrome afflicting both she and Tuesday.

"I was just making coffee, detective. Can I pour you a cup?" There was more than one way to warm up a cold fish.

Richards made no effort to disguise his scrutiny of the shop. "No, I only have a minute. I wanted to be sure my men did a thorough job of investigating yesterday."

Olivia saw his eyes rest on Hemingway's lamp. "Do you know antiques, detective?" She explained the writer's connection to the lamp.

He shook his head. "I know nothing about antiques, but I have read Hemingway, of course."

Olivia commented on the disdain in his voice. "You're not a fan?"

"Hardly. I'd like to think we are over Hemingway worship and all that macho bull. . . ." He corrected himself. "Business. But those horns could come from the blackbuck we have in India."

"Your birthplace?"

"Oh, no. I'm a Midwesterner. A suburb of Chicago. Lake Forest."

Olivia blinked. "I know it." The Billionaire Hollow of the Midwest. Hardly the breeding grounds for cops. And very, very white male oriented. She recalled Richards bristling when Mrs. Blackman referred to "you outsiders" at the police station. Olivia bet he had a story to tell. She guessed his parents were servants to one of the wealthy Lake Forest families. Lake Forest would never allow the type of small shop Indian immigrants liked to set up.

"When I visited my grandparents some years back they took me to Vallanadu because of my interest in wildlife. It's a sanctuary. The blackbuck is on the endangered species list."

Olivia started to apologize for owning the lamp. She didn't want to embarrass him by pressing him any further about his background. "Of course, in the Hemingway era, ..."

But Richards was relaxing, becoming downright chatty. "My father did an internship at a Chicago investment firm during his studies at the London School of Economics. Fell in love with the cold winters."

He misinterpreted the look on Olivia's face. "Yes, I know what you're thinking. He could have lived any place he chose. Why would a native of one of the hottest places on the planet pick one of the coldest? But stranger things have happened, I guess. When I left Harvard I vowed I would only live in sunshine for the rest of my life. Then a dream job came up back in Chicago. But that's neither here nor there. Let me get back to business and I'll leave you alone."

Olivia was at a loss for words, and more than embarrassed for her immigrant profiling. But with that background, why was he a detective in Darling Valley?

"Miss Granville, I've decided to place a detail outside your house tonight, just to keep an eye on things. I should have done it yesterday. I trust nothing else is missing?"

"Okay. No, but I haven't looked."

She noticed his bristly chin. Why hadn't he shaved? He was getting ready to leave. She touched his sleeve to ask a question, felt his arm under his jacket, a delicious sinking feeling warmed her solar plexus. What was she doing? "Um, detective, I have to ask you. Do you always start at the crack of dawn?"

"Murderers don't take any days off and neither do I. Even when the day has to start at 6 am."

Startled, Olivia said, "You think the murderer stole my things?"

Richards didn't seem to be able to maintain a lighthearted pose for long. His eyes narrowed again. "I can't understand why you are being targeted. It could be random coincidence, if I believed in coincidences. Have you noticed anything unusual lately?"

She crossed her arms, but she needed them to camouflage her whole body, not just the sad chest that her hoodie accentuated. "Actually, I have. A body in my armoire and a target on my back."

Richards shook his head in grim agreement. "A homicide puts everyone under the microscope, Miss Granville. I'm sure you can understand the need for increased scrutiny."

"I do, and I would appreciate it more if you could tell me about the progress you're making. Any clues show up at the country club?"

She was fishing for news about the girlfriend, she knew that, and immediately wished she hadn't.

"Oh, I wasn't at the auction to investigate the murder." He reached into his pants pocket and jangled his change.

No, of course you weren't. You were impressing the socks off your girlfriend with all the hot shots you know.

He didn't offer any more information, so she asked, "Well, have you made any progress, outside of the country club?"

"We're investigating some leads. Nothing I can talk about just yet. I stopped by to see if you've located your belongings. My officer said nothing seemed to be amiss when he came by yesterday. Of course, since this is still a crime scene, two thefts in twenty-four hours raises alarm bells. I was hoping you'd tell me they'd turned up."

Richards was wearing a suit. Was it the one he had on last night? She tried to remember. Yeah, it was. She detected the wine stain on the front of his shirt. He probably was on his way home from a sleepover at his girlfriend's house. That realization made her more acutely aware of her baggy sweats and helmet hair.

He volunteered that, "Tasmania lives near here and I stayed at her place last night rather than drive into Marin City."

Olivia wanted to say, "TMI, detective," but he blathered on and didn't give her an opening. Crapola. Why was her heart pounding for this guy when she was still mooning over Brooks? Maybe her birth certificate was wrong. Was she 12, instead of 32?

He continued. "So I thought I'd stop by and just see for myself."

Olivia shook her head and gave him a mournful grimace. "Sorry. Tuesday and I have torn this place apart. They are gone."

"What about your assistant," Richards pulled his notepad out of his pocket, "Mr. White. Do you think he could have picked them up? Innocently or otherwise?"

"Cody wouldn't do that. He just wouldn't. And anyway, whenever he was in the house, he was with me. He hasn't been alone in the house. Plus, he wouldn't steal from me. I know that."

"Well, if anything turns up on our end, I'll let you know. I won't keep you. I need to just go around to Mrs. Harmon's apartment and check something out with her."

"Mrs. Harmon? Why are you interested in her?"

"Confidential, I'm afraid."

"Well, she doesn't rouse herself until close to ten. I'm not sure she'd hear you knocking."

"Oh, she's expecting me.

Stunned by the news that he was not only investigating Mrs. Harmon but also that she deigned to speak to anyone before noon, Olivia said, "Well, don't let me keep you. You can go down through the back stairs if you like." She pointed towards her office.

"No, that's all right. I've disturbed you enough. Thanks for your time. Oh, one more thing? What is your relationship with the deceased's daughter?"

"I have no relationship with her. I don't know her, well, only that she exists. I believe she's a friend of Mrs. Harmon and was friendly with Cody White. But no longer from what I can gather. You know how it is with kids and dating. Easy come, easy go."

"Yes, I know that."

Oh, why so serious? Touch a nerve named Tasmania? Before Olivia could say anything else, Richards turned and opened the door, causing the little bell over the door to jingle. Olivia stopped him.

"Detective Richards, can I ask you a question? How did you know I'd be up this early?"

He cracked a faint smile that allowed Olivia to get a glimpse of his dazzling teeth. "I'm a detective, remember? You work for yourself. When was the last time you slept past 5 am."

Olivia smiled back. "Make that 4 am and you've got me."

His smile disappeared and for just a moment Olivia caught his eyes quickly scanning her down to her bare toes.

Oh my god. Is he checking me out, She wondered? He just left his girlfriend's place. Are all the men in Darling Valley slugs?

As she downgraded his good-guy rating, he slipped back into his formal, policeman's stance. "Goodbye, Miss Granville. Actually, I have a favor to ask. I let slip a bit of personal information. I feel more comfortable not talking about where I went to school and that sort of thing."

"You mean you don't have many Harvard classmates on the police force?"

"Let's just say, I prefer not to flaunt it. Not that anyone couldn't look it up. But I try fit in."

"So that's why you pretended not to know what an armoire was?"

"Oh, that's for real. I had to Google it. They don't teach you everything in grad school."

"Good bye, detective. And, oh . . . " She gestured to her sweats. "I'm sorry about the way I look. It's so early and all."

"Not at all. You look quite fine."

Arrrghhh rattled through her brain. What was wrong with her, apologizing to this, this, GUMSHOE! She closed the door behind him and watched him walk around to the side and up the driveway to the entrance of Mrs. Harmon's apartment. Well, at least he didn't hassle her about the illegal unit.

Chapter Twenty: Banking Day

Olivia wound her turquoise and ivory beads through her tangerine cashmere scarf and arranged the creation on her neck. She zipped up her cropped Alexander McQueen skinny jeans and pondered her sweater collection for a moment before grabbing a yellow cabled silk pullover, hand knit by the owner of Cobwebs and Cashmere, the yarn shop across the street. Kittie, the owner of the shop, assured her the color was made for her blond highlights. Olivia wanted to say, honey, I've been worked over by the masters of Rodeo Drive, but bought it anyway and wrote off the sweater as a public relations expense.

The reason she invested a few hundred dollars in the sweater when she had bins full in her closet was because Kitty Woolery, could that really be her name, was the first shop owner to give Olivia the time of day and she wanted to build on the favorable first impression she had made. Olivia did not knit: the sweater was a handmade sample she begged Kitty to part with, for twice what Olivia was sure it was worth. Business was business. She checked herself in the mirror. She was ready to meet Cody and anything else the day might have to offer. Why couldn't Richards arrive now?

Tuesday raised her eyebrows at the tangerine, yellow and orange get up and said Olivia looked like a citrus juice commercial. Olivia kept her mouth shut about her friend's outfit. Leather pants cut into daisy dukes, ripped fishnet stockings, a pink lace cami under a man's 1950's sport coat and tap shoes. Her hair was badly braided into four cornrows with frayed scrunchies at the tips and over it she had jammed on a pillbox hat, circa 1960. Olivia had gotten Tuesday to dress down for the auction. That was all she could expect in the way of fashion correctness for the remainder of this trip. But she did say, "A chapeau pour petit déjeuner?"

Just then a text came in.

"It's Jesse," she said.

Tuesday feigned a swoon. "The dreamy fish monger."

Olivia held up her index finger to silence Tuesday, and then read the message.

Wuts up w Queenie and Blkmr's dtr? Tt 1's a nasty pce o wrk and they r in cahoots bout smthin. We noobies gotta stk 2gthr. yr bb brudda

Olivia had to sit down to read it to Tuesday.

"Okay, what's this about?"

Olivia explained that Jesse referred to Mrs. Harmon as Queenie and this was the second time she was implicated in something with Jessica Blackman. Why was Jesse worried about Olivia's well-being all of a sudden? His attention comforted her, but she was in the dark about the reason. They'd have a friendly chat if they ran into each other around town, but that was the extent of their relationship. When she first arrived he would fill her in on some of the local flora and fauna and that's when he first referred to her tenant as Queenie. "Have you seen her carry that purse? I swear, I expect her to start waving to the commoners."

Olivia liked his warmth and sense of humor, but they had never acted on their promise to have lunch. They were both too busy getting their businesses off the ground. She teased him about being the baby brother she always wanted and he said, "I'll take that." Hence, she explained the signoff, yr bb brudda.

"I wish we would have lunch," she added. "I'd love to pick that Harvard marketing brain of his."

Tuesday licked her lips. "That's not all I'd like to do with him."

Olivia laughed. "Can we talk about one man, just one, without you being all over him?"

"Where's the fun in that?" Tuesday had her head in the refrigerator looking for jam for her toast.

"Seriously, why is Jesse worried about me? That must be why Detective Richards was snooping around here this morning. Jessica Blackman has something to do with her father's murder. Maybe Mrs. Harmon is her accomplice. Maybe it is my association with Mrs. Harmon that got me pulled into this. I need to know what Jesse knows."

Before she had a chance to reply to Jesse's message, her phone rang. She saw Elgin Fastner's name on her screen. She held it up for Tuesday to see and mouthed, "Should I answer," and immediately hit the button. "Hello, Elgin. What a surprise."

The banker's voice turned syrupy and soft, more intimate than his business voice. "Olivia, my dear. I've been thinking about our conversation yesterday and I believe I overreacted to your request."

Olivia was cautious. "Oh? In what way?"

"Well, I believe I know of some documents that you might be interested in seeing, though I would have to have your word that you would not make the information public or in way implicate me in revealing them to you."

"Confidentiality. Of course, Elgin. It goes without saying."

She mouthed, He wants to blackmail Sabrina.

Tuesday mouthed, Yes! and gave her a fist bump.

"But let me ask you, what changed your mind?" She gave Tuesday a big wink.

"Well, I certainly can't reveal her financial information. But there is a document you might find interesting. Given that you are implicated in her affairs by way of your relationship with, oh, how do I put this? Her late partner. It is my judgment that you are entitled to see an agreement they made."

"An agreement? What kind of agreement?"

"Well, I'd rather not say over the phone. Can we meet for lunch and we can talk about this further?"

After she mouth, "He wants to do lunch," Tuesday made an obscene gesture and Olivia nodded yes.

"Why that would be fine, Elgin. Shall we say noon at Hugo's?"

"Oh, no. Not Hugo's. Let's go somewhere quiet. How about the Buckeye Roadhouse? I just love their Asian tuna salad and Key Lime Pie, don't you?"

"I love the Buckeye, Elgin, but that's half an hour away, almost to the Golden Gate Bridge." She covered her mouth so her laugh wouldn't seep into the phone. "Are you sure we couldn't find a place in town that's quiet?"

"No, no. It has to be the Buckeye. I, I . . ." She could hear him thinking on his feet. "I have to go to San Francisco and it is so convenient to the bridge.

"Well, if you say so, Elgin. I'll see you there at noon."

She could hear his sigh of relief. She gave him a seductive, "Bye, Elgin," and hung up before she burst out laughing.

Tuesday plopped onto a stool. "Tell me, tell me."

"He wants to double cross Sabrina by showing me some document that must be incriminating in some way. I knew that one was up to something. He doesn't want to be seen with me in town, but, of course, he's hoping I'll, ahem, return the favor."

Tuesday said, "Then he doesn't know my Olivia."

The two women burst out laughing.

Tuesday said, "Seriously, Olivia. This murder thing is getting deep and dirty."

"I'll say. We have Sabrina, the Ice Queen partner up to something. Then Mrs. Harmon playing some kind of grandma footsie with young Jessica and that guy in the truck with Cody last night? The Gotshalk thug shouting he knew something about the other night? And people think I had something to do with the murder? We have enough suspects to start a TV crime show."

"Speaking of Cody, shouldn't he be here?"

Olivia dialed Cody's number. "Change of plans." She told him he would have make it coffee and soon. And Tuesday would come with her. "But I'll make it easy on you. Mohammad will come to the mountain. Name a place and we'll meet you there."

The threesome wedged into a red Naugahyde booth on Cody's side of town, the area skirting the meth park.

Cody started out by complaining about how long it was taking Detective Richards to return his truck.

"And my armoire, I might add." Olivia kicked herself for not asking Richards this morning when she'd get her belongings back.

"So Cody," she said. "What was that all about last night. Whose truck were you in and why was that guy beating up young Gotshalk."

He still hadn't shaven. Did he go on a bender last night? Or was the news about Jessica keeping him awake all night? He shook his head as if this was all too much for him. "Olivia, can we order some breakfast first? I'm starved."

Olivia said, "sure," knowing she would be picking up the tab. "Tues and I have eaten, so I'll just have some decaf." She rubbed her stomach. "To tell you the truth, I think I've had too much food. Not feeling that great. But you go on and order. How about you, Tues?"

"What kind of herb tea do they have?"

Cody and Olivia looked at one another, incredulous.

"Tuesday, look around. It's not an herbal tea kind of place."

Tuesday saw the bikers with tats wrapped around their necks, shaven heads and long scruffy beards. "Yeah, I see what you mean. How about a chocolate shake. I don't trust the coffee here. It's probably not organic."

Olivia said, "Tues, what was all that this morning about a cleanse and ditching sugar?"

"Clearly, I have to be in the right environment."

Cody looked confused. Olivia turned her attention to him. "Okay, let's get to it. Cody, what went down last night."

"Olivia, I'm not supposed to talk about it. Some people could get in serious trouble."

"Okay, just the broad outline."

"Well, it was a drug deal gone bad. Gotrocks owes Roger some money."

"Roger as in Blackman's Roger?"

"The same. He has a little side business, if you get my drift."

"I think I do. And he shorted Gotrocks?"

"No, Gotrocks shorted him. Roger figured he would get him to pay up at the country club so he wouldn't cause a scene. But Roger figured wrong and Gotrocks started punching him out."

"Well, what was that he shouted to Roger that he knew what he was doing the other night? I assumed it had something to do with Blackman's murder."

"I don't think I should talk about that."

"Why, because you don't know anything?" Olivia paused. "Or you do know something?" He looked so disheartened, Olivia reached over and stroked his hand.

"Well what were you doing with Roger last night? Tell me that. Are you involved with drugs? You can tell me, Cody. I don't judge. You know that."

"No, it wasn't about drugs. That's not my thing. But I don't have wheels. I told you the other day. Roger wants to do some business with me. Legit business. Helping him with my truck and stuff and he'd make sure I got some delivery work from Blackman's. After hours, you know. After I'm done with you for the day. So last night I told him I needed a ride. I had a date. He said he'd give me a lift into Darling Boulevard but that he had a quick stop to make. I didn't know he was going to shake down Gotrocks."

"A date?"

"Yeah. Well, not a real date. But I texted Jessica that I wanted to get together and talk and she said yes. I wanted to let her tell me about her marriage, see if she needed anything. You know, friend stuff."

"Jessica!" blurted Tuesday. "I hear she's bad news."

"Sweet Jessica! Who's telling tales about her?" Cody came alive, looking like he would take someone out.

Olivia told him. "Jesse, if you must know. And as far as I'm concerned, his word is good. And he's not the only one. Monica, Mrs. Blackman's assistant said some things. Hints. Intimations. And she should know."

"I don't believe it. What are they saying?"

"Cody, I don't know how to say this, but there is a rumor around that she had something to do with her father's death."

"I don't believe it." Cody looked crushed.

"Richards is investigating it. Well, he hinted that he was. I can't say any more for sure."

"It's not Jessica. It can't be."

"Cody, are you sure of Jessica? You know for sure that she's being straight with you?"

"Of course she is. Why would you say a thing like that?"

Before she could answer, her phone rang. Elgin needed to move lunch up another half an hour because of an emergency bank meeting. Olivia told him it was fine, then told Tuesday they needed to leave so she could drop her off at the house.

"You okay being at the shop by yourself again? This won't take long. And Cody, listen, when I get back why don't I pick you up from wherever you are and you can take me home and keep the truck. As long as Tuesday is here with the rented Mercedes, I have wheels. Bring it back when the PD releases yours."

"Gosh, thanks, Olivia. Just give me a call. I'll probably be home."

"Not a problem, Cody. Are you sure there isn't anything else I should know."

He hemmed and hawed. "Well, my allegiance is more to you than Roger. Nobody else knows this and he doesn't want it to get out to the police. Roger had a dustup with Mr. Blackman. He caught him stealing money from the shop. I don't know why Blackman didn't fire him on the spot, but Roger let it slip to Gotrocks that there'd been trouble. Blackman wanted to meet with him the night before we found him in the armoire. Last night Roger told me he was terrified that Blackman called the meeting because he was going to turn him into the police. But then they just talked about business, but now Gotrocks is putting it around town that Roger killed him. But I can't believe Roger would do something like that. Off Blackman?"

"But if he's dealing drugs, that can lead to really bad stuff."

"I told you Roger isn't the sharpest knife in the drawer. He tried one deal with Gotrocks that went sour. It scared him plenty. He wants out of the whole drug scene. You can't let the police know about this."

"But Cody, this gives Roger a motive and opportunity. It could clear me. Where's your loyalty?"

Cody finished up his omelet and hash browns and wiped his mouth with a paper napkin. "Roger says he has an alibi. Somebody came into the shop before he left and Blackman was definitely alive when he took off. He doesn't know who the guy was because Roger swept up like he always does and left by the back door because the two men were having a drink and he figured Blackman had forgotten about him. He reported that part to the police and they are checking it out to see if Roger's story is for real. He's just afraid if they find out about the theft part they will pin the murder on him. He's smart enough to figure that out.

Olivia scratched her head and pulled her hair back. "I don't know. This isn't working for me. If he told Richards that someone was in the shop when he left, the police would tear Darling Valley apart finding that guy. They probably found out it was a customer and that backed up Roger's alibi. Otherwise, why isn't he in jail? Thanks, Cody but false alarm. Ready Tues?"

Tuesday slurped down the last of her milkshake and the two women headed out of the diner, eyes straight ahead to avoid the stares of the biker dudes giving them the once over. Tuesday said, "I'm surprised the Sons of Anarchy weren't on Sabrina's guest list last night."

Chapter Twenty-One: A Change of Heart

The valet parking attendant at the Buckeye helped Olivia out of the Mercedes and handed her a ticket. Smiling and winking, which Olivia knew was code for how about a big tip later on. The famous San Francisco fog bank that confounded travelers as far back as Sir Francis Drake wrapped itself around the Golden Gate Bridge standing just above the landmark restaurant and Olivia shivered up the hill and into the wood paneled waiting room. The hostess came around from the bar and when she gave her name told Olivia her party was waiting.

"This way please," and she led Olivia into the back room by the huge stone fireplace to the table in the far, far corner where Elgin sat nursing a drink. He apologized for hurrying their lunch, and, though Olivia knew the reason, she put on an innocent face and asked why he didn't want to have lunch in Darling Valley.

Elgin pointed to the windows and view of the north deck of the Bridge, the city beyond peeking through the fog in places. "I love Darling Valley and all that, but once in a while it's nice to see the outside world. Don't you think?"

"Whatever you say, Elgin. This is your lunch."

Elgin started to make chit chat, but Olivia wasn't having it.

"Since you are in a hurry and I have a client waiting for me, why don't we get to the point. What is it about Sabrina that you would like me to know?"

"How well do you, I should say, did you know Mr. Blackman?"

"I keep telling everybody. I didn't know him at all. I dealt with Sabrina."

"Oh, yes. Sabrina. They were partners, you know."

"Yes, I knew that. I just was never in the shop when Mr. Blackman was there."

"Well they had been business partners for several years. Before Mr. Blackman's marriage to Greta."

"I didn't know that. The timeline, that is."

Elgin explained that, therefore, Mr. Blackman's part of the business was not community property. And apparently to assure that would not change, they wrote up an agreement specifying who would get control of the business if something untoward happened to either of them. In the event of a death, the surviving partner would get the partnership. None of it would go to Greta, or to Sabrina's husband."

"I didn't know Sabrina had a husband."

"Soon to be ex. At any rate, Sabrina obviously had a lot to gain from Blackman's death. There isn't a whisper of suspicion about Greta's involvement, of course. She had nothing to gain. Sabrina has not been married for very long, either and doesn't stand to receive much of a settlement in her divorce. As you may know, California's community property laws are no longer as favorable to women as they once were."

"How do you know this?"

"I read the newspapers."

"About Sabrina and Blackman's partnership?"

"No. About the divorce laws. Bankers can get involved in those property settlement disputes. About Sabrina, she confided in me. Plus, they asked me to witness their partnership arrangement."

"Not their lawyers?"

"They chose not to involve lawyers."

"Of course they didn't. Greta and Sabrina's husband would have known and thrown a fit."

"Perhaps. But other than Sabrina and Blackman, no one knew about the arrangement other than myself. If news of this should get out, it would put her in an unfavorable light. She doesn't have many assets of her own."

"Why do I need to know this? Greta now has access to all of her husband's papers. She will find this out. What do I get out of seeing this agreement when Greta surely has a copy now? Mr. Blackman would have kept it his in his office, which Greta has access to."

"Precisely. But I am sure the widow is too distraught to go through her husband's papers just yet. While you need, shall we say, closure. Now. And I know where Sabrina keeps her copy. If it got into the hands of the police, it would show that Sabrina had a motive."

"And what good does this information do me? Do you think I'm going to raid her office some night and steal it? Evidently, you don't know me very well. And how would I explain to the police how I got it?"

"Olivia. You asked me if there was anything I knew about Sabrina that might take suspicion off you."

"I didn't say that."

"But in so many words. Let's not quibble. If you were to find yourself in her office and looked behind the ancient map of London mounted over her desk, you'd see a small safe. If you were to look under the center drawer in her desk, you'd find a key taped there."

"And how do you know that?"

"As her financial advisor, she confided in me about certain matters."

Olivia remembered Sabrina's rebuff of Elgin the night before. Hell hath no fury and all that. But watch out for a man's wounded ego.

"Really, Elgin. You're practically asking me to steal her property. That is way beyond anything I suggested to you. I think I'll leave now. Especially since you have to get back for a meeting."

"But Olivia, we haven't had our Sesame Crusted Tuna. It's the best dish west of the Mississippi. Maybe even east of it."

"Why don't you take mine home in a doggy bag. I have to head back to Darling Valley. It's a long drive."

He tried to grab her hand to induce her to stay but Olivia eluded his grasp. She plunked a dollar into the hand of the valet guy and avoided his angry gaze as she headed back north.

Chapter Twenty-Two: Another Theft

On the way back to the house, the Marimba chords of Olivia's iPhone sitting on the dashboard rang out. She almost drove off Highway 101 when she saw that it was Mrs. Harmon. Previously, the grand dame communicated only on monogrammed, 20-pound stationary that she stuck into Olivia's mail slot. She hit the speakerphone and said a cautious, "Hello."

Mrs. Harmon didn't mince words. "Ms. Granville, I am entitled by law to the quiet enjoyment of my premises. All week I have had to put up with police cars, reporters and I don't know what else. Oh yes, and that woman who is staying with you taking over the back yard in her ridiculous outfits."

Olivia tried to interrupt but Mrs. Harmon plowed on. "If you don't remove those impediments to my comfort, I shall have to resort to legal means."

The nerve of that woman. Doesn't she realize she is under suspicion for murder. Under her breath, Olivia said, if I were you I'd lay low, girlie. And then cooed, "I'm so sorry for the inconvenience, Mrs. Harmon."

She didn't climb to the top of the partnership ladder in record time without learning how to mollify quarrelsome clients. "I'm sure you understand that when it comes to the movements of the police department, my hands are tied. And as far as the press is concerned, as long as they don't step on my property, they are legally allowed to congregate in their cars and on the sidewalk. And as far as Tuesday is concerned, I'm sure if you met her . . . "

Mrs. Harmon interrupted to bark, "If you don't handle this situation you will hear from my lawyer," and hung up.

When she got home and relayed the story, Tuesday said, "Do you think she stole those balls from a from a wrecking crane?"

Olivia shook her head in disgust. "That's all I need, a tenant dispute. I'm starved. Let's have some lunch."

"But you just came home from a lunch date?"

So while Olivia raided the refrigerator for leftovers, she told Tuesday about her meeting with Elgin, ending with, "And the worst of it, I never got any of that fabulous tuna salad.

Tuesday ruminated. "Ollie Mollie, that's not a bad idea. Looking at that agreement. It might get you off the hook with Richards. This could exonerate you. Problems solved." She swept her palms together in an all cleaned up gesture.

"Oh," said Olivia, making a sandwich of cheese and greens, "and then what will we do with it? Rush over to Richards' office and say, na na, look what I've got? And then he'd pull out his handcuffs and say, na na look what I've got. That's breaking and entering. First jail cell to your right."

Tuesday held up her phone. "We don't have to steal it. An exact reproduction would do."

"And then what, post it on Facebook?"

"First things first. Let's get a copy of the document and then we'll figure out what to do with it."

"Absolutely not. Last word on the subject or I'm throwing your herb tea in the compost pile."

"Yeah, well I hate that stuff in the first place," she joked. "Where's the Veuve Cliquot?" Then opened a bottle of vitamin water.

"You know, Tues. I didn't really know what I was going to do if Elgin forked over any incriminating information about Sabrina. But now my nose is twitching. It's time for me to take matters into my own hands. It's Wednesday and I have a boatload of work to do to arrange my sale for Saturday. If we don't figure out who did this and nail the culprit, my sale is toast, and I'll be on that plane with you back to Los Angeles."

"I'm with you girlfriend. What do you have in mind?"

Olivia the list maker reached for the notepad on the counter. Then she combed through her purse for her favorite Mont Blanc pen. She had to unload her keys, her phone, her travel makeup kit, her hairbrush, her retro packet of Sen Sen, her Chinese silk tissue holder, her mini-sewing kit, her golf ball, her roll of masking tape, her card of thumbtacks, her empty prescription bottle and an envelope of Herbs de Provence seeds with lavender. At the bottom she found her pen, then started repacking her purse.

Tuesday grabbed the Herbs and held them up with a question mark on her face. Olivia said, "For my herb garden. When I have time to plant one."

Tuesday sniffed the packet. "Are these from that trip to Provence where we visited that medieval garden and you came home wanting everything to look like an illuminated manuscript?"

"The very one." Olivia held out her hand for the seeds.

"Holy Mrs. Greenjeans! These are so old they've turned to powder." She started to toss them in the trash under the sink.

"Don't! I keep them for good luck." Olivia grabbed them out of her hand and added them to the hoard on the counter. She shook her purse into the trash container under her sink to rid it of dust and started repacking her collection of bits and pieces, stopping with a puzzled look. "Wait. Where's my flashlight?"

"Huh?"

"You know, the flashlight I used to get in last night. Didn't I put it back in my purse?" The memory of breaking into her own home came back to her. "No, you know what I did? I put my purse, my keys and the flashlight on that little pine table by the door to take off my shoes. I picked up everything but the flashlight. Hold on a sec while I get it."

Olivia ran down the stairs and trotted through the maze of furniture in the showroom towards the front door. A moment later she screamed, "TUESDAY! It's gone. My flashlight is gone."

Chapter Twenty-Three: Tummy Trouble

Was it rotten fish? Was Hugo's responsible for the vise-like cramp sending electric shocks through Olivia's mid-section? She looked at the clock. Six a.m. Too early to check on Tuesday to see if she were afflicted with food poisoning, too. But then it had been two days since the halibut at Hugo's. She crawled out of bed and tiptoed into the hallway past the guest room to pull the heating pad out from under the carefully stacked towels.

"The towels," she said to herself, mentally slapping her forehead. She had to get the towels from the dryer. Mrs. Harmon will have a fit if she needs to use the laundry and finds Olivia's towels in the dryer. But they would have to wait, she explained to herself, doubling over with a stab of pain. Back in bed, the heating pad warmed quickly, but the spreading fingers of heat only increased the intense pain in her belly. Within an hour she was gasping with each breath and Tuesday came knocking.

"What is it? I heard you moaning. What's wrong?"

Tuesday made her some chamomile tea. When she brought it into the bedroom, Olivia said, "How are you feeling? We ate the same thing."

Tuesday thumped her belly. "Fine."

The tea helped and Tuesday left her to rest and soon Olivia fell back asleep. Two hours later she woke unable to stand up straight from the cramping. She crept into the kitchen where she found Tuesday poring over an herbal text. When Olivia said she hadn't recovered, Tuesday asked it there was a natural foods store in Darling.

"I think I need some real medicine, Tues. Something's wrong. I just don't know a doctor here."

Olivia checked the contact list on her phone and punched in the number for Champagne and Cobwebs, the stitchery shop across the street. "Kitty, this is Olivia. Listen, I hate to bother you but do you know the name of a doctor? I have stomach grumpies and think I need to be seen."

Tuesday listened intently to Olivia's end of the conversation. "Oh, yes. I've heard of him. No, that's all right. Is he an internist or Family Physician? Oh, I see. Okay. No, don't trouble yourself. I can look up his number. Thanks, Kitty. No I have a friend with me, I'll be fine. Thanks a lot. Yes, you too."

Olivia put the phone down and took another sip of tea. "The stars are against me on this one, Tues. She recommends Dr. Chandler, Greta Blackman's physician. We saw him at the police department. She said otherwise I'd have to go into San Rafael to an Urgent Care Center. He's one of those private physicians who only accepts cash, no insurance."

Olivia was describing the growing practice of doctors who avoided insurance company bureaucracy and let patients file their own insurance claims. In return for the inconvenience, it was easier to get an appointment and they made themselves more available to their patients..

"You're looking green, Olivia. See if he has an opening. There's no way you can ride that bumpy road into San Rafael."

"Coming from someone who hates doctors, Tuesday, that's an endorsement. I must look pretty awful."

A few minutes later Olivia had an appointment with Dr. Chandler at 11:30. She fingered Detective Richards' card, then picked up her phone and dialed his number. He picked up on the second ring and Olivia asked if anyone suspicious had turned up. He wasn't in a chatty mood. He gave her a curt, no, how are you? When she mentioned her food poisoning, he recommended Dr. Chandler, as well, and said he had to go.

Olivia relayed this to Tuesday, commenting with a sneer. "His brunette bombshell is probably waiting."

Tuesday answered, "Tell me again how much you don't care about that guy?"

Olivia finished registering at the reception desk and joined Tuesday on a down cushioned sofa opposite a wall of tropical fish.

"Honestly, Olivia, can't doctors think of anything more original than tropical fish in their waiting rooms?"

The receptionist overheard and offered, "They did a study and found that fish are very calming. Dr. Chandler is an amateur ichthyologist."

Tuesday whispered out of the corner of her mouth, "She's got more makeup on than all the Kardashians put together," then pointed to a two-inch thick encyclopedia of exotic tropical fish on the table next to her. "I guess he is," she said for the benefit of the receptionist.

"O," she added, drawing her attention to a three-inch bright blue creature swimming by. "I could use eye shadow that color."

Again the receptionist showed off her knowledge. "Blue German Ram. Not as rare as it once was. A cichlid from Venezuela."

Tuesday mouthed, "Chiclets? Like in gum?"

The girl at the desk patted her extension-rich hair and was about to expound on South American species, but Tuesday leaned over and gave her a thousand watt smile. "Thanks, hon, but TMI." The girl gave her an equally fake smile right back.

But it was a separate tank that caught Olivia's attention and took her mind off her cramping belly for a moment. The receptionist couldn't help herself.

"That's the tank for the Scribbled Mappa. They can get rowdy with the other fish." She mouthed chomping and swallowing. "If you get my drift. So they get their separate tank."

Ever the designer, Olivia noted the few fish in a big tank.

"Yeah, they like a lot of real estate or they eat one another. At $400 a pop, it's cheaper to get them their own designer digs." She put up her hand to pause the lecture and listen to her headset. She unplugged herself and got up. "They're ready for you in the back. Come this way."

Tuesday jokingly picked up the encyclopedia and said, "I'll wait here and bone up on my, what are they?"

The assistant repeated, "Scribbled Mappas."

After a nursing assistant noted her vital signs in a brand new chart, Olivia sat on an examining table clutching a lilac paper gown around her shoulders that she was told to don with the opening in the front. While she waited for the doctor, she pondered whether she should remind him that she had seen him and Mrs. Blackman in the police department. Before she could formulate an answer, the door opened and Dr. Chandler entered wearing a black lab jacket that, if it weren't for his name embroidered over the pocket, could have passed for a summer weight sport coat. As befitting the doctor to the billionaires, Olivia guessed he had them made on Savile Row.

Chandler quickly picked up her chart and scanned his assistant's notes, eliminating the need to shake hands. He sat on a surprisingly ordinary rolling stool and said, "So, we meet again. Not that we were formally introduced at the police station."

Olivia got to the point as well. "Dr. Chandler, I know this is awkward, considering the, um, circumstances, but I have been in scary pain and you were the only doctor available in DV. I couldn't stand the thought of having to drive into San Rafael. I'm sorry. I didn't mean to slight your expertise, but given your relationship with Mrs. Blackman, it would have been better for both of us for me to see someone else. But . . ."

The doctor interrupted her. "Miss Granville, you signed a privacy statement so you understand that I take patient confidentiality very seriously. Obviously, I will not discuss any of my other patients with you, nor will I reveal to anyone else that I am treating you. Why don't we forget about the unfortunate incident at the police station and tell me what I can do for you."

Olivia described her symptoms and Dr. Chandler questioned her about her medical history. She told him she'd had several similar episodes in the past couple of years, but never this severe.

After examining her and sending her through the roof when he palpated her left abdomen, he said he thought she had IBS.

She gave him a blank stare.

"Irritable bowel syndrome. I would guess the recent stress brought it on. I have my own lab here and I'll run some tests. Your belly is tender but I don't detect any swelling or hard masses. That's a good sign. If everything is normal, which I suspect will be the case, I'll give you some medication. Even if you recover in an hour, I want to see you back here in a week. Your symptoms could mask a number of problems, some severe, such as a bowel obstruction. I don't see that yet, but if your pain gets worse, call me immediately. Even if it's in the middle of the night. Just call my office number and the answering service will find me."

He directed Olivia down the hall where a technician drew blood and offered her a glass of orange juice. She pointed to a juicer and large basket of oranges. "I squeeze it myself."

Olivia refused. "I don't think I can eat or drink anything right now."

Then the tech sent her to the front desk where the assistant tallied up her bill. Olivia looked at it and joked to Tuesday, "Glad I didn't take the juice."

The assistant said, "Oh, we don't charge for that."

On the way home Tuesday complained about the receptionist who wouldn't shut up about fish while Olivia was being examined. "If I had to listen to one more fact about puffer fish I would have jumped into the tank myself."

Olivia was about to say I didn't know they were kept as pets, but her phone rang, a blocked number. Should she risk listening to a crank call or let it go into voice mail. What else could go wrong? She'd live dangerously. "Hello?"

A female sobbed into her ear. "Hello? Hello? I can't understand you. Who is this?"

The only part of the blubbering she could understand was Carrie. "Carrie, oh my god, what's happened. Slow down so I can understand you."

Carrie gave her a sad tale of losing her mother's earrings. Her mother didn't mind if she wore her jewelry as long as she asked first. But her mother had left the house early and Carrie didn't think it would be a big deal. Turned out they had real diamonds in them.

"Do you think Tuesday could help me find them? You know, because she's like a psychic and all? I mean, like she was so right about Cody and a new guy coming into my life."

"Carrie, have you met someone?"

"No, I'm just saying. Now I just have to find those earrings."

"Okay, I can't speak for Tuesday. Come over to the house and you can ask her yourself."

Tuesday opened the door for Carrie. Olivia had locked up the shop and gone to bed with a pain pill as soon as they got home from Dr. Chandler's. When she heard Carrie and Tuesday coming back up the stairs, she came out to the kitchen to greet Carrie, who had arrived with The Salted Caramel's signature pink box full of macaroons and the heart shaped pastry Tuesday loved. She handed it to Olivia.

"You know, like, to say thank you."

She had a second paper sack from The Salted Caramel and set it beside her purse, explaining that it was a special delivery. Olivia put the pastries on the counter, explained she was unwell and excused herself, suggesting Tuesday take Carrie down to the showroom for some privacy. As they headed for the stairs Tuesday asked, "Do you have something that will swing like a pendulum? Something that you use often that will have your energy on it."

Carrie dug into the bottom of her backpack and pulled out a Minnie Mouse Disney key chain. Tuesday looked back at Olivia as they descended the stairs and gave her a whatever eye roll. "Perfect, Carrie. That will do."

Olivia's pill had started to work and after fifteen minutes, she was drowsy but pain free. She made a pot of tea and took it down stairs with a tray of mugs and plate of pastries.

Tuesday and Carrie were standing in the middle of the show room floor. She tiptoed to a corner and quietly set the tray on the floor so could pull three side chairs around a small table. She poured tea into one of the mugs and blew on it to cool it while the psychic and client finished up.

Carrie's face sagged, telescoping the results as they joined her. "It says the earrings are right here."

"What?"

While Carrie helped herself to a pastry and Olivia quickly stuck a napkin on her lap, Tuesday explained. "The pendulum said they weren't in her room or her car, so we narrowed it down to them being close to her. Then she asked if they were on her person. Got a no answer. Naturally. I said, ask if they were near her and the answer was yes. But she turned her backpack and pockets inside out."

She shrugged apologetically to Carrie. "We're dealing with the realm of mystery. Perhaps the answer will become clear after you've had a chance to sit with the session for a while."

Olivia glared at her, then Carrie said, "Listen you guys. Thanks for trying, but I gotta hustle. Let me get the pastries for Mrs. Harmon and I'll be outta here."

Olivia blinked. "Mrs. Harmon?"

"Yeah. I drop off some pastries every once in a while. The Cooks used to do it. You know, like when they lived here? They really liked Mrs. Harmon and asked if I would do it if I happened to be in the neighborhood. I've been neglecting her so I figured since I was, like, how much more in the neighborhood can I get?"

Olivia said, "But I've never seen you come by."

"Yeah, well, I use the side door. If you're in your office or upstairs, you wouldn't know. It's not like I do it every week or anything. I brought them a few days ago, in fact, but I figured with all the crime tape and everything she'd need another treat."

Olivia wondered if Mrs. Harmon had complained to Carrie about the disruption around the house. Carrie wouldn't let her get up but said, "Finish your tea. I'll run upstairs and get the pastries and let myself out the back."

"Thanks for these," said Tuesday holding up a cookie. "Sorry I couldn't be of more help."

Olivia said, "How's that cleanse working out for you, Tuesday?"

Before Carrie dashed out the back door, she called, "You guys going to the memorial service for Mr. Blackman? Word at the shop is that it's going to be a big deal. Like a show of support for his wife. She's really torn up."

Olivia said, "Yeah, well she would be. Maybe. I'll see. When is it?"

Carrie told her and was gone.

Chapter Twenty-Four: The Memorial

"Heads we don't go, tails we don't go." Thus, Olivia answered Tuesday's question about whether they should attend the memorial.

Tuesday finished up the last of Carries' pastries. "I see you're really up for this, honeybun."

"I know it would be disrespectful not to go, but she thinks I killed her husband."

Tuesday drained her tea. Out of habit, she examined her tea leaves. "Hmm, travel in my future."

"Brilliant. You're going home soon."

Tuesday ignored her. "But maybe if we go she will see you are a good person and couldn't possibly have done that. Would the killer show up at the funeral of his, or her, victim?"

"Alright." Olivia pretended to check her calendar to see if she if she had a conflict the next morning at ten, sending Tuesday into fits of laughter.

"Baby cheeks, you'd be drummed out of Beverly Hills with a calendar that blank. "

The next day, bolstered with pain pills, they set off. Olivia intended to slip quietly into the back of the Darling Valley First Episcopal church and blend in with the mourners. She figured she'd sign the guest book with something appropriately syrupy and get out before the widow saw her. Her plan was scotched as soon as she walked into the vestibule.

"Miss Granville?" She turned into the devastating eyes of Detective Richards. All heads within earshot swiveled in her direction and the elbow poking began.

"Detective Richards. I didn't realize you were a friend of Mr. Blackman's."

"Oh, I'm not. It's my practice to attend the funerals of my murder victims. Sometimes the guilty party reveals himself in an inappropriate show of emotion. Or herself."

"Thanks for the tip. I'll be sure to keep my mouth shut and a hanky over my face. But what do you mean, all your murder victims? I thought you only had parking infractions and leash law violations in cozy Darling Valley."

"I was referring to my stint in Chicago where funerals could keep me busy. That's where I worked before coming here."

Tuesday interrupted. "Didn't I say you were a traveler?"

Surprisingly, Richards smiled. "Yes, Miss Tuesday, I've been around."

He piqued Olivia's curiosity, and she said, "I'm going to put the shoe on the other foot, Detective. How long have you been here and why DV?"

"Fair question and it's a matter of public record. I arrived just a little over a year ago."

"And? You're leaving out the juicy part. Why did you leave Chicago and why DV?"

Was it the somber setting that made Richards drop his guard a bit, the subtle message that life is short and connection is all? He surprised Olivia with a candid answer. "I left Chicago for the same reason you left LA."

Tuesday said, "To start a design business?"

Richards laughed out loud. "No, an affair of the heart gone wrong. DV looked too peaceful to pass up. A position opened up when my predecessor retired to Havasu City in Arizona. And besides, the fact that my family is nearby helped seal the deal.

But Olivia remembered him saying his family was in Lake Forest. Was that story about Harvard and sunshine a lie? Who could she trust in this place? But all she said was, "An affair of the heart. So we have more in common than just armoires and arsenic."

Remembering the gorgeous brunette he took to the auction, she thought, *You didn't waste any time patching yourself up.*

Richards corrected her. "Arsenic? Oh, we haven't determined that it's arsenic, unless you know something I don't, Miss Granville."

"That's what's all over the Internet. So I take it you don't have the coroner's report yet."

"Not yet. But let's not dwell on that aspect of Mr. Blackman's life. We are here to memorialize him."

The three stood in the vestibule listening to the low chords of the somber organ music, Olivia thinking about the cause of death. Poison. That raised a flood of possibilities. How could she find out who shared his last meal? Or drink? Didn't Roger report he saw

Blackman drinking with someone in his showroom that night? Surely, poison is easily detectable. Why hadn't the ME made an announcement?

She was about to pose these questions to Richards when she spotted the widow and her two sons getting out of a limousine. She tugged on Tuesday's arm. "Well, we have to find a seat before the church fills up. Nice seeing you, detective. Oh, that doesn't sound right at a funeral, does it? Well, as long as I've put my foot in my mouth, so to speak, where are my shoes?"

"Safe in the department's evidence room. Be well, both of you." And he went off to find his own seat.

Olivia and Tuesday could hear the click of camera shutters outside. The slim DV police force was on duty to prevent the press disturbing the solemn affair. A few reporters rudely called out, "Do you know who killed your husband, Mrs. Blackman. Could you turn around and give us a picture? Those your sons? Where they been? How'd they get along with their stepfather?"

But they stayed on public property and the officers could do nothing about them until they moved onto the church steps. The children hurried their grieving mother into the church. In a moment, Dr. Chandler arrived alone. The driver of his limousine jumped out to open the door for him and he followed the family into the church.

The church filled up quickly. Tuesday murmured to Olivia, "Ten percent mourners and ninety percent gawkers." A string quartet at the altar played a Bach sonata, and then an organist blared A Mighty Fortress Is Our God, which brought everyone to their feet. Then, when nothing happened, they sat down.

Olivia could hear the widow sniffling and in a moment, she and Dr. Chandler shuffled past her pew. Actually, the doctor half carried the widow. She was crumbling from the effort of controlling her emotions. When she sagged, he put his arm around her for support. They stood for a moment while she composed herself. Olivia studied Mrs. Blackman, trying to imagine how she would comport herself if burdened with such grief. She had attended her grandmother's funeral, whose death had been a blow from which she had not fully recovered. But her grandmother was in poor health and her demise was not only expected but a relief to her daughter, Olivia's mother, who had not shouldered the caregiving duties with as much grace as Olivia would have liked.

What was it like to receive the shock that, not only was your beloved husband dead, but that he had been murdered and gruesomely stuffed into a piece of furniture and shipped off to a virtual stranger? Olivia shook her head at the horror and indignity of it. If nothing else, Mrs. Blackman had always carried herself with utmost dignity. No doubt some of the turnout was in gratitude for her good works she had thrown herself into on behalf of the community. From what Olivia was learning about her, she had an ulterior motive, acceptance by the upper rungs of society. Still, she walked the walk. Olivia speculated that, from what she was discovering about her husband, she was more loved than the deceased.

Olivia stared at the widow as though she might reveal the answer to some of the mysteries of life and death now that she was experiencing life's cruelest blow, the loss of her most loved being. Then she noticed a peculiar movement on the part of the doctor. What was happening? He seemed to slip something into

Mrs. Blackman's coat pocket, hovering over her to conceal his movements. For a brief moment Olivia saw something gleam. It was metal and caught the light reflecting off the stained glass windows. He must be passing drugs to her, more sedatives no doubt. Mrs. Blackman's two sons came up behind her and ushered the doctor away, each taking an arm. Their mother seemed too dazed to notice.

Olivia and Tuesday left before the end of the service to avoid facing Mrs. Blackman. Late in the day, Olivia felt the sharp stab of IBS again. Over the next hour it worsened and by evening she was gasping for breath, despite taking two pain pills. Tuesday overrode her objections to calling the doctor.

"Tues, he's probably with the family. You know he hasn't left Mrs. Blackman's side. Surely she needs him more today than I do."

Then she doubled over and Tuesday grabbed the doctor's card from the kitchen counter and dialed the number herself. The answering service said they would pass the message on to the doctor. Tuesday guessed he would have a colleague on call to advise Olivia. To their surprise, Chandler called back almost immediately. He reassured Olivia that she had done the right thing in contacting him.

"But, I'm afraid I'm leaving town unexpectedly for a day or two, and I won't be in my office. Would you be able to come by my house? I can check you here and if I think you need emergency care, I'll arrange for paramedics to come and transport you to the hospital in San Rafael."

By now the streetlights had come on, helping Tuesday navigate her Mercedes to the doctor's house. He greeted them at the door and helped Olivia into his living room. While the doctor settled Olivia on one of the leather couches, Tuesday studied the three aquariums around which the room had been designed. The larger one dwarfed the tank in his office with two smaller aquariums bookending each side. The doctor began to palpate Olivia's abdomen.

"I'm concerned, Miss Granville, but your belly is soft, which is a good sign. I'm going to send you home with a stronger pain med. Vicodin. I have some samples for you. Should you take a turn for the worse and your abdomen feels tight and hot, call the paramedics immediately. These IBS episodes can be damned unpleasant, but we don't want to over treat if it resolves itself soon."

Both Tuesday and the doctor helped Olivia sit up. "I hate to rush you, but I do have to get on my way."

Olivia thanked him profusely. "Of course, we won't take up any more of your time."

Chandler hurried them out the door and Tuesday made Olivia comfortable in the front seat. They were around the block when Tuesday realized she had left her scarf in the doctor's living room.

"Ollie, we have to go back. He's going out of town and I might be back in LA before I have a chance to get it. I can't do readings without it."

"No, let's go home. I'll call him and leave a message with his service to see if his office assistant will hold it for you."

"But what if she doesn't have a key to his house? No, it will only take a sec." Before Olivia could offer up another argument, Tuesday executed a U turn with a squeal of rubber. Off in the distance, they could see a car pull up in front of the doctor's house. "See, that's his limo taking him to the airport I bet. Just in time."

But as they got closer they gave one another stunned looks. Mrs. Blackman was getting out of the car, walking quite well under her own power. They watched her pull something out of her purse, a key, and unlock the front door.

"That's what I saw him slip into her pocket today! I told you, Tues, I saw him give her something on the QT."

A light came on in a back room, highlighting the doctor coming to the front door. He put his arms around Mrs. Blackman in an embrace they didn't teach him in medical school.

Tuesday whistled. "Holy cuckold, Mr. Blackman. Look what the merry widow is up to."

Then the woman pushed the doctor away and they began what appeared to be an argument, their moving figures through the blinds like Javanese shadow puppets.

The pain pill had started to work and Olivia said, "Tuesday, out of here. Now. We don't want them to see us."

"But Ollie. My scarf!"

"Tues, I'll buy you another. Where did you find it, in the two for a buck bin at Goodwill?"

Tuesday was offended. "A dollar each," she said as she peeled away from the curb.

At home, Tuesday helped Olivia up the stairs and into the kitchen. Olivia insisted she was able to sit at the counter. "Would you make some chamomile tea? I'm going to see if I can figure out what's going on."

She flicked on her iPad. A quick Google search revealed the doctor's home page, Facebook page, medical society listings and professional CV. He credentials were impeccable, a Yale B.S. and Harvard med school graduate and, amazingly, he seemed to have gotten this far in his career without a malpractice charge against him.

Olivia said, "Well, we can assume he has a great bedside manner."

Tuesday said, "He's a saint."

Olivia sipped her tea. "Hmm. Methinks Saint Full of Shit."

Tuesday came to his defense. "So he does the down and dirty with Mrs. Blackman. From what we've learned about Blackman, she's entitled to a little TLC."

"Tuesday, there is no bigger shark pool that the one we know well in LA. These financiers didn't make their money making nicey nicey with each other. And they all play in the same sandbox."

She typed some more phrases into the Google search box.

"Bingo. I knew it."

Tuesday rushed to look over shoulder.

"Classic. Can't these guys come up with something new?"

"What do you mean, Ollie?"

"I wondered why Blackman would settle for a restoration shop when surely he had enough connections with these players to get in on some good action. I mean these guys," Olivia extended her hand to include all of Darling Valley, "built Silicon Valley. Well, it says here that he once had a biotech firm. Gotshalk was a partner, Cook, who used to own this house. Mr. Harmon, deceased spouse of my tenant. They were all in on it. And the medical director was none other than . . ."

Tuesday imitated a drum roll.

"You got it. Dr. Chandler."

"So what happened?"

Olivia said, "I bet Chandler keyword stuffed his good sites so this stuff would show up on page two zillion."

She did some more searching and found what she was looking for.

"The enterprise went bust. Blackman, Harmon and Chandler were out, but Gotshalk, Cook and a few others invested in a startup that sounds eerily similar to the original company. My guess is that those three guys were aced out but why would they come to DV?

And that doesn't give Chandler a motive, since he was left holding the bag just like Blackman."

Tuesday volunteered her opinion. "This gives us squat. Maybe the doctor isn't such a nice guy and the widow is a hypocrite. But what's new? If you're liking them for the murder, why? I'm betting on Roger. He's demonstrated that he's violent, and he certainly had a motive. Blackman was going to out him to the police."

Olivia closed the laptop. "You're probably right. Anyway, I'm getting woozy from that pain pill. I need to take a nap."

Just then the front doorbell rang. The two friends looked at each other. Tuesday patted her hand. "Rest. I'll go."

"No, I'll lock up while I'm down there. I bet it's one of those reporters who recognized me at the service." She winced when she got up but assured Tuesday she could make it downstairs.

She hobbled across the showroom trying to see who was out on the porch. Too dark, she turned on the porch light. When she saw who was there, she screamed "TUESDAY! WHAT HAVE YOU DONE? GET DOWN HERE."

In the yellow glow of the bug light on the porch, she saw a very tanned Brooks Baker waving a bouquet of red roses and a bottle of champagne at her.

Tuesday came up behind her. "I told you a man with dark skin was coming.

Chapter Twenty-Five: The Leaves Don't Lie

It took Tuesday a full twenty minutes to convince Olivia that she had not invited Brooks to Darling Valley. He looked devastated as she helped herself to his $500 bottle of Dom Perignon. Olivia couldn't enjoy any because she was high on painkillers. She nursed a glass of iced lemongrass tea Tuesday had prepared for her while she asked Brooks to explain himself.

He turned to Tuesday. "Can you give us a moment?"

Tuesday shook her head. "I don't know, Brooks. Are you sure you want to be alone with her? I'd frisk her for lethal weapons if I were you."

Olivia nodded that it was okay, and Tuesday departed for the spare bedroom with the another glass of Brook's champagne.

Brooks began with an apology so abject, Olivia almost melted. "What a fool I've been."

Olivia agreed.

"Letting you go was the worst decision of my life," he said with a cracking voice.

"You got that right, buster." The painkillers gave her a confidence that surprised them both. Gone was the, *Oh Brooks, I knew you'd come back* Olivia that had negotiated their last three breakups.

Brooks led Olivia into the living room. He put his glass on the coffee table and moved over to the couch where Olivia had stretched out. He lifted her feet onto his lap and began tenderly stroking the bottom of her foot, a move they both knew had often been the prelude to hot sex. Olivia abruptly pulled her knees to her chest.

"You know," he said, regrouping after the rebuff, "I've been feeling lost lately, out of sort, out of focus."

Out of habit, she picked up Brooks' champagne glass and drained what was left of it. In the old days, they used to joke that they were like monkeys grooming each other, feeding each other, drinking out of each other's glasses.

"Whoa," he said, taking the glass from her hand. "Don't mix that with your meds," but the last drops were gone.

"What made you think of me now, after all this time? You could have given me this speech months ago while I was still in LA and saved yourself a plane ticket."

"You know, with all that has been happening to you and having it all over the web and cable news, well naturally they would pick up on our fifteen minutes of fame. I began seeing us everywhere. The LACMA opening, the party to launch that museum I did in Brazil, the night we had dinner with Brad and Angelina. I couldn't get away from us. It was like a message from the universe. We belong together. I made a mistake. There, I said it. You know how hard it is for me to admit my fallibility, but I finally couldn't avoid it. You were all over the news and I wanted to be with you."

Olivia snuggled down into the pillows. The pain had eased but the soft glow from the narcotic and the brief taste of her favorite champagne wrapped her in a sweet cocoon. And best of all, Brooks, here at last. He'd come back to her. Finally. All that misery was behind her. If pining for him for those months, uprooting herself from LA and putting her in financial limbo instead of on top of the heap as she had been down south was what she had to do to get him back, then by golly, it was worth it.

Brooks leaned over into her face to kiss it. "What did you say love?"

"I didn't say anything." She closed her eyes to receive his kiss.

He leaned back to look at her. "No, you said something about it was worth it? What did you mean? What was worth it?"

Oops. Olivia realized she'd been talking her thoughts. Please no. Don't let Brooks know how badly he had broken her heart. A girl's gotta save face. How much did she say out loud? How much did he hear? Before she could answer herself, her head fell back, completely conked out.

Chapter Twenty-Six: Free At Last

This was why Olivia hated drugs. They drugged her. For days. She always said she'd make a lousy drug addict. She'd never take the damn stuff. Oh, she remembered last night of course. Up until Brooks laid her on the bed. But how did she get into her Goofy nightshirt? She certainly didn't remember that. Oh no! Did she spend a night with Brooks, FINALLY, and not remember it? That would be layering injustice upon indignity, the injustice losing Brooks in the first place.

Voices drifted down the hallway from the kitchen. Tuesday and Brooks must be having coffee. Yup, she sniffed it. That roused her in a hurry and she made it in and out of the shower and into clean clothes in record time. Blessedly, her hair fell into place without a struggle and a swipe of blush and lip-gloss made her reasonably presentable. The wood floor felt wonderfully cool and grounding under her feet so she kicked aside her flip-flops.

In the kitchen Brooks greeted her with an all-encompassing hug. How thrilling to be reminded of his big, comforting arms, the scent of his imported cologne and the tease of his soft lips.

Tuesday banged the kettle to get their attention. "Hey, you two. Red alert! There's a lonely old maid in the house. Don't rub it in with PDAs. I should say get a room, but you've just had one. Knock it off anyway."

Brooks released Olivia. "You? lonely! That's not the Tuesday I remember." Brooks laughed and for a moment it was just like old times, the three of them laughing, teasing, comfortably preparing good food.

"Tuesday," Olivia said, sniffing the air like a bloodhound. "Where did you find the bacon?"

"I sent Brookie Boy to Paymoor to exchange a pound of flesh for a pound of bacon."

Brooks shook his head. "And it just about cost me a pound of flesh. Where does that place think it is with those prices, Beverly Hills?"

Brooks poured Olivia's coffee and sat her in the window seat at the table. "There's more to this town than meets the eye," Olivia told him. "Like lots of the green stuff."

"I guess," he answered.

Oh, yes, this was the Brooks she had longed for all these months. And he was back. But that room business. What exactly happened after she passed out? In the old days, she would have laughed and just asked him and he would have mimed the pathetic lover whose advances are so easily forgotten. But this was both familiar and new. Perhaps because his arrival was so unexpected and her head was deeply stuck in her problems that she couldn't quite connect with him the way she would have expected. There was a little wall between them. Not big enough to erase their easy intimacy, but enough so that she needed to hold something back. Oh well. Probably the drugs. She wasn't quite herself yet.

After scraping up the dregs of the creamy scrambled eggs and caviar that Tuesday had whipped up, Brooks cleared the three plates to the sink. He looked out at the garden for a moment. He was a feast for her eyes. The cricket sweater made for him by his great grandmother in Sussex with washed cargo shorts, the touch of casual elegance. The loafers buffed to a blinding shine. All Brooks, all day.

He turned to Olivia with arms outstretched. "Baby, isn't it time we started doing the Brooks Baker boogie again." He punctuated his plea with a buck and wing.

Olivia laughed at his signature dance move. He came over and wrapped her in a hug again, then turned serious. "Babe, I've got plans. First, we have to get you in front of this media circus. I'm going to call my agent. Have her get Jannie Peters on it. You remember her, my press go-to gal. We'll have her come up here and do an in depth interview, focus not on the murder but the challenge of moving from the city where it's all happening to a little burg like Darling Valley. Pitch it say," he held his hands up like a marquee, "LA design whiz finds her soul in Northern California."

The wall, as if it had a will of its own, started to grow. Olivia crossed her arms as though protecting herself from an attacker.

"Have you started a blog? What's happening with your Facebook page and Twitter feeds. We'll get some pros on board to grow your fan base and post regular updates. And of course we'll get my profile on it. Lots of pictures of you showing me around town, cooking together here. Real homey. Once the press sees me in the picture it will take the heat off you."

Olivia winced, as though something had smacked her on the head. "Well, if you think so."

Tuesday drained her coffee and stuck the mug in the dishwasher. She had a tight line around her mouth.

She pulled a very conservative terry cloth robe around her and stared at the clock.

Brooks rushed over and pulled up his chair next to Olivia's. "That's my girl. Listen. I knew you'd be on board with this so I called my rep this morning and had her arrange a jet for Jannie. She'll be here in an hour. We can find a B&B or something for Tuesday. We'll put Jannie in the spare room so she can keep eyeballs on the scene 24/7."

Tuesday broke in. "In case you hadn't notice, I'm sitting here big as life in my comfy robe. Can't miss me. You might to ask if I want to stick around for the media circus you're proposing."

Brooks turned to her. "Oh, sure, Tuesday, if you'd rather head back to LA. I'll arrange for Jannie's jet to take you on the return trip."

And to Olivia, "See how easily things are falling into place? What would you do with out me?"

He leaned over and kissed her nose and then pulled his iPhone out of his pocket.

Tuesday shrugged her shoulders and said, "'Scuse me, you lovebirds. I have to rotate my tires," and walked to the hallway.

Olivia said, "You know, I'm still a little woozy from the drugs. I need to lie down for a bit."

Brooks said, "Sure babe. Whatever you need. And then you can change into one of your five star outfits. Something elegant, but San Francisco casual. We want to keep a bit of a city aura. Don't want to lose our fans who love seeing us around town. Nothing that smacks of Mayberry, you know what I mean?

You gotta work those paparazzi to get them on our side."

Tuesday followed Olivia down the hall and closed the bedroom door as Olivia fell back on the bed. "How you doing, sugar babe? Has the pain come back?"

"No, my tummy's okay. Maybe this whole thing is catching up with me. You know, the murder, the money worries, the drugs and then Brooks showing up."

She put her hands over her face and starting sobbing.

"Sweetie, what is it?" Tuesday sat down on the side of the bed and stroked Olivia's hair. "I would have thought having Brooks here would make all your worries go away. I know that's what you've wanted since the breakup. Even though you deny it. You two are like bonded at the soul level. You're in transition. You know what that's like, one foot on one side of a canyon the other reaching for solid ground. It's hard. Of course, he still has that it's my world and be glad I let you live in it vibe going on. But hey, if it works for you . . ."

Olivia sat up on one elbow. "Tues, did we sleep together last night? Did we do anything? You know what I mean."

"Whoa, girl. You were there. What do you think?"

"But that's just it. I don't remember. I woke up this morning in my nightshirt and don't know how I got here. Where was Brooks when you got up?"

"In the kitchen making coffee. You know how he is, can't sit still for two seconds. His hair was wet so he had showered. I assumed he had slept with you. I mean, where else would he sleep?"

Tuesday let out a big sigh. "You know, I think Brooks is right. I should leave. With all that's going on, I'm in the way now. I'll pack up my things and take that jet back to LA. He can use the Mercedes and drop it off at the airport before he comes back. I'll let the rental company know."

Olivia put her arm on Tuesday's, stroked her robe. Terry cloth! The towels. She'd have to get them out of the dryer as soon as she got up.

"But I don't want you to leave, Tuesday. I want you here. I couldn't have functioned the last few days without you."

"Yeah, but now you have Brooks. I done my duty as I saw it, captain. Go to sleep." She gently pressed Olivia down into the soft pillow and waited until she closed her eyes. She tiptoed out of the room.

Olivia's cell phone jangled her awake. "Hello?" She was half in and half out of a light sleep.

"Miss Granville? Did you get my message about lunch?"

She was about to say who is this, when a bell went off. The garage guy! Mr. Bacon. He'd left a message specifically saying he wanted to meet for lunch today. Had she said yes?

"I just wanted to check that we are still on for Hugo's at noon."

Nothing in Olivia's being wanted to meet him or anyone for lunch today. But this could be a goldmine of a client. She sat up, shook her head to wake up. "Of course we're on. I have some ideas for you that I think would not only show off your car, the Trident."

He corrected her. "Talbot, Miss Granville. Nineteen thoity-eight Talbot."

"Of course, slip of the tongue. We want to show off the car, protect it and showcase its historical context."

She didn't know how she had pulled that out of her hat, but as she heard herself describing this sudden vision of the perfect garage, it sounded pretty good. Juke box, little soda fountain in the corner.

"That's what I'm talkin' about Miss Granville. See you at noon."

"Can't wait." She gave a little laugh. "I'm hungry already." She looked at the clock. Nine-fifteen. Hmm. What should she wear? Then she flopped back down on the bed and promptly fell asleep.

Brooks woke her with a soft kiss. She opened her eyes and moved into his embrace. He stretched out next to her and took her in his arms. As he began the familiar moves with his hands and his tongue, she came fully awake.

"Wait. What time is it?"

"Ten. We have lots of time before Jannie gets here. She texted she was going to be late. The jet couldn't get a clearance until noon. An hour flying time, then a what, half hour ride in the limo from the airport?"

Olivia sat up. "An hour with traffic. But I have a lunch meeting."

Brooks said, "Cancel it. We have things to do." Then he gave her a sexy grin and kissed her again. "And I don't just mean creating a public relations strategy."

Olivia pushed past him and stood up. "No. I can't cancel. I've put this guy off what, three times now. He could be my biggest client. I won't be more than two hours."

"Wait a minute. Olivia. Let's get our priorities straight. I've lined things up that will turn all this around for you. You have to get out from under the suspicion of murder. We have to put some good spin on you. Get you back to LA and away from this Keystone Kops scene. You don't need clients up here anymore. You need them in LA. We're together again. Like old times, only better."

She sat up and moved away from him. "But I don't live in LA anymore. I live here. I have commitments. And I don't want your press gal whitewashing my story. I want to find the killer and clear my name. So there will be no doubt about my innocence. And I can't do that from LA. And I can't pass up valuable leads. This guy is looking for someone to design a space for a hundred vintage cars. You know what that could do for me?"

"Yeah. I'll design the building and you do the interior. The two of us together and it would be a bombshell for the design community. I've never done a space for cars, but it can't be much of a challenge. Not after that museum in the African bush."

Olivia turned to him, outraged. "You want to take my gig away from me? I make the connection because of the work I've done establishing myself in this town and you want to steal my thunder?"

"Babe, look. Face it. We know who's got the juice here. Nothing against you, but how many times have you been on the cover of Time? This would be good exposure for me. We're in this together, aren't we?"

The fog of drugs and intoxicating presence of Brooks lifted. Olivia saw thing's clearly now. She faced Brooks.

"I see what you're doing. We weren't in this together when you were out with your starlets and models and calling me your client. Now, whether I like it or not, the media is after me for, what are they calling it, the crime of the century. Murder in Billionaire Hollow. And you want in on the action. You've got your people on it. But did you ask me what I wanted?

"How dare you throw Tuesday, my friend, out of my own house? How dare you set up blogs and tweets and media stories without asking me? And what's going to happen when the media storm is over and the guy who did this is caught and then I'm just the same old antiques dealer and designer of bathrooms and the next model of the month drifts by? Did you even ask me if I wanted you here? You just assume you can walk back in my life whenever you feel like it.

"God I hate feeling like I'm in a soap opera. And I'm not going to. You'll be on the jet back to LA, with your go to publicity gal. You left me to handle my life on my own. And that is what I am doing. Thank you very much. Now I have to get dressed for a business meeting. TUESDAY? Unpack your bags. You're not going anyplace."

"STOP! YOU'RE KILLING THEM!"

Olivia raced into the yard and grabbed the hose out of Tuesday's hands. It whipsawed into the air like a green snake on steroids, dousing both of them before it finally fell into the dirt, pouring water down the driveway.

Tuesday, her clothes plastered to her skin, mascara spreading in a coal black river down her cheeks, fake eyelashes hanging off one lid, hair a bright pink wet beanie stuck to her scalp, was spitting out the rivulets of water dripping from her nose and upper lip.

"What the . . ."

Olivia ran to the spigot to turn off the flood, screaming, "You aim the water at the roots, not blast the roses to kingdom come with a water canon!"

She pulled her sopping hoodie away from her chest and pointed to the naked branches and carpet of waterlogged petals under them. "Look, there's nothing but hips left on that one. It was my prize floribunda!"

Tuesday was near tears, peeling off her eyelashes. "How am I supposed to know? I have plastic flowers. I was just trying to stay out of the way."

Olivia came to her senses and ran back and hugged Tuesday. "So sorry, so sorry, SOOOOOO sorry." Now she was crying. "It's not your fault. I'm a prizewinning bitch for going off that. It's just. Well, could the house be more uncomfortable? Brooks went for a run to kill time until Jannie arrives. But that's three hours away. Some delay with the plane. He told her not to come, but they were already on the runway. So she gave him what for--believe me, you don't want to be around her if she so much as has to wait for a light before she crosses the street. Then he turned on me," she shivered at the memory of Brooks bellowing at her, "and now he's parked in front of the TV sulking."

The two friends looked at one another. Olivia quoted her grandmother. "Do him good," and they burst out laughing. Olivia said, "We're good?"

Tuesday flicked her eyelashes into the roses and giggled, "We couldn't be more good. Let's get cleaned up. I feel like channeling Cher."

Olivia stopped her. "Not Turn Back Time. DV isn't ready for that."

"Course not. That's evening wear. How about Mary Tyler Moore, then. I have some bell bottoms with me."

Half an hour later, Olivia passed Brooks in her skin tight, low cut, knock-em-dead-at-the-client-meeting dress with the do-me shoes, zillion inch heels and straps wrapped around her ankles up to her knees. He avoided looking at her as she strutted by, but she heard him stretch his neck to check her out as she picked up her purse and went down stairs.

On the way to the Mercedes, she saw Tuesday hunting for her eye lashes under the drowned rose bush. "I didn't bring an extra pair," she explained, then stopped Olivia. "You can NOT go out in that dress without some bling. I've got the perfect scarf. Wait here."

Before she made it to the end of the driveway, Olivia playing deaf, was starting the engine.

In the rear view mirror, she saw Detective Johnson pull up behind her, the cadre of paparazzi pulling up. They had caught the scent of Brooks Baker.

"What can I do for you, detective," she asked when he came to her side window.

"Miss Granville, I'm afraid you'll have to come with me."

He pulled handcuffs out of his pocket. "I hope I won't need to use these."

Oh god. What kind of miscalculation had she made in sending Brooks and his media team packing?

Chapter Twenty-Seven: Hands Behind Your Back

Olivia, handcuffed in the back seat, insisted Johnson explain her arrest. But he remained silent on the way to the police station. Once there, he led Olivia past Officer Ridley's desk, where the woman watched her argue with Johnson halfway down the corridor and into the cafeteria. There, at the end of a long Formica conference table, two of the officers Olivia recognized from the investigation at her house were trading jokes on their coffee break. She heard, "So the horse says to the bartender," but the scrape of her chair on the cement floor as Johnson pulled it out for her obliterated the punch line.

Johnson undid the handcuffs. She rubbed her wrists and said, "These were not necessary."

"I could have had you for resisting arrest."

"MY NEIGHBORS WERE WATCHING!"

"Calm down and sit down." She chose option number two.

The officers did not acknowledge her. Johnson said, "Coffee? Water?" He looked down at the officers and added, "Champagne?" They sniggered into their coffee mugs and gave Johnson a thumbs up.

Olivia was curt. "No thank you, but an explanation as to what I am doing here is in order."

Johnson said, "Cool your jets, ma'am. I'll be right back," and left the room.

Twenty minutes later he returned and sank into a chair opposite Olivia. "Do you know the penalty for filing a false police report?"

"No. Why would I need to?"

Johnson pulled a sheet of paper out of his breast pocket and shoved it across the table at her. "That your signature?"

Olivia read the beginning of the first theft report stating her netsuke had gone missing. "Yes, that's my signature."

Johnson reached into his coat pocket and retrieved another folded sheet of paper. He set it on the table. "Do you know what this is?"

Olivia put as much hostility into her voice as she could muster. "I assume it is the report of the theft of my Imari bowl."

He reached into his other pocket and Olivia said, "If you are retrieving the theft report of my flashlight, don't bother. Yes, I filed it and it has my signature on it."

She heard one of the police officers whisper bingo, and his partner guffaw.

Johnson said, "That's what I need to establish ma'am. That you filed these reports."

"And the point is, officer?"

"Detective, ma'am. Detective Johnson."

"Detective."

"Ma'am, in the State of California the penalty for knowingly and willfully filing a false police report carries jail time. The stakes are higher when you add filing a false insurance claim."

"But I haven't filed an insurance claim. I'm depending upon your department to find the culprit."

"Miss Granville, I'm just saying that if you *were* to file an insurance claim . . . "

"But I didn't. Why would I do that? Those items had tremendous sentimental value. I made every effort to find them . . ." Olivia was warming up to her argument, but Johnson stopped her.

"I'm sure you did. But we have a situation here. A body is discovered on your property dead under suspicious circumstances. You file robbery reports. Three robbery reports. In three days. Your business is in danger of going under. Wouldn't it be convenient to recoup some of your losses through the insurance company?"

"That's laughable. If I were to receive reimbursement from the insurance company for those items it wouldn't even pay for my utilities bill."

"So maybe you were just starting out. Testing the waters, so to speak."

Olivia thumped the table. "Detective, I resent this. My integrity has never been questioned. Under any circumstances."

Johnson was abrupt. "There's always a first time. Look, we got this situation. The night before last night we had officers watching your house from dusk to dawn. Nobody, I repeat, not one person was seen going in or out of your premises during that time, except you and Miss, uh, you know, your guest."

"Tuesday."

"Yeah. And then yesterday you report another theft. So what I don't understand is, if we had eyeballs on your house, and nobody went in or out, how could somebody sneak in and steal your stuff?"

"But Detective Richards said surveillance would start last night."

"Well that's what he said. But it started the night before last night. So what do you have to say to that? Catch you by surprise?"

A shock of fear humbled Olivia. "Detective, please. I don't know how to prove my innocence, but I swear to you, my things were stolen. I had nothing to do with their disappearance. Give me a lie detector test. Take my fingerprints. Do . . . all the police things you do to catch criminals and prove a person's innocence."

Johnson's cell phone rang. "Yeah? Uh huh? Okay." He snapped the phone shut and gestured to the two other officers. "Outside."

Olivia could hear loud voices and was sure one of them belonged to Richards. After a few moments, Johnson came back into the cafeteria. "You can go. I'll have one of the officers give you a ride home."

"That's it?

"You want to stay I can find a cell for you."

"No, thank you. And I'll walk, detective. I don't need my neighbors seeing me in a police car again."

She made a point of glaring at his belly. Plus, exercise is good for you."

Olivia hurried out of the room and found Richards in deep conversation with the two officers, who appeared to be defending themselves against some charge. She heard him say, "You don't do that without my . . ."

As she reached the end of the corridor and headed for freedom, she said icily, "Trouble in paradise, detective?"

Chapter Twenty-Eight: The Heist

"Don't you love Della Robbia?"

"Della who?"

Olivia and Tuesday stood in the business end of Blackman Restoration, the front area containing the money pieces. The gilt mirrors, Napoleon campaign chests, Della Robbia water features.

Olivia explained. "Smart marketing to have a showroom like this. It convinces clients that Blackman seals the deal when it comes to restoring their treasures."

They looked around but couldn't see anyone in the shop. This was Olivia's third trip to Blackman's so she knew the layout. In the back Sabrina and Blackman had divided a storeroom into two small offices, each with a view to the workroom. There, out of sight of customers, a small team of woodworkers stripped finishes, sanded tabletops and replaced pieces of trim so exact the owner couldn't tell the difference between the replacement and the original. This acclaimed attention to detail had sold Olivia on Blackman's when she realized she needed work done on her pieces.

Olivia called out *hello* as a table with heavily carved legs caught her eye. "Nice copy. You'd almost say it was a Grinling Gibbons, except British museums and churches own all the surviving pieces. If you want to see a choice Gibbons collection, you must go to Petworth House."

Tuesday was checking her outfit in a ceiling high distressed painted mirror that Olivia had coveted since her first visit to the shop. Tuesday pursed her lips like a naughty 1920's flapper. "Ooo, honey. Petworth House."

Then she went back to admiring the clown suit effect of her super short balloon-like top with Day-Glo polka dots in various colors and sizes over faux leopard leggings and studded and zipped wood, aluminum and macramé six-inch platform sandals with retractable rollerblades that Olivia had said when she unpacked them were smokin' hot. If you were going for the orthopedic appliance look. She'd said, "You could hook a ladder on the side to get you up to the top bunk."

Today Tuesday had slicked her hair back with enough bobby pins to build a miniature space ship. Satisfied with the Emmet Kelly look, she said, "How you can tell one piece of squiggles from another is beyond me," referring to the ornate spray of birds, flowers, shells and cherubs on the table legs. "But I'll take your word for it. If you say the dude rocks, the dude rocks."

Olivia slipped into her docent mode and explained that in 17th century London, Gibbons set the bar for carved renderings of the natural disorder of flora and fauna, adorned, of course, with his signature cherubs. She was finishing up her story about Gibbons' habit of including a peapod in all of his carvings, left open to reveal baby peas if he had been paid for the commission, and closed if he had not, when Roger walked into the showroom covered in sawdust.

They had planned this visit intending merely to case the joint. They assumed Olivia could distract a sales person with some blather about making an appointment with Sabrina to discuss the invoices for her pieces still in possession of the DVPD, while Tuesday skulked around figuring out how to access the safe. Cody had told Olivia that she would likely find Sabrina at her desk from 10 am to noon and they timed their visit for 9:15 am to be sure her office would be vacant.

Roger introduced himself, not aware that both women recognized him from the altercation at the country club. He began with a dull-witted apology. "Sorry, but nobody's here. Just me."

Olivia and Tuesday each shook his hand but did not identify themselves.

From his slack-jawed, glazed-eye expression, Olivia half expected him to stick his thumb in his mouth and say, duh. Where was the fire she saw as he pummeled Young Master Gotshalk and drove out of the parking lot raging at Cody? Was he high? Or suffering the mother of all hangovers?

Olivia began questioning Roger about Sabrina's schedule and his opinion on how long it would take for Blackman's to repair a table leg with a crack down the center. As soon as Tuesday heard Roger say he was home alone, she slipped into the workroom. Several minutes later she re-emerged to find Olivia and Roger deep in a discussion about the difficulty of sealing wood to protect it from insects. Olivia saw Tuesday give her the thumbs up, and she cut Roger off.

"Thanks for your time. I'll just call Sabrina for an appointment."

Back in the car, Tuesday explained the heist. First, she spotted Sabrina's office from a framed photo on her desk feeding wedding cake to her groom. Tiptoeing inside, Tuesday could see the far wall with the antique map of London over the desk, just as Elgin had described it. Though her mission was merely reconnoitering, she decided to seize the moment. She slipped her hand under the desk drawer and found the key taped there, peeled it carefully to preserve some sticky so she could replace it, then slid the map aside. There it was, the safe begging her to open it. She inserted the key into the lock, quietly opened the door and found a bonanza.

The safe contained several small boxes and two documents in bank folders. The labels identified the partnership agreement between Sabrina and Blackman and the side agreement Elgin had described. To be certain it was the correct document, Tuesday checked the witness signature and bingo: Elgin Fastner's scrawl. She photographed the one page agreement and, as she slid it back into place, noticed a CD with a post it: *JB re mny Indring*. Without thinking, Tuesday stuck it in her purse, covered her tracks and rejoined Olivia.

Olivia exploded. "YOU STOLE IT? That wasn't the plan! Do you know what we can get for breaking and entering?" She felt a chill as she realized it was déjà vu all over again. Detective Johnson had threatened her with almost the same words.

Flustered now, Tuesday's hands started to shake. "I know, I know. But it was there and, well, I didn't think. Look, if it was that easy to lift it, it will be that easy to put it back. Let's just see what's on this and then we'll decide what to do."

"No. I don't want anything to do with it. Turn around. We are going to put it back. Now, before Sabrina comes to work."

Tuesday turned practical. She waved the CD at Olivia and said, "In for a penny, in for a pound. If that post it says money laundering, then you need to hear this."

Olivia relented and slipped the CD into the slot while Tuesday turned onto Darling Boulevard to return home. The silky smooth mechanism of the Mercedes swallowed the disc soundlessly. In a snap, sounds of an argument flooded the car. Olivia recognized Sabrina shouting at a man she addressed as John. She was angry; he was loud. Olivia leaned in to listen, trying to determine something about the man's character from his voice.

Sabrina was on the warpath. "John, don't lie to me. You're smuggling drugs and I don't know what all. Don't you see how that is putting me in jeopardy?"

Footsteps, the male voice walking closer to Sabrina. "You stick to managing the business and keep your nose out of mine."

Sabrina again. "Now I know why you want to focus on imports from Asia. You're hiding heroin in the furniture shipments. Are you out of your mind? How long before customs sniffs you out? And then what?"

"You don't know what you're talking about."

"I should have known what kind of man you are. After all, you cheat on your wife."

"Well, it hasn't bothered you all these months."

A few seconds of silence passed before Sabrina spoke again. "Who else did you cheat on? Those rare lamps you were accused of switching . . .you did it, didn't you? Does Greta know? Oh, knowing the kind of shit storm she can throw, I bet you've kept this quiet, haven't you? Or does she know? And you're sharing your stash with her? If this gets out you're not taking me down. I won't cover for you this time. Not like at Silicon Biotech."

Voices in the background signaled someone had entered the room and the conversation switched to a business discussion about how much to charge for refinishing a dining table. Olivia ejected the CD and stared wordlessly at Tuesday.

Tuesday was the first to gather her wits about her. "This is dynamite, Honeybun. Let's make a copy at home and slip this back into the safe. If we hurry we can get her done by ten. Isn't that when Sabrina's due in her office?"

Olivia was flummoxed. "But what are we going to do with the information? If we show this to anyone, we're guilty of theft. I can't risk that. And what really does it prove about his murder? I don't see how this clears me or fingers anyone else."

"Let's figure that out after we copy it and return it. But the first thing that comes to my mind is a motive for Sabrina."

Later, after the switch, Olivia poured ice tea for both of them and unwrapped cheese for their lunch. She washed grapes and strawberries to calm herself down and arranged them artfully around the cheese, her designer genes operating on autopilot. The two settled at the kitchen table, still an uncomfortable spot for Olivia where she could see the crime tape whiffle in the light afternoon breeze.

Olivia peeled back the wrapping on a Brie she had left to soften on the counter before they left for Blackman's. "We have to figure this out. So what do we know?"

Tuesday accepted a hefty slice and helped herself to a chunk of sour dough. "Well the widow is pretty darn good at shedding crocodile tears."

Olivia nodded. "Yeah, she's got that act sealed and delivered. Seems to have the doctor fooled, too." She snapped her fingers. "That reminds me. I have to make a follow up appointment with him."

Tuesday popped a ripe strawberry into her mouth. "I thought you said you were feeling fine."

"I am, but he said to come back for a checkup no matter what."

Tuesday groaned. "That means I'll have to listen to another puffer fish lecture."

"What are you talking about? Puffer fish?"

"You know, those special fish in his tank. The ones he keeps separate from the others. The Scribble Scrabbles or something. They are a variety of puffer fish. The receptionist said he has a matched pair in his aquarium at home. He's breeding them or something."

"Puffer fish? You mean the poisonous ones? Tuesday, remember that guy who dropped dead in that Japanese restaurant?"

"In West Hollywood? Oh yeah, the one they shut down when the Health Department said they hadn't prepared the fish properly. I'm not sure they were even supposed to serve it because it is so deadly."

"That's the one. And, Tuesday, that's it."

"What's it, Nancy Drew? You've lost me."

"Let me spell this out and see if it makes sense. We have a dead man but nobody can find the cause of death. Greta's doctor thinks it's a heart attack after some kind of altercation and that's why he gets stuffed in the armoire. Can't figure out why he would be sent to me, yet, but let's keep going. There are three other suspicious deaths. One is called an out and out heart attack, the others have no obvious cause of death. Hence, the curse."

"Yeah, but where does the girl with a broken neck from a so-called fall down the stairs come in?"

Olivia drained her tea. "I'm working on my feet here, Tues. Just stay with me. Mr. Harmon and the shirt duo. Three deaths. All called heart attacks in certified healthy people."

"Okay, I'm waiting for the punch line."

"All of them have a connection to Blackman. All of them claimed that Blackman cheated them. The girl is an outlier, unless we can tie her into this mess."

Tuesday tilted her head skeptically. "Okay. But the three who might have a motive for killing Blackman are, and isn't this just too inconvenient for words, very dead. And if Blackman slipped them some puffer fish, which is what you are suggesting if I'm getting your drift, he is also very dead."

Olivia stood up. "Grrrrrrrr. Why isn't this easy? Want some ice cream? Salted Caramel Fudge from Paymoor's or Massimo's Limoncello?"

"Did I hear someone say fudge?"

"You got it, girlfriend. Oh, that reminds me. Mrs. Harmon. Don't let me forget to get my laundry out of the dryer. I keep forgetting to get those towels. The mood she's in about all the disruption around here? She'll be on a rampage if I don't grab them by the time she needs to use the dryer."

Tuesday cleared the lunch plates while Olivia scooped ice cream into bowls and retrieved the whipped cream dispenser from the Subzero and jar of The Salted Caramel's homemade hot fudge sauce."

Tuesday's face lit up. "That's what I'm talking about. Going hard core."

Olivia held up the fudge sauce. "This stuff is better than smack. Not that I'd know the difference. Just saying if I knew the difference, I know The Salted Caramel's would come out on top."

Tuesday laughed and said, "Your secret is safe with me. Hey, are you rationing that stuff? C'mon. One more scoop." She lifted the all but overflowing bowl of goodness. "Just the thing for crime stopping." She took her first spoonful. "Chocolate understands me."

Olivia put the perishables away and headed for the living room, already digging into the gooey wonder. "You mean it feels your pain?"

"Yes it does."

Olivia winked. "There's more where that came from. But, I warn you, first bowl is free. Once you're hooked, you're mine for life. Now let's get comfortable. Oh, wait." She grabbed her iPad off the counter and tucked it under her arm before she followed Tuesday into the living room.

They settled on the couches and tried to pick up the thread of the conversation, but before long, they slid their empty bowls and spoons onto the coffee table, wiped their mouths and fingers with DVD&A cocktail napkins and slipped into ice cream and fudge-fueled comas.

Chapter Twenty-Nine: Going Fishing

Olivia jerked awake first with a crick in her neck from sleeping sideways on the couch. While she was out, Tuesday had quietly folded herself into the fetal position in front of the fireplace. Olivia didn't want to wake her friend; the sugar binge probably meant that the overindulgence in alcohol the night before still had a death grip on their metabolisms. She slipped off her shoes, stretched out on the couch and adjusted soft pillows under her head. She stared up at the beamed ceiling and allowed the CD conversation to fill her brain.

What did that all that stuff about drug deals mean for her? How could she use it? How could she hide the fact that she was an accessory to robbery? An idea popped into her head and she did some Googling, read Wikipedia for a few minutes, then went over what she remembered from the CD.

Blackman and Sabrina had a very close partnership that included sleeping together. There is a chance that the wife found out about it. Hell hath no fury and all that. Plus, Blackman was apparently smuggling dope. Who else knows about that? Was he hiding it from the wife to keep the proceeds for himself? Sharing the bounty with her? Or protecting her from the consequences if he got caught? Hmm. He was smuggling drugs. Did that involve Roger?

On top of that, Harmon and the shirt couple threatened to sue Blackman, which would not be good for Greta's social standing. Several sources have confirmed that she's a social climber. Olivia continued to run the facts or pseudo facts through her head . From what Sabrina said, it looked like Blackman was dirty dealing in that biotech firm blowup. Tuesday groaned, interrupting Olivia's thoughts. She rolled onto her back, then sat up.

"Oh," she moaned, holding her stomach. "Why did you let me do that?"

"Water," Olivia advised. "Gallons of it to dilute all that sugar. I'm going to get some. Want a glass?" She struggled up and out of the clutches of the soft, down cushions. Tuesday followed her into the kitchen and headed straight for the refrigerator. "I think I'll have a little hair of the dog," and snatched the fudge sauce before Olivia could grab it back.

"Tuesday, you'll hate yourself. You know you will."

"Maybe," she said licking her spoon, "but it hurts so good right now."

Olivia put her hands on her hips and pointed to Tuesday's collection of pharmaceuticals on the counter. "Is this your idea of a cleanse?"

Tuesday nodded her head, a dreamy look of ecstasy sliding over her face. "You better believe it, Betty Crocker. What have you been up to?"

Olivia with her water and Tuesday with her poison slid onto stools at the island. "Just trying to make sense of it all. Here's what I've been thinking. Stay with me because I'm making this up as I go. The widow's beloved doctor raises deadly puffer fish and let's say he has told his favorite patient how poisonous they are. So she gets a brainstorm. She has potential troublemakers in the shirt couple and Harmon who, for the sake of argument, are planning to sue her husband. Oh, think of all the party givers who will strike her off their guest lists if that comes out. So she feeds the sue-ers some puffer fish and their deaths pass as heart attacks. Then she finds out about Sabrina and her husband, and maybe the fact that he's hiding drug millions from her, and she decides to off her husband, too, and slips puffer fish into his hot milk."

"Or scotch."

"Whatever. I'm just saying. According to Wikipedia, the coroner wouldn't find the puffer fish toxin in the bodies without a special spectrometer. It doesn't leave a trace and the effects mimic a heart attack. But this isn't puffer fish country. No fishmonger sells it, no restaurant serves it, and so nobody suspects puffer fish or Greta. The couple accidentally fell into the lake and drowned with no other cause of death and Harmon was running too fast for his age and collapsed. Heart attacks? Makes sense to the ME. Then we find out Greta's a sailor."

Tuesday licked her spoon and said, "We do?"

Olivia pulled up the text from the New York Times news alert on her iPad and showed her the extensive story about Greta's skill and impressive track record in races on San Francisco Bay. "Who would know how to tie those complicated knots that were around the armoire? A sailor. How's that for a theory?"

Tuesday wiped the fudge mustache from her upper lip. "Well, I think that is brilliant, Sherlock. It ties everything up in a neat package. It really does."

Olivia beamed.

"Except for 27,000 teeny tiny questions. Where does she get the puffer fish? How does she figure out how to use it? How does she get them to eat it? Why does she send the body to you? This has been my question all along, Dick Tracy. If it's the perfect crime, and feeding puffer fish to a victim sounds like it could be, why does she make it look like murder?"

Olivia put her head down on the table in frustration, then looked up. "You would have to bring that up. Okay. One thing at a time. Let me call Jesse, my favorite authority on sea creatures."

Her smile faded during her conversation with him. "Thanks, Jesse. Sorry to bother you. Yeah, sure. See you soon."

"So?"

"Jesse doesn't know very much about puffer fish, except that you have to be very skilled at preparing it or it's curtains. Therefore, outside of Japan, where it is a delicacy, no restaurant serves it. He had no idea where somebody would get hold of puffer fish around here. He could ask his suppliers, but doesn't think it's available locally. So," Olivia's eyes brightened again, "maybe she imported it?"

"But Ols. Why go to all that trouble? Why not make the deaths look like muggings or something and blame them on the drug trade in meth city?"

Olivia corrected her. "Meth park."

"Whatever. I just don't get sending the body to you where everybody will know it was murder. Once murder has been established, it's always the spouse that comes under suspicion if there are no other suspects. Why would she take that risk? And why isn't your darling detective, pun intended, going after her? I haven't heard anybody mention her as a suspect. So nobody knows what we know, but also perp-wise, she seems to be clean. I mean, we still don't know why they hauled your pretty butt in, but if they are down to looking at you as a suspect that must mean they have ruled her out."

Olivia gave up. "Let's do something counterproductive for a change. Let's make new labels for furniture that isn't going to sell at the sale that nobody in Darling Valley will be caught dead at. Metaphorically speaking."

Two hours later, with only half of the showroom furniture tagged, Tuesday slumped into one of the wing chairs. "Olivia, why did you make me eat that ice cream?

Olivia opened a new package of furniture tags and undid the knot that held the strings together. "I warned you"

Tuesday closed her eyes, clearly suffering from her overindulgence. "You did not. You opened my mouth and stuffed it down my throat like I was a goose you were raising for foie gras. You probably could sell my liver for top dollar."

Olivia walked over to her and rubbed her shoulders. "You don't have to do this, honey. Why don't you take a break, sit out in the sunshine." She looked out the window. The fog was drifting in. "What's left of it."

Tuesday gave her a pitiful look. "I think I need your doctor. Seriously. I'll even brave the puffer fish."

Olivia shooed her out of the showroom. "Go, rest. I can finish up."

Tuesday did as she was told. Olivia tagged a few more items and then threw down her red pen and tags. Oh my god," she said to herself. Then screamed, "TUESDAY! I've GOT IT."

She ran through the showroom, up the stairs to the loft and into the guestroom where Tuesday lay on the bed with her arms crossed over her eyes.

"Tuesday!"

"What?" she asked sitting up.

"It's not Greta who does the murders. It's the doctor!"

"What? A doctor is a mass murder?"

"It's happened before. Who was that guy in England? Howard Shipman? Harold somebody? He killed hundreds of his patients. Anyway, Chandler's got the puffer fish. He's tight with the widow so he kills the couple and Harmon because, I don't know why. Has something to do with that biotech deal. I'd bet on it. And he gets rid of Blackman because, oh, I don't know. I've done this much. You come up with something, Tues."

Tuesday lay back down, thinking. "Maybe we don't have to come up with everything. If you go to Richards with your suspicions, he can have the ME sample Blackman's tissues for puffer fish toxin. The doc has puffer fish and a grudge against Blackman. That should be enough. And one more thing, Olivia. Chandler's receptionist made a huge point of telling me that he had a matched pair of those special puffer fish at home because he was breeding them. When we went to his house the other night and he was examining you? I was looking at all of his fish. He had a special tank just like in his office for the puffer fish. But there was only one fish there."

Olivia said, "You're kidding."

"I'm not. I can't believe I even noticed it, but I didn't want to stare when he was checking you out so I looked at his fish. It didn't mean anything to me at the time, but I swear to you, babykins. There was only one fish in that tank."

Olivia spoke slowly. "He fed the other one to the deceased."

Tuesday nodded her head. "That's what I'm thinking. Tell Darling Valley's finest that when you saw Chandler's puffer fish, you remembered seeing a customer die of what looked like a heart attack at the time, but later was determined to be puffer fish. Let police figure out the rest. This way, you won't have to say anything about what we heard on the CD. What difference does it make whether Blackman was a drug dealer. You just need to find out who killed him. And why he was sent to you."

Olivia went into the kitchen, dug into her purse for her cell phone and a business card, then dialed a number. A moment later she said, "Detective Richards, please."

Chapter Thirty: The Catch

"Coffee?" said Richards. Without waiting for an answer he offered chairs to Olivia and Tuesday, closed the door to his office and took his seat behind his desk. "Now, what is all this puffer fish business about?"

Olivia explained her theory and then backed it up with more of her argument. "I've been going crazy trying to figure out how I'm involved with this man's death. And I still don't understand, but a big piece of the puzzle is what killed him. Your reports to the press are inconclusive, except there are no signs of violence. The easy poisons are traceable, so last I heard, poison was ruled out and you were looking at some kind of sex thing gone wrong that gave him a heart attack."

Richards nodded. "Nothing's conclusive, but it has been put forth as a theory."

"Well, I never would have put two and two together if Tuesday and I hadn't been in a West Hollywood restaurant last year when a customer collapsed and died of his puffer fish entrée. Huge scandal in the restaurant scene."

Tuesday added, "Which, in LA, is not to be trifled with."

Olivia continued without missing a beat, twisting her hair into a ponytail when she saw a tray of rubber bands on Richards' desk. She grabbed one, "Do you mind?"

"Help yourself, he said," which she did as she got on with her tale while she anchored her hair.

"Well, it was hard on me because I'd never seen a dead body before. You know, in the restaurant. I mean," she grimaced, "he was at the next table."

Tuesday added a throwing up gesture.

"So when I got curious about the puffer fish, I checked out Dr. Chandler on the internet. I was flying blind, and it took some digging, but I found out that he was aced out of a juicy development deal with Blackman back when they both worked in Silicon Valley for a biotech company."

Richards was busy making notes with his Bic and yellow pad. "What else?"

Olivia gestured with her hands. "Well I don't have anything else." She looked over at Tuesday for confirmation. "Except for this. I've mentioned to you that I had a stomach ailment." She described the scene she and Tuesday had witnessed when Greta Blackman let herself into to Chandler's house.

Richards' shook his head. "Interesting. You're sure it was her?"

"Detective, I'm sure I'd recognize a woman who has publicly accused me of murder."

Richards whistled the air out of his cheeks. "I'm going to have to do some more investigating. But I can tell you this because will be on the Internet before nightfall. We have pretty good evidence that Blackman was involved in smuggling drugs. Roger Hatfield, an employee of his, finally admitted to us that he found a stash of drugs when he unknowingly unpacked a table or something that he found in Blackman's office. The guy threw a fit, threatened to fire him and expose his drug use—Hatfield is an addict—if he didn't keep quiet. Blackman kept his mouth shut by supplying him with drugs. You're new here, but Darling Valley has just as much of a drug problem as any other city in the country. But we are on it and, while we have a small police force, it's highly trained. When we heard that, we had Hatfield as a suspect. Plus, someone gave us a tip that he had done the murder."

Curious, hot with suspicion, Olivia leaned closer. "Who would that be?"

"A guy name Forrest Gotshalk."

Olivia gave an I thought so look to Tuesday. "Yes, I know who he is. His mother is a client of mine."

"Well, he overheard something at a club and wanted to do his civic duty. But we checked out Hatfield and it didn't fit. Especially when he told us that he had swept the porch before he left work the night before Blackman was killed. He left the shop and never saw him again."

"So what does that mean?"

"Well, we were careful to keep this out of the press, but we found two sets of prints where the chest, your amory was left on the porch."

Tuesday was putting the pieces together. "Yeah, but lots of people work in that shop. I'd think you'd find many fingerprints."

Richards spoke slowly, stretching out the suspense. "I didn't say fingerprints. Prints. Footprints. Shoe prints to be exact. A man's shoe and a woman's."

Olivia snapped her fingers. "My Jimmy Choos!"

"Exactly. Well, I was going over some of this with Tasmania, you remember meeting her at the auction, right?"

Olivia's stomach didn't know what to do with this information so she just let it flutter a bit. "Sure, we remember her, right Tues?"

Tuesday smiled at Richards. "How could we forget?"

"And she told me to check with Shoe Candy. That store on Darling Boulevard."

"Oh, I know it, detective."

"I know you do, Miss Granville."

Olivia wondered if they would ever get on a first name basis. But then with Tasmania on the scene, what did it matter?

"We had someone from the shoe store look at photos of the woman's prints and they narrowed them down to a few brands and styles. Then we asked who had bought them recently and among others, apparently it is a popular style, you, Ms. Chase and Mrs. Blackman showed up in their customer database."

Olivia's face fell. "Is that why Detective Johnson arrested me yesterday?"

Richards apologized. "I'm sorry about that. Your shoes were the wrong size. I'd told him that but he got hung up on those thefts. We still can't figure out who is responsible but, he's top notch at his job, but that's what he was putting together. When I found out, I was out in the field when he brought you in, I told him to let you go."

Olivia chuckled. "In no uncertain terms as I remember."

Richards said, "Mistakes happen."

Tuesday broke in. "So who did the dogs fit?"

Richards squinted. "Dogs?"

"The shoes."

"Oh, yeah. The three of you wear different sizes. They fit Mrs. Blackman."

The name hung in the air.

Richards explained. "She would have every reason to be in the shop and have her footprints there. We never figured her for this. But now, after what you've told me? We need to talk to the widow. Why were her prints around the armoire after Mr. Hatfield had swept the porch?"

Olivia chewed on her bottom lip and considered the consequences of withholding information in a murder investigation. After all, she watched Law and Order and NCIS, too. "Detective, I can't reveal my sources, but I think there is a possibility that Blackman and his partner, Ms. Chase, had a, shall we say, special relationship."

Richards waved her statement away. "Oh, we know all about that. Hard to keep that kind of thing quiet in a small town."

Olivia didn't know specifically what he was referring to, but she decided she was off the hook about stealing the CD and reporting what she and Tuesday and heard on it.

"I think that's it, Ms. Granville and Miss Tuesday. I'll let you know if I need anything else."

Olivia and Tuesday got up to leave, then Olivia stopped. "Detective, can I take down the crime scene tape."

He shook his head. "Sorry. We're not finished here."

"How about my shoes?"

His face was impassive. "Have a nice day."

Finally, Olivia got some Internet love. By six o'clock the cable news blog texted that there was a break in the case. Olivia called for Tuesday to come into the den. "Hurry!"

Then she flipped on the TV. The cable station's newest anchor, all fifteen inches of blond hair, half-inch of makeup and killer biceps shown to advantage in the requisite sleeveless dress female TV news personnel wore these days, was announcing that doctor to the billionaires, Ross Chandler, was being held for questioning. Details not yet available. The program buzzed with speculations as to why the doctor was implicated, none of them correct. At 6:27 the station flashed huge Breaking News banners across the screen. The blond shared a split screen with a young man standing in front of an official-looking building that Olivia knew for sure was a fake set. "What do you have for us, Trevor.

The field reporter, with looks that would qualify for People Magazine's Worlds Sexiest Man issue, announced that, "Behind me, Aurora, in bucolic Darling Valley's city hall, the deceased's wife, Grace Blackman, was being arraigned for the murder of her husband, former Silicon Valley venture capitalist and reputed Darling Valley drug smuggler.

"Shocking, Trevor. What do we know?"

Olivia flicked off the TV. "The only thing that's real in that segment is the drug smuggling. Darling Valley's city hall doesn't look like a 1960's communist apartment block. Blackman was never a venture capitalist, but a high level financial officer. Briefly. The wife's name is Greta not Grace and the hair, boobs and teeth are fake."

Tuesday said, "On which one?"

Olivia said, "Both. And this station is number one in the ratings?"

A few minutes later she turned the TV back on to a local station. There was a shot outside the Police Department. Olivia recognized Officer Ridley looking out through the lobby window at a reporter interviewing Detective Richards."

"There's not a lot I can tell you at this moment, Jay. We have a person of interest that we are questioning. But I do want to thank the great citizens of Darling Valley for their unbelievable cooperation during this investigation. Now if you'll excuse me."

Richards ducked back into the police station through the door that Officer Ridley held open.

The reporter stared into the camera. "KTZV, your number one place for news in Darling Valley, has learned that one of the citizens who was particularly helpful to the police in this case was our own Ms. Violet Granville, along with her partner, Miss Tuesday. We don't have a last name for Miss Tuesday. Ms. Granville, I'm sure you all know, is the owner of Granville's Antiques on the west side of town."

Olivia threw the remote at the TV and shouted into the plasma screen. "VIOLET? GRANVILLE"S ANTIQUES? I'M ON THE NORTH SIDE OF TOWN YOU IDIOT. AND TUESDAY IS NOT MY PARTNER."

Tuesday picked up the remote. "But it's nice to know that finally Darling Valley is claiming you as its own."

Later, after Tuesday opened a Pinot Grigio and they toasted the end of Olivia's nightmare, Olivia remembered her towels in the dryer. Tuesday was heating water for tea. "No reading," she promised, "just a cuppa."

Olivia shouted, "I'll be right back, "and she ran down the stairs. Before opening the door that led down to the laundry and Mrs. Harmon's inside door, she stopped at her desk. It had been what, four, five days since the grisly discovery in her armoire? It seemed like a lifetime. She decided that she and Tuesday would order pizza from the Italian place with the brick oven and super thin crusts as good as Mozza's and have a quiet night. There was nothing more she could do. It wouldn't take long to finish up labeling the furniture for the sale, and tomorrow she would corral Cody, he had been noticeably absent since yesterday, and they would arrange the showroom and plan what they would put out on the lawn. She would sell her soul to the devil if necessary, but she was determined to convince Richards to remove the crime scene tape, still flapping on the front porch, if only for the duration of the sale.

If Tuesday were not waiting for her upstairs, she would stop and sit at her desk and sketch some ideas she had for the elusive Mr. Bacon's garage. Should he ever return her calls. As soon as she left the police department after her arrest, she apologized profusely into her phone about missing yet another appointment with him, without mentioning the reason for her standing him up yet again. But he had not returned her calls. Probably, he had written her off as a flake.

Working at her desk, this beloved desk that had followed her from college to Manhattan Beach to LA and here to Darling Valley, gave her a sense of security she could not describe. She believed that people should do what they were born to do. And making the world both functional and beautiful was what made her feel whole, human and ultimately at peace. But she had to finish her chore. She owed Tuesday a long soak in her sumptuous, standalone bathtub and a stack of soft, lavender-scented towels.

The one part of the house that never felt completely hers was the basement and laundry room, in part because it had been renovated to accommodate the unit for Mrs. Harmon before she bought the house. There was no room to put her unique stamp on the space., so she left it as is. Part of this unease was the fear of being discovered there by Mrs. Harmon, childish she knew but a real feeling nevertheless, perhaps connected to the reality that Mrs. Harmon and Darling Valley did not make her feel that she belonged. So she slipped off her shoes so Mrs. Harmon wouldn't hear her. Barefoot, she opened the door to the basement and continued on down.

The new appliances were quiet in all respects, and she was sure Mrs. Harmon, should she be in her kitchen, near the door, or just out and out eavesdropping, would not hear her open the dryer door and lift out the cloud of warm, ivory towels. She tiptoed over to the folding table and began making order out of her tangled laundry. She quickly became lost in thought about what the next few days would bring. Possibly a murder indictment against the doctor and a successful sale on the weekend. But then, if this week had taught her anything, it was that things were almost never what they seemed and she should quit thinking she had the future nailed down.

Deep in thought, a sudden creaking sound made Olivia jump out of her skin. She whipped around, but it was just Mrs. Harmon opening her kitchen door with a bag of trash in her hand. However, when Mrs. Harmon, equally surprised, saw Olivia standing there, she tried to slam her door closed.

Too late. Olivia saw what she was trying to hide. Simultaneously shocked and furious, she leapt across the five feet of laminate flooring separating them and pushed the door wide open, knocking the old woman unceremoniously into the doorjamb. She marched into the kitchen wildly pointing. "Mrs. Harmon! That's my Imari bowl on your table!"

Chapter Thirty-One: Sold

Olivia handed a Paymoor's shopping bag full of crime scene tape to Detective Richards in exchange for the box containing her Jimmy Choo shoes.

"Thank you for keeping these safe."

Richards gave a little bow. "My pleasure. But you'd better check them before you sign on the dotted line. We did have to take them out of the box to compare them to the print found at the crime scene."

Olivia broke in. "The REAL crime scene, I might add. Not my shop."

Richards laughed. "Yes, the scene where Mr. Blackman was killed. By the way, I'm sorry we couldn't get your arMOIRE back to in time for the sale. But Forensics is still working on it to make sure we get every bit of evidence we can to put these two away. We don't want them getting off on technicalities."

"That's the only reason I'm not complaining. Between them they've committed four murders. That makes them mass murderers, right?"

Richards shook his head. "Technically no. Mass murderers kill many in a single event. Sandy Hook Elementary School, the Aurora movie theater massacres. While serial killers act on one victim at a time, usually for the thrill of the kill. Son of Sam and Ted Bundy. Our pair killed for expediency. Not sure what crime writers would call them."

Olivia turned up her nose. "Murder as a business skill set? Gawd. Well I thought, when I get the armoire back I'd have to do an exorcism before I'd be able to sell it. But would you believe I've had six offers from collectors of the macabre? One woman offered twice what I hoped I'd get at the sale. So it looks like I'll have to have an auction for it."

Richards shook his head. "People."

"Well," Olivia said, tucking her beloved JC's back in the box and signing for them on Richards' small pad, "we saw on the news last night that you have officially arrested the doctor and widow for murder."

"We did. They will be charged later today when the judge arrives back from vacation. She cut it short so we don't have to hold them over the weekend. The DA wants an arraignment today. She thinks they will try to plead it out. But that's out of my hands. It was an easy case as these things go."

Olivia burst out, "Are you kidding me? This has been the worst week of my life."

Richards gave her a wry grin. "I don't know what to say about that. I can only imagine."

His smile calmed Olivia down. "Detective, one more question. Why was Mr. Blackman sent to me?"

"It's complicated." He gestured to the crush of people climbing over her lawn, down her driveway to the Garden Center in back and pushing in and out of the showroom through the porch door. "I think you have enough on your hands with your sale. We can go over all this another time at the station."

Olivia had trouble focusing on Richards as Cody and Tuesday were constantly interrupting them with questions about prices and provenance. However, when Tuesday realized to whom Olivia was talking, she backed away and stayed away.

"Detective, I will end the sale now if necessary to get the answer to that question."

Richards shook his head. "Well, okay. You won't believe this. After the doctor spiked Blackman's drink with the dried puffer fish toxin, he was the man Roger saw with him that night, he left thinking it would appear that he'd had a heart attack. . . you were right. The doctor got cheated out of a sweet options deal at that biotech company and blamed Blackman for it. Some kind of dirty dealing we haven't figured out yet. So after he texted the widow that Blackman was dead, she came back for an act of revenge. She had seen Blackman with his partner steaming up the back seat of his car in Hugo's parking lot when he was supposed to be at a meeting in San Francisco. She couldn't let it go, even though she knew she was going to have all his drug proceeds to herself. Well, aside from sharing it with the doctor. Yeah, she knew about the drug smuggling. She knew about everything. She knew where he kept the key to his safe deposit box. He had taken his proceeds in diamonds. She wanted to teach Sabrina Chase a lesson and cast suspicion on her at the same time. It wasn't a very well thought out plan. Late that night she went back to the shop and put her husband into the armoire. The door kept opening so she tied it shut. You're right. She's an expert sailor."

Olivia saw Mrs. Harmon come walking down the driveway, smiled and waved to her as Richards continued. Olivia waved back, then asked, "But where do I come it? I still don't get why she sent it to me."

"Greta didn't know the armoire was supposed to go to you. Roger had taped a note for Cody on a pizza delivery flyer. He wasn't enjoying all of his faculties, if you get my meaning and was sloppy about using the correct delivery form. That Greta would have noticed. But to her it just looked like a pizza delivery flyer or maybe she didn't even see it. It was late, not much light. Her label, with instructions to deliver it to Sabrina Chase apparently fell off during the night, or sometime before Cody picked arrived. Or maybe Cody knocked it off while he moved it and didn't see it. At any rate, we found it on the floor. To us it was nothing. Sabrina Chase was an owner. Her name was on everything. So you got it. Bureaucratic mix-up."

Olivia's mouth dropped. "I went through all that because a hophead couldn't get his act together?"

Richards said, "Fraid so. If he had put the proper form on the chest in two places as Blackman's required, this never would have involved you."

"Detective, I need a moment to take this in. Wait until I tell Tuesday and Cody.

Richards looked around to allow Olivia time to absorb the news. "You know, the doctor was furious when he saw on the news that Blackman ended up on your doorstep, so to speak. He rushed over to see if he could have him declared dead of a heart attack. He didn't want anyone doing any exotic testing and find the puffer fish toxin in his tissue. Blackman never had a heart condition. He made up a phony chart and put another patient's EKG and lap tests in it. It was his idea for Greta to do the weeping widow act and blame you."

Olivia flashed on the day she went to his office and lay on his examining table, half naked. She shuddered. "Detective can't I bring a malpractice suit against him for treating me as his patient while setting me up for murder?"

Richards gave her a commiserating smile. "Up to you ma'am. Now we just have to figure out what happened to your bowl and other items."

Olivia stammered. "Oh, detective. Forgive me. In all the confusion and the sale, well I forgot to notify you that they were in the house all the time after all."

He narrowed his eyes. "Seriously? But we searched everywhere."

"I know. So did I. But there they were all the time," she crossed her fingers behind her back, "just under my feet."

She was not going to involve Mrs. Harmon in any of this. The poor woman was desolate about losing her husband and then the Cooks who had befriended her. She wouldn't allow herself to warm up to Olivia and then have her go out of business or something and move away. And then when Olivia told her she was a customer of Blackman, who had cheated her husband, thereby, as she believed, contributing to his heart attack, she snapped. Her only revenge was to steal her things.

Olivia thought she had locked her out in the renovation. But Mrs. Harmon knew how to wiggle the door to get any lock to slide open. She grabbed only what she could carry. The pendulum was right. Olivia was standing on her treasures. So was Carrie. Her earrings had fallen out when she delivered cookies to Mrs. Harmon. The tenant found them in her living room, but didn't know they were Carrie's. The girl was so excited to get them back, she volunteered to help with the sale.

Just then, before Richards could quiz her any more, Olivia saw a familiar figure get out of a BMW 751 in a Prada workout suit she recognized from the Neiman's catalog. It was Tasmania of the lush, cascading hair and sweeping eyelashes waving and rushing over to greet them. Olivia didn't know what Richards' girlfriend did for a living, but if she ever asked Olivia for career counseling, she'd tell her to apply to cable TV as a news anchor. Tasmania came up behind Richards and put her arms around his waist. He half turned, drew her close and kissed her forehead.

Olivia knew Richards was dropping off the shoes today. A good faith gesture considering what she had been through. But Tasmania? What was she doing here? Cody caught a look at Tasmania and hustled over to ask Olivia if there was anything she needed, all the while staring at the beauty. Olivia had no choice but to introduce them.

"Tasmania, this is my assistant, Cody White. Cody this is Miss Tasmania . . .I'm sorry, but I've forgotten your last name."

Both Richards and Tasmania gave her an odd look. "Why, Richards, of course. Same as Gurmeet's."

Olivia flushed. "Of course, I'm sorry. This is Detective Richards' wife."

Friggin frig. How could she not have figured out that he was married. Just her luck, though what was she thinking anyway. Both she and Tuesday agreed he was definitely not a MAD man.

Richards was shaking his head and for once, flashing Olivia a blinding smile. "No, not my wife. My sister."

Chapter Thirty-Two: BFF's

Olivia tallied up her proceeds while Tuesday started packing. She was taking a six am flight in the morning from SFO to Burbank to make her nine am Monday morning standing appointment with Holley Wood, star of Warner Bros. latest blockbuster about aliens taking over the body of a time-traveling princess. Tuesday had said when she told Olivia, "God's truth. She showed me her birth certificate. I could slice her in ribbons. She got the name first. But she probably needs all the help she can get. She calls them alients."

She zipped up the last of her cases. "Well, I guess that's it. The only thing left is for you to tell me what's up with the shoes."

Olivia bent over into a downward dog, straightened up into warrior pose and said, "I've got to get back into yoga. I have so much tension in my back from all this. The shoes. You won't believe this."

She explained the tortured murder plan and, out of jealousy, Greta's foiling what would have been a perfect crime.

"Over a man she conspired to murder. That's some serious crazy. Oh, don't let me forget my herbs."

Olivia said, "Puleeze don't forget them." Then she went on to explain how they nailed the doctor when they found the sliced up puffer fish in his freezer and vials of toxin he had been able to extract.

Olivia did an *I don't get it* eye rolling head shake. "Who even knows how to do that? Anyway, Richards told him that they could trace the DNA from the fish to the DNA in Blackman's tissues. Richards pulled that one out of a hat, but it worked. Chandler bought it and caved and gave up Greta in the process. They'd been getting it on since Blackman cheated everyone out of the biotech deal. He was really just into Greta so he could figure out a way to get back at Blackman. She killed her husband for the diamonds. She wouldn't share them with him but was willing to give half to Chandler because, get this: She believed he loved her."

Now Tuesday did the eyerolling thing. "When will they learn?"

Olivia explained that Chandler moved to DV and set up a practice for the rich and richer to be closer to Blackman, keep an eye on him. Then the others showed up. The shirtmakers and Harmon. They weren't just after Blackman. The doctor's hands weren't any too clean in the deal either and those three were after both Blackman and Chandler.

Olivia stretched out on the floor and threw her feet behind her head, then moved into a shoulder stand. She huffed and puffed as she spoke. "So he did his first experimenting with puffer fish, he really is an expert, on Harmon. ME said heart attack and he knew he finally had a magic formula. He then slipped it to the shirt couple, apparently it's not hard to smear it on something and it seeps into the skin. He really isn't sure how they got into the lake. They should have just collapsed on the ground." Which is what she did, rolling herself down and touching her heels to the rug again.

"Then when Greta told him she'd heard through the grapevine about the drugs and confronted her husband, I don't know what grapevine she hangs on, but he admitted it, Chandler had his solution for Blackman. But hell hath no fury. If Greta had left well enough alone, they would have gotten away with it. Blackman told her about the drugs, the safe deposit box, the works. She probably was on him for losing so much money in the Silicon Valley deal. So she decided to have the diamonds to herself and then Chandler swept her off her feet with his bedside manner and they thought they had it made. But Roger got high and was complicit in unknowingly helping her send the body to an amateur sleuth."

Olivia sat up and shrugged innocently. "That's where I come in. Who knew?"

Tuesday sat on a case to zip it shut.

"How much do you have to pay for all that luggage?"

"What's money for? So everybody's happy, now, right? Richards has the killers, Cody has Jessica. How did he figure out Mrs. Harmon was BFFs with the wrong Blackman sister?"

"He asked her. Funny how communication works. The daughter I heard about was adopted. Once Jessica was born, she took center stage. Apparently, Brenda, the adopted one, wanted their father to make a business loan to her husband and he refused. The husband took a powder and she blamed it all on her father. She found a willing listener in Mrs. Harmon. They knew each other from when they all lived in Silicon Valley. So that's it. Last thing. Richards and Mrs. Harmon are tight because she and her husband lived in Mumbai for a while and she befriended

Tasmania. Mrs. Harmon is like everybody's favorite mother. Could have fooled me."

The two friends said goodnight and hugged goodbye, promised there would be no tears, hugged some more and raced each other for the box of tissues.

"Tuesday, I'd beg you to move up here with me but I know you would hate it."

"And I'd beg you to come back to LA but I've looked deeply into Detective Richards' eyes. It would be cruel and unusual punishment to tear you away from those brown beauties."

Olivia pooh-poohed that idea. "Seriously, he's not my type and I have a business to get off the ground and a car museum commission to snag."

"Did you finally hear from George Clooney, er Mr. Bacon?"

"Yeah, he came to the sale. Figured it was the only way he could talk to me. I looked for you to introduce you but you must have been in the house. We have an appointment next week."

"Now there's an interesting proposition," Tuesday said seductively.

"No, it's not like that. He's a widower still grieving for his wife."

"And I know just the chickadee to cheer him up."

"Honestly, Tuesday, if that came out of anybody else's mouth I'd never speak to them again. Have you no respect? And you know how he got his money? He won the country's two biggest Powerball lotteries, three years apart. Three hundred million and change in the first one and four hundred million and change in the second one. Before that he was a dispatcher on the Hoboken public transit. His wife died just before he won the first one. He can't get over her."

Tuesday shook her head. "What I have is a deep and abiding wish for my best friend's happiness. Now give me one more hug and let me get some sleep. Promise me we'll get together again before Christmas."

Olivia crossed her heart. "Promise."

Tuesday said, "Preferably so I can catch your bouquet."

Olivia threw a pillow at her and then blew kisses all the way out of the room. "Travel well, Tuesday."

"Stay out of trouble, princess."

"Which one of us will fulfill those wishes?"

"You better."

"No, you better."

"Love you."

"Love you more."

"I give up. Let me sleep."

The End

About the Author

Cassie Page is a prolific writer of tasteful and humorous mysteries set in Northern California and other exotic locations. She resides in a small town near Darling Valley where she raises rare orchids and perfectly behaved children. Her soufflés rise effortlessly, her skirts are always the correct length and she only tweets with the best people. She fraternizes with gruesome murderers and backstabbing lowlifes and reads quantum mechanics for relaxation. Her editor says she has a breathtaking mastery of the semicolon—the colon not so much. If you pass her on the street, she begs that you do not ask for an autograph. Please respect her privacy; the paparazzi have worn her to a frazzle.

Cassie Page Books

The upcoming books in the Darling Valley Mystery series features designer/clothes horse/sleuth extraordinaire Olivia M. Granville; the winsome if bizarrely dressed Tuesday, the tiresomely righteous Mrs. Harmon and the deliciously distant Detective Richards.

Future titles include:

Groundbreaking Bodies

Death is in the Details

A Second Coat of Murder

Tea For Two Murders

Designed for Death

Now you can enjoy Tuesday in her own breakout series by Cassie Page. Available now.

A Corpse in a Teacup: A Tuesday's Tea Leaves Mystery, Book 1

Free Gift and Updates About Future Books

Sign up for a free gift and updates on future books, discounts and tidbits about what Olivia and the residents and scoundrels are doing, eating, wearing and buying.

Go to the link below to sign up. And remember, we NEVER share your email address with ANYONE. So your secret (email address) is safe with Olivia.

http://www.cassiepage.com/?page_id=30

Contact The Author

While Ms. Page has worked tirelessly to execute the perfect murder mystery, mistakes happen. Should you find one or wish to communicate on a higher plane, she would be thrilled to hear from you. You can reach her at cassiepagebooks@gmail.com

Follow The Author

https://www.facebook.com/cassiepagebooks

http://www.cassiepage.com

@cassiepagebooks

Fiction Disclaimer

This book is a work of fiction and solely the product of the author's warped imagination and twisted sense of humor. Any resemblance to actual people, living or dead would be a huge surprise to the author and wholly unintentional. If you feel you resemble any of the characters, honestly, I'd keep it to yourself. You know how rumors start.

All rights reserved.